WINTER'S FURY

BY TOM THREADGILL

WINTER'S FURY BY TOM THREADGILL
Published by Lamplighter Mystery and Suspense
an imprint of Lighthouse Publishing of the Carolinas
2333 Barton Oaks Dr., Raleigh, NC 27614

ISBN: 978-1-64526-249-7
Copyright © 2019 by Tom Threadgill
Cover design by Elaina Lee
Interior design by Karthick Srinivasan

Available in print from your local bookstore, online, or from the publisher at:
ShopLPC.com

For more information on this book and the author, visit: www.tomthreadgill.com

All rights reserved. Non-commercial interests may reproduce portions of this book without the express written permission of Lighthouse Publishing of the Carolinas, provided the text does not exceed 500 words. When reproducing text from this book, include the following credit line: "*Winter's Fury* by Tom Threadgill published by Lighthouse Publishing of the Carolinas. Used by permission."

Commercial interests: No part of this publication may be reproduced in any form, stored in a retrieval system, or transmitted in any form by any means—electronic, photocopy, recording, or otherwise—without prior written permission of the publisher, except as provided by the United States of America copyright law.

This is a work of fiction. Names, characters, and incidents are all products of the author's imagination or are used for fictional purposes. Any mentioned brand names, places, and trademarks remain the property of their respective owners, bear no association with the author or the publisher, and are used for fictional purposes only.

All Scripture quotations, unless otherwise indicated, are taken from the Holy Bible, New International Version®, NIV®. Copyright ©1973, 1978, 1984, 2011 by Biblica, Inc.™ Used by permission of Zondervan. All rights reserved worldwide. www.zondervan.com. "NIV" and "New International Version" are trademarks registered in the United States Patent and Trademark Office by Biblica, Inc.™

Brought to you by the creative team at Lighthouse Publishing of the Carolinas (LPCBooks.com): Eddie Jones, Shonda Savage, Darla Crass, Sally Shupe.

Library of Congress Cataloging-in-Publication Data
Threadgill, Tom
Winter's Fury/Tom Threadgill 1st ed.

Printed in the United States of America

ACKNOWLEDGMENTS

When I wrote the first Jeremy Winter novel, I wasn't sure there'd be a sequel. I wasn't sure I *wanted* a sequel. I don't know about other authors, but by the time I finish writing a book, the last thing I want to do is start on another novel with the same characters. I mean, I've just spent the last several months (years?) with these imaginary people and it's time for a break, right? At least that's what they keep telling me.

But here we are with *Winter's Fury*, the third book involving my make-believe friends. As is always the case, a few fine folks helped out considerably in getting this novel to market.

Linda S. Glaz, agent extraordinaire, has stuck with me for years. Her encouragement and confidence (and promise of fudge—where is it, Linda?) have kept me plodding along. This book's for you, Linda.

Darla Crass, my managing editor at Lighthouse Publishing of the Carolinas, pushed me to write and rewrite until the novel was ready. To paraphrase a popular saying, if your editor ain't happy, ain't nobody happy. Rewrites are excruciating and every author hates doing them. However, the benefit of having to spend so much time going over the same book you've already written is that you come up with some great names for the next novel. Carla Drass, prepare to be the first victim of my antagonist. I'm thinking first page.

Finally, my wife Janet is a constant source of inspiration. A lot of the banter between Jeremy and Maggie flows from conversations Janet and I have. Love you, babe. Always have, always will.

for Linda S. Glaz
thanks for believing

CHAPTER ONE

Shane Kingston pulled the closet door shut, shoved a couple of old towels against the light-leaking gap at the bottom, then scooted until his back pressed against the wall. Dress shirts, each ironed and hanging with its matching tie, brushed his face and he pushed them toward the other end, down where the polished shoes rested in their cubbyholes, and the creased pants waited on their wooden hangers.

Outside, the TV blared commercial-free recordings of *The Jerry Springer Show* just loud enough for the on-screen ruckus to creep through the door. Indistinct voices talked and screamed in a never-ending cycle of confrontation.

Most of the day was booked, with a funeral starting soon and then off to his second-shift job at the call center. Adulting left little time for play. Better get right to it. He closed his eyes as they adjusted to the lack of light. With darkness came peace.

His hand inched along the baseboard until he found what he sought, right where he'd left it yesterday. Hard plastic, nearly a foot tall with pop-out wings, buttons for lasers, and a broken retractable helmet. No batteries, of course. Buzz Lightyear never spoke. Never zapped anyone. Never went to infinity and beyond.

But his day would come.

Too dangerous to make a sound now. There could be no noise from the closet until the yelling on the other side of the door stopped.

Shane hunched over Buzz, took a deep breath, pressed the button to extend the toy's wings, and flew him in slow, gentle figure eights before bringing him to a soft landing in his lap. Buzz always enjoyed his flights and kept his toothy grin, a stark contrast to Shane's pounding heart and beading sweat. The space ranger's right wing broke off years ago, probably kicked or thrown in the final confrontation between Shane's parents. After that, Mom was gone. Dad was happy. And Shane grew. Accepted the inevitable. Embraced it.

Jerry Springer's guests continued their screaming while the studio audience roared their approval, and Shane scooted lower until he was lying on his side, his back to the door. He popped Buzz's wings back into their retracted position and placed him on the floor so they faced one another. They couldn't see each other. Couldn't talk either. But it didn't make any difference.

Shane chuckled. What would a psychiatrist have to say about this routine? Lots, most of it probably correct. No question he had issues, but what thirty-three-year-old over-educated under-employed man didn't? You deal with what you've got. Maybe not in a way society approves of, but at least in a way that is productive, efficient, and creative.

He sighed, put Buzz back in the corner, and checked his phone. The funeral began in an hour. Such a waste of time. He didn't want to go but felt obligated. The widow, Brenda Clancy, was one of his employees, and he needed to represent the company and her coworkers. No doubt she was still traumatized. Her husband's death had been especially brutal. Words like *grisly* and *gruesome* came to mind. Rumor had it a firefighter threw up at the scene. A horrible, painful accident.

Just the way Shane planned it.

CHAPTER TWO

Jeremy Winter held his coffee mug toward the light and squinted. No question about it. Maggie washed the thing. He'd have to start taking the cup back to his apartment every day. After filling it halfway and wiping the drips off the counter, he limped to the sofa and placed the steaming mug on the end table, then plopped onto the couch and massaged his left leg. The stiffness and aches used to be random, but the incident in Texas changed that. In the struggle with Cody Talbot, Jeremy had been stabbed in the shoulder and injured his already damaged leg. The knife wound healed fine, but the doctors said his leg wouldn't get any better and might get worse. A lot worse. Nothing he could do about it except wait and see. Maggie bought him a wooden cane to replace the sterile-looking aluminum one the hospital gave him, and she kept on him about using it. On bad days he did, but his theory was that the less he used the walking aid, the stronger the leg would become. The physical therapist said that wasn't true, but doctors were wrong all the time, right?

The earthy scent of his coffee woke his taste buds, and he took a sip of the dark Sumatran blend. Down the hall, the weekday morning ritual was well underway. His girlfriend, FBI agent Maggie Keeley, was locked in a battle of wills with Rebecca, her seven-year-old daughter. Every you-have-to-get-up-now was met with a grunt, moan, or muffled "I'm too tired." The routine warmed him better than the coffee.

He cleared his throat and raised his voice. "Beks, honey, get up now and we can swing by the donut shop on the way to school, okay?" *Beks.* They'd both decided that sounded more grown-up than *Rebecca.* Maggie wasn't a fan but tolerated the nickname. Jeremy dabbed a drop of coffee off his lower lip. If there was a response from the girl's room, he didn't hear it, but Maggie's approaching footsteps told him he'd succeeded.

She passed behind him and went into the kitchen. "I wish you'd stop bribing her. She needs to learn responsibility."

Uh-oh. "Sorry, just didn't want anyone to get in trouble. Won't happen again."

"Says the man who pushed her bedtime back an hour last night because she finished her homework without complaining."

He scrunched down in the sofa and clutched his coffee to his chest.

She chuckled. "I can still see you. Comfy?"

"Will be once you bring me some breakfast."

"You're going to be waiting a while. Tell you what. Tomorrow's Saturday. You come over early, and I'll let you fix pancakes for us."

"Deal. Got to be here anyway to watch cartoons with Beks. Trying to work in a little Roadrunner and Bugs Bunny when I can. Bring her up on the classics." He motioned toward the TV. "News says Diane Morgans is ahead by three points."

"Dumping Cronfeld didn't hurt her any, that's for sure."

Jeremy shook his head. Colonel Ramsey Cronfeld, the former husband of presidential candidate Diane Morgans, now spent his days avoiding the public and assembling a high-powered legal team. Homa Nezam's eyewitness accounts of the colonel's activities in Afghanistan turned the man's dreams of power into a nightmare of desperation. Many in the press expected charges of war crimes would be leveled against him any day, though Jeremy doubted it. Things like this tended to fade away in DC. Ugly memories from an angry time.

Maggie pulled on her jacket. "You gonna vote for her?"

"Morgans? Stick me in with the rest of the undecideds."

She grinned. "Oh? Won't vote for her because she's a woman? You know what that makes you, right?"

"Yep. A charter member of the he-man-woman-haters club."

"What?"

"Little Rascals? No? Nothing? I'll add it to Beks' to-watch list."

"Um, no. Not happening. I think we decided they're racist."

"We? Who is we? And is there like, I dunno, a website or something that lists all the words and shows and people I'm not allowed to have anything to do with anymore? I can't keep up."

"Yeah, go to w-w-w the world is leaving you behind dot com." She grabbed her purse. "I've got to go to work. Get the munchkin to school on time."

He arched his eyebrows. "Munchkin? Are you sure you're allowed to say that?"

"No, but here's what I *can* say. If you don't get up off your—"

He set his mug on the side table and extended both hands, palms facing her. "Get her to school on time. Yes, ma'am. Want me to pick her up too?"

"Nah, let her go to after-school care. She needs to spend time playing with the other kids. The therapist said that would help."

He clenched his teeth and inhaled deeply as his chest tightened. The little girl had come close to death after being kidnapped. She'd be dealing with the trauma for years, maybe the rest of her life. Moving to Haymarket in upstate Virginia had at least changed the scenery, though not the memories, and the commute time to Maggie's office in DC was less than half what it had been. His apartment was just around the corner from hers and stopping in every morning was part of the daily routine.

"Got a big day planned?" she asked.

"Find some cardboard and a marker, then choose a street corner. Getting tired of being unemployed."

She bent forward and kissed him. "Maybe you should actually look for a job, huh?"

"What fun would that be? Besides, the pension pays my bills. Actually, I thought I might take another run up to Frederick."

"Did you hear something new?"

After so long, there'd be nothing new to hear. His wife and unborn daughter had been killed shortly after 9/11 in what police suspected was an attempted robbery. He'd been in Afghanistan when they died. The guilt and pain and anger had eased thanks to the woman now standing before him, but the emotions still randomly flared. And justice had not been served. The killer remained unknown, a mockery Jeremy was determined to correct.

Finding the murderer wouldn't bring closure. No such thing. No peace or comfort or satisfaction. How could there be? People he loved were dead. Catching the killer wouldn't change that.

But it would allow him to move forward. To remove that sword hanging over his head and begin this new part of his life without constantly looking backward. He'd promised Maggie that once he'd done everything he could to find whoever'd killed them, he'd be able to turn loose of the past. Until then, it wouldn't be fair to her or Beks to take their relationship to the next level. She accepted that and said she wanted whatever was best for him.

But Maggie wouldn't wait forever. She'd never say that, of course, but he knew. One day she'd wake up and understand that his promise might never be fulfilled. That he couldn't let go until the killer was rotting in prison, or better yet, six feet under.

"Hey," Maggie said. "Hello? I asked if you heard something new from the Frederick PD."

"Something new?" he said. "No, just want to talk to Detective Pronger again."

She bit her bottom lip and nodded. "Third time's on your side, right?"

He stood, placed his hands on her hips, and kissed her again. "Something like that. Call me when you get home tonight, okay?"

"Will do. Take your cane today. And better go get Rebecca moving. She'll spend an hour deciding what to wear to school. I swear, for a seven-year-old she sure is particular."

He arched his eyebrows. "Wonder where she gets that from?"

Maggie shook her head and moved toward the door. "Not me. I'm not that picky. Look who I hang around with."

CHAPTER THREE

The church sanctuary echoed with low whispers and sniffling, mostly from women clutching wads of tissues. A good turnout. The newly widowed Brenda would be pleased.

Shane never attended the funerals of his victims. Loathed the very idea of it. Why go when you didn't know the widow and only met the deceased once, and then just long enough to kill him? Today was a necessary exception. He *did* know this widow. The planning of Bo Clancy's murder indicated this was a probable outcome, and Shane's presence here validated the accuracy of his analysis.

He lowered his head, clasped his hands, and inched forward in the line of mourners. A white ceramic urn sat atop a table at the front of the church. Flowers and photographs surrounded the man's remains and provided false evidence of a life well-lived. Brenda stood to the side and dabbed a Kleenex at her nose and eyes as the somber crowd paraded by, each person pausing to express their sympathy.

Oh, the irony of the man choosing to be cremated. Shane faked a low cough as an excuse to hide the smile on his face. Such an appropriate outcome, but maybe it was more from necessity than choice. No telling how much of him was left by the time the firefighters arrived.

This death was one of Shane's favorites, and today was Brenda Clancy's reward for the creativity of the plan. Her husband's workshop, his retreat from the world, gave him a quick ending. Far better than he deserved. The fire investigators had it all figured out. The sweet, woodsy odor of gum turpentine fumes masked the propane leaking from an old tank stashed in a back corner. Sawdust and lumber covered every available space and served as fuel. The man lit a cigarette and triggered his personal pyre. An excellent theory, really, except that Clancy had been unconscious when all of it happened.

He shuffled forward another few inches in the queue and examined the wreath of flowers next to him. Based on its large size, the arrangement was probably the one from her coworkers. The circle of white carnations, lilies, and roses looked too perfect to be real. Was it bad form to peek at the tag and see who'd sent it? He'd chipped in a twenty which gave him the right to sign the sympathy card as well. It would be nice to know what his money bought.

The line moved forward again, and he abandoned the thought. Three people ahead of him. Should he plan what to say or just wing it? The urn was within reach now, and he had a sudden urge to lift the top and peek in. How odd that a man the size of Bo Clancy fit into such a tiny jar. Wonder if Brenda's going to scatter them somewhere or put them on the mantel? Doesn't seem like she'd want anything in the house to remind her of the man, but you never know.

One guy ahead of him now. The widow looked good, aside from the puffy redness in her face. The dark semicircle under her right eye was barely noticeable, a far cry from the bruise's appearance a week ago. As usual, she'd worn her sunglasses at work. Eye strain from the fluorescents, she said.

The man moved on, and Shane paused to frown and shake his head. "Brenda, I'm so sorry." He lightly hugged her, careful to keep his hands high on her back. Even though she was almost fifty and they weren't at work, no sense risking a trip to HR.

"Thanks for coming, Shane. It means a lot."

"Of course. Everyone at the office said to tell you they were thinking about you."

She sniffled and nodded. "I'm planning to come back next Monday."

"Are you sure? Take all the time you need. Your job's not going anywhere."

"Thanks, but I really don't want to be alone. I think it would do me good to be around people and get back in a routine as soon as possible."

He pasted on a sympathetic smile. The couple had been married for over twenty years and never had kids. Her coworkers would be her family now. "Whatever you think is best. Listen, I can't stay for the service, but if you need anything, anything at all, you be sure to let us know, okay?"

"I will. Thanks again for coming. You're a good boss."

"If you change your mind about coming back so early—"

"I won't," she said. "See you Monday."

He wrinkled his forehead, pulled his lips into his mouth, and tilted his head to the side. An expression of sympathy, though she'd be better off without the ash-man. It might take time for her to realize that, but she'd get there. And she'd never know how fortunate she was, being the only employee he'd ever be able to help. Couldn't take a chance on anyone making a connection. Better to keep all the victims far apart.

He clasped his hands again, then turned and ambled out of the church and into the late afternoon sunshine. A breeze took the edge off the upper-80 degree temps. The weatherman said the heat was at the high end of normal for Charlotte in late August, and autumn seemed a long way off. He stretched and wandered toward his car. Time to head back to work.

The hundred or so employees he supervised on second shift at the call center would want an update on Brenda. First, he'd pull through Chick-fil-A, order a spicy chicken sandwich, and top it off with a glob of Buffalo sauce. Ramp up the heat enough to bring on sniffles and watery eyes. He'd eat it on the way back to the office and go in and sit at his desk without speaking to anyone. After a few minutes, some employee would tap on his door and ask if he was okay. He'd nod and say how bad he felt for Brenda, then excuse himself to go splash water on his face. When he came back, he'd put on a brave face and try to work for a while, but soon decide he needed the rest of the evening off. One of the other supervisors would cover. On the way out, he'd halfheartedly wave and tell everyone to have a good evening. Maybe even choke up a little.

The drive back to the office would take less than twenty minutes at this time of day. He knew of at least three Chick-fil-A's on the way, each of which would be busy. Down in this part of the country, the restaurant was basically a license to print money. He pulled into the drive-thru lane at the first one he came to so he'd have time to eat before arriving at work. The woman on the speaker announced that it was her pleasure to serve him today, and please pull around to pay and pick up his order. Such a happy voice. They were all that way. The Stepford employees of the fast food industry.

At the window, the woman—Natalie according to her name badge— took his money and handed him his order. Her perpetual smile broadened her somewhat narrow twenty-something face. "Hold on just a sec for your change," she said.

He nodded and checked the rearview for any rowdy hairs before cinching his tie tighter.

"Here ya go," Natalie said.

He held out his hand, and she counted out his change, coins first, then the bills on top. Her forearm. A series of ...

"Sir?"

He jerked back to reality. "I'm sorry. What?"

"Will there be anything else?"

"No. No thank you, Natalie. Have a great day."

"You too. Come back soon."

He pulled away from the window and dumped his change in the cup holder. Come back soon. A cry for help. He'd seen the four dark splotches on her forearm. Bruises from someone's fingers. No wedding ring either. A boyfriend?

After easing into traffic, he pulled the sandwich from the bag, added a generous amount of the Buffalo sauce, and took his first bite. The heat flared in his face, and he inhaled deeply to cool his mouth. He teared up almost immediately. The plan was solid. Good thing, since he needed to leave work early.

Come back soon, Natalie said.

He would.

It would be his pleasure to serve her.

CHAPTER FOUR

Jeremy cinched his jacket tighter as he hobbled toward the red brick building that housed the Frederick, Maryland, police department. According to the display on his vehicle's dash, the temperature was in the mid-70s, nice for this time of year, but the light gray clouds and steady breeze sent a chill through him. His cane remained in the car, and by the time he made it out of the parking garage, his chest ached, and breaths came hard. The exertion raised beads of sweat on his forehead. His leg complained with each step, and the two donuts this morning weren't doing him any favors either. His exercise routine, what little there was of it, disappeared after the latest injury. The result was an extra twenty pounds. The physical therapist had prescribed a workout regimen, but he'd never committed himself to it. That needed to change soon. He jaywalked across the street and hobbled inside.

A receptionist greeted him, and he showed her his ID. She phoned to get approval for him to carry his weapon in the office, then escorted him to the same small room he'd waited in on his prior visits. The off-white walls and dim lighting did nothing to warm him, so he left his jacket on and buried his hands in the pockets before sitting. Two other chairs were on the opposite side of the square metal table. Not an interrogation room but might as well be. He glanced in the upper corners. No cameras as far as he could see. Nowadays they probably put them in the light switches or thermostats or something.

The door opened and a man, early 40s, trim, starched white shirt and blue-striped tie, rubbed his hands together and nodded. "Good morning, Mr. Winter. How are you?"

"Morning, Detective Pronger. I was up this way and thought I'd stop by and get the latest."

The man shook his head and eased into a chair. "Damp chill in the air this morning. Makes my bones feel twenty years older. You ever get that?"

Jeremy pulled his hands from his pockets and placed them on the table. "Not really."

"Must be an age thing, I suppose. To answer your question, no, I'm sorry, but there's nothing new. Like I said last time and the time before that, your wife's case is active, and we're continuing to investigate. There's nothing more—"

"What exactly does that mean? 'Active' as in we have people actually looking for the killer or 'active' as in the case is still open, and if someone calls in a tip we'll investigate?"

The detective sighed and leaned forward. "Look, Mr. Winter. Do I wish I had something to tell you? Of course I do. But with your background, you know how this works. It's a cold case. We only get one or two murders a year, so I can tell you this is still a priority, but the department has done everything it can, and until something new pops up, we simply do not have the manpower to assign someone to it. Even if we did, it wouldn't make a difference. There are no witnesses we can interview again. No video from security cameras we can enhance through the latest software. No DNA from the shooter, no bullet or casing, nothing to compare to any database in the hopes something's turned up since the last time we checked. Do I wish it wasn't that way? Yeah, but those are the facts."

Jeremy scratched his forehead just above his nose. The officer's habit of asking himself questions and then answering them was beyond annoying. "You start with motive. Attempted robbery, right? Then why was her purse not taken?"

Pronger stiffened. "I've been doing this a long time. I know how to investigate a case. We think it was an *attempted* robbery. If her purse had been taken, it would have been an *actual* robbery. We arrived at that conclusion based on the statements *you* gave us when you returned from Afghanistan. Your wife had no known enemies, no secret life we could find, nothing that would make her anything other than a random target. I wasn't the original investigator, but there's nothing in the file that I don't agree with. Based on what we know, the murder was a street crime. Nothing more."

Electricity bolted through Jeremy, and he jumped to his feet. "Nothing more? Well, it's *more* to me."

The detective held up his hands. "I'm sorry. I worded that poorly. Please, sit."

Jeremy hesitated, then sat. "It's different when you're on this side of the case."

Pronger cupped his hands around his mouth and sneezed. "I understand. I'm sorry I said it that way. What I meant was that, again, based on what we know, your wife's death was unintentional. I wish I could tell you that we have fresh leads and are confident something will break, but after so long …"

"No similar crimes around that time? Nothing that might expand the search?"

"Sure, there were other robberies, but nothing we could ever connect back to your wife's case. And none of them involved a shooting."

Jeremy stretched his injured leg under the table and twisted his foot left-right several times. "In other words, you're at a dead end. So why not let me take a look? What could it hurt?"

"Can't do that. What you do as a private citizen is your own business as long as it doesn't interfere with us, but I can't give you access to the full file. Goes against policy. Do I wish it wasn't that way? Yeah, I—"

Jeremy flicked his hand. "Yeah, you do. You don't have to give me access. Just bring it in here and take a long bathroom break. Nobody will know. Call it a professional courtesy."

Pronger intertwined his fingers on the table. "This isn't about what I want to do. If it was, I'd be back there running off the copies for you myself. I can assure you there's nothing in the murder book I haven't shared with you, and that's pushing the boundaries of what I'm allowed to do."

Boundaries. The lines that were supposed to keep everything nice and clean and legal. Only problem was criminals didn't care much about boundaries. And now that he was free of the restrictions of his FBI job, stepping over the line didn't seem so bad. Not as long as you did it for the right reasons. "And if it had been *your* wife and daughter?"

The detective's face flushed, and he stood and extended his hand. "Have a nice day, Mr. Winter. The Frederick Police Department puts maximum effort into solving every crime, whether our family is involved or not."

"I didn't mean to—"

Pronger dropped his hand to his side and moved to the door. "Oh, but we both know you did. Next time, please call instead of dropping by. I might not be here."

Jeremy slouched in his chair as the door closed behind the detective. Don't call us, we'll call you. Great. One thing was certain. His people skills hadn't improved since he'd left the Bureau. Any camaraderie he'd built with Detective Pronger was gone. If he wanted a look at the murder book, he'd have to find another way. Get someone else to help. Someone with the authority and ability to request a copy without pushback. Have to be from the state or federal law enforcement community and willing to take a chance for him.

Someone like Maggie.

CHAPTER FIVE

Jeremy popped open a Sam Adams and made the cycle through the channels again. Nothing on but scripted reality TV shows. No history on the History Channel. No learning on TLC, the Learning Channel. No music on MTV, though that counted as a blessing. He grunted and shifted on the couch. Maggie said he'd become more cynical lately and was in danger of becoming a forty-eight-year-old curmudgeon. He'd replied that she was in danger of becoming an almost-forty-year-old nagger. Not one of his better decisions.

Still another hour until the hockey game started. Tonight was the preseason opener for the Capitals. This was the year they were going to take the Cup, and he was determined not to miss a minute. Maggie and Beks were coming by in a bit to watch the game with him. They'd be wearing the jerseys he bought them with their names across the back, but Maggie wore hers as a concession more than as a fan. Despite his best efforts, she showed no interest in the Caps or any other hockey team, her one fault as far as he could tell. She'd read or do her nails while he and Beks cheered their team on to victory.

Might be a good night to talk to her again about his visit to Frederick, but the more he thought about it, the more hesitant he became. It had been a few days since he'd spoken to Detective Pronger, and Maggie hadn't volunteered any assistance other than listening. Asking her to use her FBI influence to get him a copy of the murder book could cause problems. If she asked permission, the denial would be swift. If she did it on her own and got caught, she could get in serious trouble. And since they both knew that, if he asked her to help, how would their relationship be affected? Didn't seem likely the outcome would be positive. Better to find another way. He still had friends in other places who could prove useful, but those favors might be better called in on something more … what? Important? What was more important than catching his wife's killer? Not losing Maggie and Beks, that's what.

Muted voices drifted through the door, and he grinned. The girls were here. The doorknob turned slowly, and he sank lower onto the sofa. Normally, he'd rest his hand on the Glock holstered on his hip, but a muffled giggle eased his tension. He placed his beer on the side table and closed his eyes just as the door clicked open.

Four foot-stomps later, the little girl barreled into his lap. "Gotcha!"

He wrapped his arms around her. "What? How did you get in here?"

Maggie held a neon pink fishing tackle box in her hand, the container for her nail products. She closed the door and turned the deadbolt. "Keep your door locked."

"Yes, ma'am." He hugged Beks and kissed the top of her head. "Ready for the game?"

"Caps all the way, right, Jeremy?"

Maggie frowned and shook her head. She'd abandoned any hope of her daughter calling him "Mr. Jeremy."

He squeezed her again, and she slid to the sofa next to him. "All the way, Beks. This is our year. You hungry? Popcorn's already in the microwave. You know what button to push, but let me get it out when it's done. Don't want you to burn yourself."

Wrinkles appeared on the girl's forehead. "I'm not a baby."

Amazing how much she'd grown in the three years he'd known them. "No," he said. "You're sure not. But I'll still get the popcorn out when it's ready."

She slid off the couch. "Whatever. Can I get something to drink?"

Maggie set the tackle box on the table. "You know I don't like it when you say "Whatever." And yes, you can have some milk, water, or juice."

"Chocolate milk?"

"Honey, that's got a lot of sugar in it."

Beks planted her hands on her hips. "But I like it."

Jeremy motioned toward the fridge. "Chocolate syrup's next to the milk, but don't use too much, okay?"

"M'kay."

Maggie's lips and eyes narrowed. Uh-oh. Seemed like he'd done a lot of uh-ohing lately.

"Don't do that." She lowered her voice. "I have enough trouble getting her to behave as it is."

"Sorry, Maggie. Just wanted her to feel like this is a special place where—"

"Where she gets whatever she wants? Uh-uh. I'm trying to raise a daughter, not a princess. Her father already spoils her too much. I don't need you doing it too."

He held his palms out. "Okay, okay. I'll back you up from now on. Promise."

She sighed and flicked her hand at him. "Scoot over so I can sit next to the table. And I don't need you backing me up."

He slid over to give her room. "But you said ... so you don't need ... what exactly do you want me to do?"

She sat and shifted to face him. "What do you want for Rebecca?"

Where was this going? "What do I want for her? The best of everything."

"Uh-huh. Well, me too. So how's she going to get that? By having people hand her everything she wants? That's not the way the world works."

"But while she's still so young it—"

She sighed and rolled her eyes. "Decide. Right now. You can be her friend or her father, but you can't be both."

His heart fluttered, and heat flashed through his face. Was that a proposal? "Wha ... I mean, are you ... wait. What?"

She tilted her head downward and arched her eyebrows. "I'm waiting for an answer."

He rubbed his chin. "Um, yes. I mean, father. I want to be her father."

She grinned. "Sorry, we come as a package. You don't get one without the other."

The hair on the back of his neck stood. "Don't want one without the other." He kissed her, hard, and pulled away until he was only inches from her face. "I love you, Maggie. Beks too. I promise I'll—"

A ding from the kitchen area interrupted. "Popcorn's ready! Come get it out. I spilled some milk, but I wiped it up. And the chocolate syrup's all gone."

He kissed Maggie again. "Coming. Don't touch it or you'll burn yourself."

"Hurry up. Mom said she didn't care who wins."

Maggie brushed a hand under her eyes. "That's not entirely accurate. I said I hope the Capitals win, but I won't lose any sleep if they don't."

"Same thing," Beks said.

"You're not losing any sleep either. School night, remember? Winning or losing, you'll be home and in bed by ten."

"But Mom, that's not even—"

Maggie crossed her arms. "It's an hour and a half later than normal. Any argument and we'll go home now."

The girl widened her eyes and looked at Jeremy. He shrugged. "Don't expect me to help. I'll be lucky if she doesn't make me go to bed too."

CHAPTER SIX

S hane backed into the Chick-fil-A parking spot and watched the crowds cycle through the restaurant. Nearly eight p.m. and the place was jumping. He'd taken his lunch break as late as possible, but there were still lines inside. Natalie wasn't at the drive-thru window, so hopefully she'd be working the registers tonight. Today was the third time he'd tried to find her, and if she wasn't there, he'd have to move on to someone else. Too many other women needed him.

He wandered into the restaurant and stopped inside the door. Four employees worked behind the counter, none of them Natalie. He sighed, joined the shortest line, ordered his nugget combo meal—extra Polynesian dipping sauce, please—and found a table where he could keep an eye on everything. He barely got seated when a young man brought his food.

"Can I get you anything else?" the employee asked.

Shane took his food off the tray and peered at the worker's name tag. "No thanks, Artie. I'm good."

"Enjoy your meal."

"Will do. Hey, is Natalie working tonight?"

Artie took the empty tray and smiled. "Sorry, I'm new. I don't think I know her."

"Got it. Well, thanks anyway."

"My pleasure."

Poor Natalie. Perhaps if their paths crossed again, he'd be able to help. Until then, she'd have no choice but to fend for herself. Time to move on.

He dipped a nugget and plopped the morsel into his mouth. The sweetness of the Polynesian sauce almost, but not quite, overpowered the chicken. Perfect. So who would be next? Finding another woman to save was never difficult. Arrest records were posted online, and a few of the area newspapers and TV stations even ran daily features with all the mugshots from the day before. Plenty of options, especially since the situation never improved on its own. The women stayed for whatever reason. Maybe hoping things would get better or something, but they wouldn't. His own childhood taught him that.

If ignoring the problem didn't make it go away, then common sense dictated that another way must be found to resolve the issue. As he'd learned while earning his business degree, conflict required resolution, and of the five possible approaches to solving the matter, competing was the appropriate choice. These women's situations dictated an aggressive response. Compromise or collaboration wouldn't be effective. He had to stand his ground until the conflict was resolved and recognize that if the men went away, so did the problem. And thus far, many men had gone away. The supply was unlimited.

"Sir?"

The new guy was back, probably checking to see if he needed a refill. Shane shook his head. "I'm good."

"Yes, sir. Uh, I asked one of the other employees and Natalie is working in the kitchen tonight. Do you want me to give her a message?"

Well now. "That's okay. I'll catch up with her later. Appreciate you getting the info though."

"My pleasure."

Shane raised a finger. "Do you guys get in trouble if you don't say that?"

The kid straightened and peered up front. "I, uh, well … see, we're supposed to … uh …"

"Forget I asked."

His shoulders dropped, and he hurried to the opposite side of the restaurant.

Shane finished his lunch in peace and checked the store's closing time on his way out. Eleven p.m. Same time his own shift ended. If Natalie was working the kitchen, she'd probably have to stay and clean too. That meant midnight or later before she got off work. Plenty of time for him to get back here and follow her home. Once he had that information, doors would open, and the real work would begin.

First, he needed to confirm her husband or boyfriend was truly abusing her. It wouldn't do to kill an innocent man. There were few enough of those around as it was. Once he verified the man was guilty, that's when things got especially interesting. The death had to look like an accident or at least a random crime. There could be nothing linking the victim back to him. Sadly, that meant the women he saved might never know who'd rescued them. Such was the price to be paid.

Sooner or later though, he'd be caught. No point in being naïve about it. A true analysis of the strengths and weaknesses of his activities included the possibility that something would go wrong. There was simply no way to cover every potential variable. The best he could do was minimize the risk as long as possible. Not for his sake, but for the women waiting on him to step forward.

He pulled out of the parking lot and headed back to work. Things were slowing down at the call center, what with Christmas only a few months away. That was par for the course for the collections industry. People were interested in adding to their debt, not paying it off. It'd be that way until February or so when tax refunds started coming in. Then there'd be a frenzy for four months as the agencies negotiated with debtors to offer onetime deals to pay off what they owed. Until then, it would be business as usual, with each shift struggling to meet their quota while upper management sent memos encouraging everyone to just try harder. Sure. Maybe when you start sharing your quarterly bonuses with the rest of us.

Moving up the corporate ladder was a faded dream. Work hard, they said. Apply yourself. Get noticed. Perform and be recognized. There's no limit to where you can go. All solid advice until you watch your boss' hunting buddy with a GED and no college get promoted ahead of you. Mention it to HR and get labeled as a troublemaker. Quit for greener pastures and learn that it doesn't matter where you go. You'll find the same situation everywhere.

No worries though. Employment meant a paycheck. A way to pay the bills. Nothing more. No job was going to define him. That was his father's generation. These days it was all about finding a balance and maintaining social responsibility, and he'd done that. Some might call it a sense of purpose, but that would be underselling the idea. It was the sole reason he lived.

And the sole reason others died.

....

Shane got lucky. Natalie left work a little after midnight, and he watched from a back spot in the parking lot as she broke off from the small group of employees and climbed into a waiting car, an older goldish-colored Camry. The vehicle passed in front of him, pulled out of the lot, then paused at the red light and turned right. A man drove the car, but was it him? The one who'd left the bruises on her arm? It was too dark to get a good look at the guy. Could've been her father or brother or boyfriend.

There were a few other cars on the road, though most of Charlotte slept at this time of night. He maintained a safe distance, but close enough he could keep up if they sped through a yellow. Less than five minutes after leaving work, the driver of the Camry switched on the left blinker and turned into an apartment complex.

Shane continued straight, passed the car, and eyed the huge complex. Had to be at least a dozen large buildings back there. If he didn't stay close, he might never find her. He made a quick u-turn at a 7-11 and pulled into the complex's entrance. Off to the right, taillights crested a hill and disappeared from view. He followed them, bouncing over speed bumps as he tried to catch the car. All parking seemed to be around the buildings, rather than in a garage, so he'd have a chance of spotting them. He came over the rise in time to see the brake lights go off ahead and to the left. He slowed as he approached, careful to not look directly at the couple as they got out of their car.

The lights around the building, most of them actually working, gave Shane a good look at the couple. The man seemed to be older than Natalie, though not so much that he couldn't be her boyfriend. He was almost as thin as she was and wore clothes that were at least two sizes too big. It reminded him of a picture one of his employees kept on her desk. A Shar-Pei. Too much skin, not enough dog. The pair walked toward the closest building, oblivious to Shane as he eased past. A few steps into their journey, the man placed his hand on Natalie's back. His sudden movement caused a reaction in her so brief that the untrained eye would've missed it.

But not Shane. He'd seen it, and that was all he needed to know. Natalie had flinched.

The man had to die.

CHAPTER SEVEN

Jeremy didn't get much sleep. The girls left before the game ended, and the Caps pulled out a victory, though he couldn't tell you any of the details. His mind filled with questions after Maggie's proposal. What kind of wedding would she want? A justice of the peace would work just fine for him, but her? And the ring? Should he buy one or let her pick it out? Was he supposed to arrange everything? His first wife, Holly, had done all the planning back when they got married, leaving him blissfully unaware of what was involved. Would Maggie want to do the same thing? And did they need to do some sort of formal announcement? Or was it supposed to be a secret? As if he had anyone to tell. Neither of them had many friends, and any family was of the second-cousin-twice-removed variety. Maggie went home last night without any further discussion on the issue. In fact, it was as if nothing had changed other than his heart rate.

She'd be at work by now and would call soon. Should he bring it up if she didn't? The proposal was clearly unplanned. Maybe. Have to make sure she's still okay with it today. Lord knows he was.

After the trauma of the last few months, things seemed to have turned a corner. They'd settled into comfortable routines and allowed optimism to creep back into their lives. Maggie's reduced commute helped, and so far, her travel time had been limited. Janice, Director Bailey's former assistant, had retired and become an on-call babysitter, though most times it was she who phoned and asked if it was okay to watch Beks. And now that he was semi-retired, life seemed easier. No more bureaucracy. No more long nights spent in some motel. No more Cronfeld headaches.

Only one thing still bothered him. The promise. The unfinished business with Holly's murder. Getting married now would mean his past still hung over him. Maggie knew that and still chose to move forward, but could he do the same? Maybe, at least for a while. Maggie's proposal made it clear, not in so many words of course, that he should not forget what happened, but realize there was nothing he could do about it. With her help, the guilt had eased somewhat. The pain would never go away, and sometimes flared at the oddest moments, but the emotions no longer consumed him. Still, it felt like a chapter in his life with no closure. Like a book with a page torn out right at the end. It pecked away at him, stealing moments of peace.

Maybe Maggie was right. She was so much stronger in her beliefs. Things he hadn't thought about since he was a kid in Sunday school. She'd said that Holly and Miranda's justice would come. God would see to it. The real question, she said, was how long would it be before he could accept that some things were beyond his control? It was a question he still hadn't answered, and until he saw the murder book, he *couldn't* answer. If there was any chance he could move the investigation forward, he had to know. And he had to know *before* they got married. It was only fair, right?

He massaged his temples in tiny circles. Fair to whom? Him or Maggie or Holly? All or none?

Right on cue, the phone rang, and he took a deep breath before answering. "Morning."

"Hey," Maggie said. "Sleep well?"

"Sure. You?"

"Liar."

"Had a lot to think about, you know?"

The silence lasted for several heartbeats. "Listen, I didn't mean to put you on the spot last night. If you want to—"

"No take-backs. You asked, I accepted. End of story. Truth be told, I was getting tired of you chasing me anyway. I guess you wore me down."

"Right. I figured we'd both die of old age before *you* got around to asking. So how do we ... I mean, what do you ... argh. How does this work?"

"Well, I've got a pretty good government pension and a couple of thousand in savings, so I guess I need to see a lawyer about a prenup first."

She laughed. "Idiot. If I had any friends, they'd tell me I could do better than you."

He rubbed his hand across his chest. "And they'd be right."

"No, Jeremy. They wouldn't be. I see you with Rebecca, and I think

..." She sniffled. "You're going to ruin my makeup."

A wave of lightness flowed through his body. "We're really going to do this, huh?"

"Yeah, we are."

"You talked to Beks about it yet?"

"Nah. Haven't planned that far ahead. We'll tell her together after we get a few things worked out."

He cleared his throat. "Um, were you planning to ask when you came over, or ..."

"Or what? Spur of the moment of truth? Call it a mix of the two. Does it matter?"

"Not to me," he said. "But I don't want you to feel like you blurted it out and now you're stuck with me."

"Jeremy Winter, do you want to be my husband or my friend?"

He grinned. "Can I be both?"

"Yeah," she said. "You'd better be."

After a few more minutes of teenager-in-love talk, they said their goodbyes. Maggie said she'd call again after work. Maybe at lunch if she had time. He said he had some running around to do anyway, and both agreed to keep the weekend open to start figuring out plans.

After hanging up, he sat on a barstool at the kitchen counter and dragged his laptop in front of him. He had to write the chapter ending on Holly and Miranda before getting married. It was the only way for his future to be unwritten. While the computer booted, he reached and grabbed the coffeepot. Cold. The two-hour timer had shut the unit off. He glared at the microwave and shook his head. Years ago, he'd reheated his coffee one time. Never again. If microwaving cold coffee wasn't a crime, it should be. A felony, not a misdemeanor. The computer waited for his input, and he typed his password. After the whirring sound stopped, he opened his web browser and searched for the Frederick Police Department. If all went according to plan, one more meeting with Detective Pronger was all he needed. After that, he'd have access to everything the investigators knew about the deaths.

He couldn't ask Maggie to help, and Pronger would offer no more assistance. Jeremy had no choice.

He was going to steal the murder book.

CHAPTER EIGHT

Jeremy browsed the diner's menu and decided on the special: crab cakes with two sides. He'd arrived early so he could get a table in the back corner and position himself for a good view of Detective Pronger's arrival. It took some convincing, but the cop had agreed to meet him here for dinner, Jeremy's treat. A way to ask just a couple more questions, maybe get a look at one or two photos of the murder scene, then be out of the officer's life forever.

A quick bit of research told him that the Pronger family lived in Middletown, a decent drive west of Frederick. He chose this restaurant because it was far closer for the detective to head home from here than to stop back by the station. The place was more than half full, so the sounds of dishes clanging, people chatting, and the occasional cough or laugh would cover their talk. The noise also masked the rumbling from his stomach as the smell of fried whatever wafted from the kitchen, over the display of fresh pies, and across the dining area, before finally settling on him like a heavy dew.

Headlights swept across the diner's windows as a dark sedan pulled into the parking lot, found a spot, and stopped. Pronger stepped out and pulled on his suit jacket. He strode toward the restaurant, a thick binder in his hand. Despite the clear weather, he paused to shuffle his feet on the indoor/outdoor carpeting at the entrance. Jeremy raised his hand, the two men made eye contact, and the detective nodded before sitting and laying the binder on the table.

"Thanks again," Jeremy said. "Just got to scratch that itch one last time, you know?"

"I do appreciate how difficult this must be for you, especially with your background in law enforcement. As I told you on the phone, it's a very gray area even allowing you to look at some of the photos, but since you're not a suspect, well ..."

"Professional courtesy?"

"No. One husband to another. I thought about it, and I know what I'd do if it was my family."

The waitress dropped off a couple of glasses of water and clicked her pen. "What can I get you?"

Jeremy pointed at his menu. "I'll have the special."

"Comes with two vegetables," the waitress said.

"Surprise me."

She scribbled on her pad, then peered over her glasses at Pronger. "Fried chicken, mashed potatoes, and corn?"

He winked at her. "You know me too well, Gayle. And yes, I'm aware the chicken takes an extra twenty-five minutes, but it's worth it."

Jeremy held up one finger. "Check comes here."

"You got it," the woman said. "Save room for blueberry pie. The berries are still fresh."

She refilled the water glasses at the next table before heading to drop off their order.

"She's right," Pronger said. "Save room for dessert. They make their pies from scratch. My kids would eat a whole one if I'd let them."

"Will do. Hate to be blunt, but can I take a look at the photos before we eat? I don't want to keep you here late. I know what being a cop is like, and the sooner we're done, the sooner you can head home to your family."

The detective placed a couple of napkins on top of the folder and slid it across the table. "No prints, okay? Nothing comes out of the binder. Keep it on the table, and if Gayle or anyone else comes close, shut it. Oh, and keep your phone in your pocket."

He's got a cop's paranoia. Jeremy used the napkins to flip open the binder. First impression was that he'd seen a thousand just like this one. Official forms mixed with scraps of paper mixed with photos mixed with newspaper clippings. Only thing was, none of the others he'd seen had pictures of his dead wife in them. He skipped through the forms, figuring Pronger already told him pretty much everything that was in them. The articles from the paper were the same ones he'd read dozens of times. He paused before flipping to the photos.

He'd pictured them a million times in his mind, but his words to victims' families echoed. Don't look. Remember them as they were, not as they are. Once seen, the images stayed with you forever. He knew it was true. The images he'd seen of strangers over the years were still with him.

Pronger reached for the binder. "May I?"

Jeremy drew both lips into his mouth, exhaled loudly through his nose, and nodded.

The detective held the folder below the table's edge and flipped a few pages before sliding it back. "Start from there. If you want to see photos of the vic—your wife, they're all before that one. The autopsy report is right after the last photo."

"Tha—" He cleared his throat. "Thanks."

Jeremy studied each photo. There were several of the parking lot from various angles. The crime scene tape was still there, and it appeared nothing had been moved other than the bodies. A shopping cart rested against the bumper of a red SUV. Four large cartons of diapers filled the basket, and the rack underneath held an oversize rectangular box with a new car seat atop it. He ran his hand over his mouth. The cardboard box contained a crib, waiting for him to put together. It still sat unassembled somewhere in a police evidence room.

He swallowed hard and turned to the next photo. There were plenty of other vehicles in the lot. He hovered his finger over them one at a time and stared as if they could reveal what they'd seen.

"I know what you're thinking," Pronger said. "Did we run the tags on all of them? Of course. Nothing stood out."

Jeremy moved on. A few photos of the crowd followed, obviously taken covertly. Was the killer in there somewhere? Maybe, but probably not. With this many people, too risky that someone had seen something and could point him out. Even though no witness had ever come forward, someone knew. Had to. Someone always knew. Either they saw the murder or heard about it when the shooter got too drunk or too high or too stupid.

He flipped a few more pages and saw more of the same. Generic photos. No help. The truth might be in there somewhere, but he wasn't going to find it in the few minutes before his dinner arrived. He'd already seen the autopsy report years ago and skipped over it for now. The last few pages were handwritten notes, presumably from investigators. On the inside back cover of the binder was a plastic pouch containing a USB flash drive.

"What's this?" he asked.

"Copy of the 911 call. They get deleted after a year unless we manually back them up. You heard it, right?"

He had, and like everything else with this case, it wasn't helpful. The flash drive did create a problem though. Unlike all the other material in the folder, he wasn't going to be able to photograph the 911 call. He'd have to take it and make a copy.

The waitress headed their way with plates of food, and Jeremy pushed the binder back across the table. "Be right back with more water," she said. The crab cakes were good, the fried chicken looked better. The waitress' selection of coleslaw and creamed corn as his sides was spot on, a point he made when she came back.

The men ate mostly in silence, avoiding the shoptalk that cops often shared. The bond between members of law enforcement was as undeniable as it was sketchy. We may not know each other. We may not like each other. We sure don't always agree with each other. But push comes to shove, I've got his back and he's got mine. You mess with one of us, you mess with all of us.

The waitress returned after a while and smiled. "Sure you won't have any dessert?"

Jeremy patted his stomach. "Can't do it, but if you'd box up a blueberry pie for my friend to take home, I'd appreciate it."

"Oh, no," Pronger said. "That's quite—"

Jeremy held up his hand. "I insist. How about a tub of ice cream to go with it?"

The waitress scribbled on her pad again. "I'll go get them both ready."

The detective checked his watch. "That's very kind. My waistline doesn't appreciate it, but my wife and kids sure will."

"Least I can do. I know what a headache I can be. You're a patient man, and I am truly grateful for your help."

Pronger shrugged. "Sorry I couldn't do more. I hope this gives you some closure or at least lets you move on without worrying there's something you don't know about the case. Listen to me. 'The case.' Like that's all it is."

"No sweat," Jeremy said. "I get it. Hard not to see it that way after so long. It's not a knock on you. I do—did—the same thing back at the Bureau. To us, it was a case, not a memory. Doesn't mean we forget the people involved. Just means we found a way to deal with it."

"I can't imagine. I read up on you, you know? Some of the cases you were involved in?" He shook his head. "Do the things people do to each other still surprise me? You bet they do."

The waitress placed her hand on Pronger's back and set a bag on the table. "You'll want to head straight home with that if you don't want cold pie and melted ice cream."

The men stood and shook hands.

"Thanks for dinner," Pronger said. "I promise I'll call the instant we get any new information."

"No problem. Thank your wife for me, would you? I know you miss enough dinners at home without some crotchety old guy making you miss another one."

Pronger waved his goodbye and headed out the door toward his car. When he'd pulled away, Jeremy motioned for the waitress. "Tell you what. I think I will try a piece of that blueberry pie. No ice cream though. And some coffee."

She gave him a look and retrieved the check. "Decaf?"

"No, the hard stuff please."

It was going to be a long night, but there was no sense hurrying. He knew where the detective lived.

CHAPTER NINE

Jeremy parked down the street from the Prongers' home and walked toward the house. He'd opted to bring the cane to keep his heart rate low, and he winced each time it clacked on the pavement. There were no sidewalks, but there was a curb, and he stayed near it and moved at a steady pace. Close to midnight. Just a guy with a limp out for a late-night walk. A few of the homes had porch lights on, but there were no streetlights. He scanned the area regularly for any sight of headlights that might indicate a patrol car cruising the neighborhood. The houses were on the small side and most, like the Prongers', had only a one-car garage. Jeremy's plan hinged on a couple of important details.

First, the detective's car needed to be parked outside. The Google satellite image showed him all he needed to know, so he hadn't risked a drive-by. If the vehicle wasn't outside, breaking and entering a garage wasn't a crime he was prepared to explain. Second, the murder book had to still be in the car, which was highly likely since it wasn't the type of thing you wanted to bring into a house with kids. If the binder was there, he'd grab it, then drive somewhere to photograph the contents before returning everything to Pronger's car. The USB drive was a problem. He didn't think to bring his laptop so he had no way to copy it. Not much of a thief.

As he got closer, he could see that the first hurdle was overcome. The dark sedan sat parked in the driveway. Good man. Let your wife park in the garage. Easier for her on those cold mornings. The porch light was on and created an arc of brightness into the yard and onto the driver side of the car.

He forced himself to keep his mouth closed and breathe through his nose in an attempt to control his heart rate. He could turn around, walk back to his car, and drive home now and no crime would have been committed. No crime other than knowing that he'd never be able to let it go. That his past would always taint his future, and that wouldn't be fair to Maggie or Beks.

Maggie. What would she say if she had any idea what he was considering? He could hear her voice telling him he was an idiot. That he jeopardized everything they had together. What if he got caught? If he was charged with anything, he felt pretty sure he'd only get probation based on the circumstances. Unless Pronger wanted to push it, that is. And if he wasn't caught? Should he tell Maggie about this when, one way or another, he was satisfied he'd done all he could to bring justice to Holly and Miranda? They'd agreed there'd be no more secrets after he told her about Afghanistan. He'd have to tell her, and he'd have to do it before they were married. And why, if the questions were so big, was he still standing in a stranger's driveway contemplating a theft?

His gloved hand slid along the car's side, and he bent to peek inside the windows. Too dark to see much. Didn't look like the binder was in there, but it could be on the floorboard. Did the vehicle have a security system? If he tried to open the door and an alarm went off, he'd have to run. Not a fun thing for a man with a cane. And what if there was no alarm but the doors were locked? What then?

He checked the house again. Still no lights on inside and no sign of movement.

He squatted and edged his thumb under the front passenger door handle and swallowed hard. The point of no return.

His heart raced as he eased his hand upward, waiting for the click of the door opening and the blare of an alarm sounding.

Nothing.

He raised the handle again. The door was locked, but no alarm went off.

A get-out-of-jail-free card. He could walk away now, knowing he'd done what he could.

Unless the driver's door was unlocked.

He scanned the area again before half-standing and moving to the other side of the car. From here, if anyone peered out the home's windows, he'd be in clear view. No time for stealth. He clenched his jaw and raised the door handle, hoping for the click.

He got it. The interior light came on and he scanned the inside.

Nothing front or back. He ran his hand under each seat. Old french fries, a few coins, a straw wrapper, and a used Kleenex. *That settles that. Pronger must have taken the file—*

Maybe it's in the trunk.

He found the release button and pushed it. The trunk popped open, and he closed the door as quietly as he could before moving to the rear of the vehicle. He lifted it just enough so the light came on.

There. The binder lay next to a long-handled ice scraper, a mangled roll of crime scene tape, and a fire extinguisher. He grabbed the file and pushed the trunk until he heard it latch, then hurried back to his car. Once there, he pulled away to find someplace to park and take photos of the contents.

He jumped on I-70 heading west and exited when he spotted a 24-hour McDonald's. There, he backed into a spot, laid the folder beside him, and began snapping photos with his phone. When he came to the first of the pictures of his wife's body, he froze. *Focus on the job at hand. Take the photo and move on. There will be time to deal with the emotions later.*

When he'd finished, he pulled the flash drive from its pouch and struggled to come up with a way to copy it. Only one solution he could think of. Replace the binder in the trunk, then drive home, copy the drive, and speed back to replace the original in its pouch. Still plenty of time before Pronger would head to work. He dropped the drive in the cup holder and headed back to the detective's home.

Forty minutes. That's how long he'd been gone. A couple more minutes and the folder would be back in the trunk. His mind ran through scenarios. What if something happened, and he didn't replace the USB drive before Pronger left for work? Not much he could do except hope the detective didn't check the binder before placing it back in the file cabinet. And what if Jeremy's investigation uncovered new information? Would he share that with the cops, and if he did, how could he do it without letting on that he'd copied the file?

Don't see how criminals do it. Too much to worry about. Too many things could go wrong. He scratched his chest and took a deep breath as he turned onto Pronger's street.

One step at a time. Don't get ahead of yourself. Replace the binder in the trunk and—

He braked and looked around. Right street. Right house.

But Pronger's car was gone.

Jeremy pulled around the corner and stopped. He wiped the back of his hand across his forehead and squeezed the steering wheel. What now? Nearly two a.m. Where was Pronger, or more importantly, his car? A missing flash drive might go unnoticed, but an entire folder? No way.

Maybe the detective got called out on a case. It'd have to be a shooting or something pretty bad, or he would've waited until morning. That didn't seem likely though. Pronger said they only got two or three murders a year, so what were the odds one would happen tonight?

He drove away from the neighborhood and headed back to Frederick. If he cruised around, maybe he'd spot the flashing blues somewhere. No idea what he'd do then, but as Maggie liked to say, he'd cross that bridge over troubled water when he came to it.

Two hours later, he pulled into a Sunoco and filled his tank. No sign of any police activity. He'd seen a couple of patrol cars, but neither was in a hurry to get anywhere. Pronger's vehicle wasn't at the police station as far as he could tell, but the cops had a private parking garage so the car might be in there.

A little after four. The detective probably went to work around eight. Plenty of time to make one more trip past his house just in case he'd returned home. And if the car wasn't there?

Better start working on a good lie because there'd only be one suspect in the theft.

Wonder how Maggie would feel about a jail wedding?

CHAPTER TEN

"Hey. You awake?"

Jeremy grunted his response into the phone. Maggie's call came earlier than usual, and he was exhausted, worried, and afraid. Pronger would arrive at work soon, and when he checked his trunk, he'd discover the binder was gone. Things would go bad quickly.

"So, can you?" Maggie asked.

"Can I what?"

"What's with you this morning? Can you watch Rebecca today? She's running a low-grade fever, and I want to keep her home from school."

He used his thumb and forefinger to rub his eyes. "Yeah. No problem. Let me grab a quick shower and then I'll head over."

"You sure? I can call Janice if I need to."

"No, no. I'll handle it." He stood, stretched, and yawned. "Be there in a few."

He laid the phone on the table next to the murder book. What to do with that thing? He couldn't leave it out in the open, but hiding the binder made him look like, well, a thief. Would Pronger get a search warrant? Could he? No doubt Jeremy had committed a crime, but what? Theft of government property, maybe? In the hierarchy of criminal activities, this had to be somewhere near jaywalking, but he'd done that too. If he were ever charged with anything, a slap on the wrist would probably be the outcome, especially after he explained the reason he needed the information. Truth be told, it wasn't the police he feared.

He needed to tell Maggie what he'd done. The worst would be if something happened and it came as a surprise. He placed the folder high on a bookshelf, well out of Rebecca's reach. He'd tell Maggie this morning before she left for work. Give her time to settle down before she came home at the end of the day. She'd understand. Not approve, but understand.

But if that was true, why was he so afraid?

. . . .

Maggie's face reddened, and her voice shook. "You're kidding, right? Tell me you didn't do that."

He avoided her gaze. "Maggie, I'm sorry. I just wanted—"

"What? You wanted what? To screw everything up? Because that's what you did, you know."

Everything? What does that mean? "I wanted this behind us. I didn't want to spend the rest of my life wondering if—"

"*Your* life. What about *our* lives? Remember that? You, me, Rebecca? And don't you dare give me that 'I did it for us' garbage."

"What do you want me to say? Tell me what you want me to do, and I'll do it."

She jabbed her finger at him. "Uh-uh. No way you get out of this that easy. How can anyone be that stupid? Fix it. Whatever you have to do, fix it. You know I'm now an accomplice, right? You told an FBI agent you committed a crime. What am I supposed to do with that information?"

He sighed and stretched his neck. "Do whatever you have to do. If it'll make you feel better, turn me in."

She threw a sofa pillow across the room and low-yelled through clenched teeth. "You selfish son of—"

Beks' cough interrupted the tirade. The little girl stood in the hallway, her eyes wide and a stuffed giraffe clutched to her chest.

"Hey, baby," Maggie said. She walked to her daughter and placed her hand on the girl's forehead. "You're supposed to be in bed."

Jeremy stood and wiped his palms on his jeans. "She still feel hot?"

"Not too bad. She's due for more cough medicine at nine." She turned and narrowed her eyes. "Think you can handle that?"

His chest hollowed. "I'll take care of it."

She kissed Beks and guided the girl back to her bed. After a moment, she returned to the living room, snatched her purse off the table, and headed toward the door. "Figure this out, Jeremy. Today."

"I'll—"

The door slammed behind her.

CHAPTER ELEVEN

It'd been almost a week since Shane followed Natalie and her boyfriend home, and he now had everything he needed to move forward. The man's name was Eddie Rodman. He worked as a self-employed auto mechanic. An oily job for an oily man. He operated his all-cash and likely unreported business out of a metal shed a few miles away from his apartment. The building sat among a dozen other similar structures, most abandoned, down a gravel road behind a strip mall.

Eddie's work allowed him the flexibility to set his own hours, giving him the opportunity to hang with his friends whenever he wanted. Natalie, on the other hand, spent her evenings—and sometimes mornings too—at Chick-fil-A.

Shane shifted lower in his car's seat and glanced at the clock. Nine-thirty in the morning. If Eddie was going to his shop today, he'd be leaving soon. Natalie worked the late shift last night so probably wouldn't head in until later today. If that was the case, her boyfriend usually returned home in time to give her a ride.

The apartment door opened and Eddie staggered out wearing ripped jeans splotched with grease stains and a matching T-shirt. The back of his sleeveless denim jacket had an oversize patch of a naked girl silhouette, the kind you sometimes saw on the mud flaps of semis on the highway. It was his normal work outfit, though truth be told, it wasn't much different from his non-work outfit. The man coughed violently and spat on the ground before climbing into his Camry and pulling out of the lot.

Shane counted to ten before following Eddie and watching him turn left toward the shed. It'd take the man fifteen or twenty minutes to open his shop and get to work. Enough time for Shane to grab a late breakfast at a drive-thru. He swung into a Bojangles and ordered two steak biscuits and a small coffee with two creams and three sugars, then cruised toward the mechanic's shed.

He parked beside the strip mall where he could keep an eye on things. The building was older, so no security cameras outside. Nothing but empty fields on either side of the place. Plenty of traffic passed on the street behind him, so anyone paying attention might see him parked there, but no one paid attention anymore. And even if he was seen, so what? Per standard operating procedure, he'd removed the battery from his phone before leaving home and wouldn't turn the device back on until he was miles away. If anyone ever went looking, he had proof he was nowhere near the scene.

The Camry was in its usual spot beside the shed, and the building's lift-up door was wide open. Inside, a vehicle—late-model Honda of some sort—had its front end jacked high above the packed dirt floor. A pile of greasy rags sat in one corner, begging to be lit. Shane shook his head. Too soon for another fire.

Eddie was leaning against an oil drum and smoking a cigarette. After a minute, he flicked the butt outside the shed, next to two ancient-looking vehicles that had long ago given up hope of being repaired. The mechanic arched his back and yawned, then knelt and scooted under the Honda on his back.

Shane took a bite of biscuit and checked his surroundings before pulling on a pair of gloves and stepping outside. A line of gray clouds filled the western horizon, a promise of the late August storms headed their way. Better hurry and get it done. Don't want to get mud on my khakis.

He jogged along the gravel road, head tilted downward, and veered off to the side once he neared the shed. If Eddie came out from under the car, he wouldn't be able to spot his stalker. The Honda's radio blared AC/DC's "Highway to Hell" at a level the speakers couldn't handle. Highway to hell. Karma. If he'd been a religious man, he might even call it a sign from God. But, unlike most of the Bible belt, he didn't even claim to be a believer, much less actually buy into the propaganda. Watching your father beat your mother tended to drown any God-fearing inclinations you may have.

After a quick peek behind him, Shane hunched lower and crept behind the two abandoned cars, his attention focused on the ground. Broken glass, rusted metal, and empty beer cans were strewn everywhere. He made a mental note to check the last time he had a tetanus shot, then skulked behind the shed.

AC/DC gave way to "Stairway to Heaven." The DJ must be really bored if he's trying to pair songs like that, though "Don't Fear the Reaper" would be a good choice for the next tune. But as lengthy as the current song was, chances were he'd be long gone before it ended. The clank of metal against metal, followed immediately by a muted stream of profanity, confirmed Eddie was still at work.

Shane edged along the building's side until he could barely peek inside. No worries. A pair of legs extended from under the front passenger side, directly under the Honda's engine.

He leaned farther and affirmed his suspicion. The car's front end was held up with a pair of old jacks. Great for keeping the vehicle elevated. Not so great if there was any side-to-side motion while the car was raised.

From this point, he'd have to move quickly. If Eddie spotted him, things could go south in a hurry, but it was unlikely he'd be able to get out from under the car before being hit by the knowledge of what was about to happen.

Shane grinned. *Before it hit him hard.*

He pulled his gloves tighter and took a deep breath. He'd need enough momentum to make sure the car fell on the first attempt, and the angle he approached from was tight. There was maybe two feet between the driver's side of the car and the shed wall. At five-foot-ten and a hundred sixty pounds, he'd need all the speed he could muster.

He peeked behind him, then took a few steps back. Led Zeppelin was barely halfway through their classic rock song. No one else around and—

Eddie's right hand appeared from under the Honda, patting the ground, likely searching for some tool that wasn't there.

No time.

Shane ran toward the vehicle and thrust his body against the car's front. The mechanic screamed as he saw his destiny rushing toward him.

The Honda rocked side-to-side, but it wasn't going to be enough to unbalance the jacks. Eddie, given a second chance at life, chose to make the worst decision possible. Instead of scrambling backward out from under the car, he scooted toward his attacker.

Shane placed his back against the car just above the tire, planted his feet on the shed's wall, and pushed.

The mechanic finally realized the fate that befell him. "What the—"

The vehicle gave way to gravity as the angle of the jacks grew. Eddie's scream was cut short as the Honda's front bumper impacted the ground, then made three or four more bounces, each smaller than the last.

Shane straightened and placed his hands on his hips while concentrating on slowing his breathing. "Hey, Eddie," he said. "The owner wants to know if you can take a look at the shocks while you're under there."

He circled the car and squatted to check the body. It was an unnecessary step—you don't live through something like that—but one he felt obligated to perform, though he gained no satisfaction from it. Dark blotches already formed an aura around his torso and head as blood soaked into the dirt. Hard to be sure, but it looked like Eddie had been staring straight up when the vehicle hit him.

Shane coughed and fought the urge to vomit. Death didn't bother him—it was the only acceptable outcome after all—but the gore teased bile up his throat. His reactions were always physical, never emotional. The things his father did emptied whatever place Shane's feelings came from. For a while, he'd hoped taking care of people like Eddie would refill the emotions. Now he knew better and accepted it as a gift. Emotions clouded objectivity and were a threat to continuing success.

Besides, the men who died didn't warrant sorrow or grief. A nanosecond's suffering by Eddie was never going to balance the lifetime of abusive memories Natalie would harbor. He stood and backed away.

He shuffled back the way he'd come, careful to obliterate any shoe prints. "Stairway to Heaven" still flowed from the radio, but the song was nearing its end. Time to go.

Still no sign of anyone else nearby. He hurried along the gravel road to his vehicle and drove away from the strip mall. Eddie was dead. Natalie was safe. And he still had time for a nap before work this afternoon.

All in all, a good morning. His thigh muscles ached a bit from the strain of pushing—

The wall. His shoe prints were on the shed's wall.

His heart raced, and he licked his lips. Why hadn't he foreseen this as a possible weakness in his plan? Days of plotting, including site surveillance, and he'd never anticipated not being able to drop the car on the first push. A poor effort on his part. When his employees made mistakes, he used them as a teaching experience. Too many errors though, and he had to fire the worker. He wouldn't be so fortunate if his mistakes were caught.

No big deal. Learn from it and move on. Besides, no one would be looking for something like that at an accident scene.

But better safe than sorry, right?

He pulled through a McDonald's and drove back toward Eddie. No hurry. The important thing is to make sure you're not seen. Aaaand ... of course I'm going to hit this red light.

He turned off the radio and drummed his fingers on the center console. Slow. Down. There's no danger, so don't create any.

The light changed, and he cruised to the strip mall. A few cars were parked out front now, probably employees since the shops opened in a few minutes. Shane edged his car along the side of the building far enough to get a view of the shed. Nothing appeared to have changed. He stepped outside and casually scanned his surroundings. No worries. Hustle down there, erase the prints, then get out of here.

The sputtering of an engine sounded from behind him, and he waited as another employee pulled into the parking lot. The car had seen better days. Its mismatched panels, cracked windshield, and smoky exhaust were telltale signs of the struggle to—no. Surely they weren't here to see Eddie. What were the odds of that? His karma was good, right?

The car backfired, jerked, and came to a stop. No.

The driver cranked the engine several times before it fought its way back to life. Shane caught a whiff of burning oil and turned away. He had to get out of there before anyone saw him.

He scooted into his car and circled behind the building. In his rearview mirror, he watched as the junk car crunched along the gravel road and stopped in front of Eddie's shed. Nothing he could do about it now. If the police took photos, and surely they would, returning later to erase the shoe prints would only highlight their importance. Disposing of any evidence was his best bet.

He stared at his feet. *Man, I really liked these shoes.*

CHAPTER TWELVE

Beks' fever was gone, and the antihistamine in the medicine kept her asleep most of the day. Maggie had texted twice to check on the girl. No phone calls, which could only mean she was still steaming.

There'd been no contact from Pronger either. He must have forgotten the folder was in his trunk or, more likely, was waiting for Jeremy to make the first move. He could call him. Explain what he'd done and ask for forgiveness. The detective was a by-the-numbers kind of cop though. He'd want to file a report, which meant somebody higher up could decide to press charges even if Pronger didn't.

Jeremy twirled his cell phone in his hand and stared blankly at some game show on TV. He needed to make progress on the problem before Maggie got home. She didn't get angry often, but when she did, it was every man for himself. A few days in jail might be the safest place to be right now. He exhaled a steady stream of air. Whoever said that confession is good for the soul must not have been familiar with America's judicial system. Or with Maggie.

He dialed Pronger's number, waited three rings, and got voice mail. "Hey, Detective. This is, uh, Jeremy Winter. Listen, I think we need to talk. Give me a call, would you? Sooner's better than later. Thanks."

He tossed the phone on the sofa and stared at the ceiling. Nothing to do now but wait. He checked the clock. A little after noon. Time to wake Beks and get some lunch in her. Maybe try to call Maggie and smooth things over. His phone buzzed, and he answered on the first ring. That didn't take long.

"Mr. Winter?"

"Hello, Detective Pronger."

"Yes, sir. I'm returning your call."

That's it? Does he not know the binder is missing from his car? Or maybe he does and just wants me to incriminate myself. "Uh, yes. Thank you. Listen, I need to talk to you about, um, a problem I have. We have."

A too-long pause followed. "Mr. Winter, *we* do not have a problem. You do. As I'm sure you're aware, the murder book on your wife's case has gone missing. Theft of official police property is a serious offense. One that could easily lead to jail time. Care to guess who my only suspect is?"

Fess up or hold out? "Why don't you tell me?"

A heavy sigh came through the phone. "You called me, remember? Do I think you took it? Yeah, I do. Now, I was up half the night working a B&E downtown, so I'd appreciate it if we could move this along."

"Yeah, okay. Let's say, hypothetically, I did take the file, but had every intention of returning it? What kind of agreement could we reach in a situation like that?"

"I'm not sure I understand. When a crime is committed, my job is simply to locate and arrest the suspect. The DA would be the one to discuss any deals, not me."

"Of course. But, one cop to another, isn't there—"

"Mr. Winter, we agree that a crime has been committed, do we not?"

"Yeah, but in the grand scheme of things, is this really something you want to pursue? I mean, come on. No harm, no foul, right?"

"Yes, I believe that's in the Constitution somewhere. No harm, no foul."

Was that supposed to be humor or sarcasm? Either was a surprise. "Detective, I'm sorry. Really. I know I've put you in an awkward position. Tell me what I can do to fix this."

"Come into the station. Let's talk about it and go from there."

Right. So I'll be in Maryland, and he can arrest me. He closed his eyes and leaned his head back. Think. There has to be a way out of this. "I screwed up big time. The opportunity presented itself, and I took advantage of the situation. I'm asking for your understanding."

"The opportunity presented itself? Really, Mr. Winter? I'm not buying it. You had Gayle toss ice cream in with the pie. You knew I'd have to go straight home. The whole dinner was a setup. You played on my sympathies."

Jeremy closed his eyes and let his head flop backward onto the couch. "I did, and I'm sorry. Look, I'll return the murder book as soon as I can. Tomorrow morning, okay? Nothing's missing. It's all there. Can we—you—forget all this ever happened? Please?"

"Where is the line, Mr. Winter? The line that says it's okay to break this law, but not that one? I know what you think of me, but look at this situation from my perspective. You broke into an official police vehicle and stole from it. Not only that, but you committed the crime at my house. *My house*. Would you be angry if something like that happened to you? Yes, I believe you would be."

He gritted his teeth. "What do you want me to say, Detective?"

"Bring me the folder tomorrow morning, and we'll discuss it further."

"Fine. Tomorrow morning. Say nine o'clock?"

"Make it ten. I'm working late tonight."

Again? It was becoming a pattern, and patterns meant something. Last night, the detective had been up half the night working a B&E … in downtown Frederick, an area Jeremy reconnoitered at least twice looking for the man. He tapped a finger on his forehead. Downtown consisted of no more than a half-dozen blocks. All one- or two-story buildings. If there'd been police activity, he'd have seen it. Didn't mean anything, really. But was he curious? You bet he was.

Pronger cleared his throat. "Are you still there, Mr. Winter?"

"Yeah, I'm still here. If you don't mind me asking, everything okay at your B&E? They get much?"

"What? Standard robbery. Turned out not to be that big of a deal. Probably someone wanting to score meth with whatever they stole."

"Downtown, right? Seems like a nice area. Guess you never know, huh?"

"No, you don't. Tomorrow morn—"

"See, here's the thing. Last night I drove around looking for you. Cruised every street in downtown several times but didn't spot any active crime scenes. No lights. No tape. Nothing."

Pronger paused before answering. Not long, but enough.

"What's your point, Mr. Winter? We're not the FBI. We don't make a show out of every investigation."

"Right. So what's the address?"

"The address?"

Jeremy leaned forward. "Yes, the address. You know, of the break-in?"

"Why would I share that information with you? Frankly, I'm offended by your questions. Perhaps it's time I talked to our DA about the theft of your wife's file. See what he thinks we—"

"Feel free. And perhaps it's time I made a few calls of my own. Started asking some questions about why a detective at the Frederick Police Department would lie about where he was in the middle of the night. Honestly, I can only come up with a few scenarios, all of them illegal except one. And you'd never do anything illegal, would you? No, I think I only need to make one call. To your wife."

Pronger remained silent for a few seconds before responding. "I don't believe that will be necessary."

"Then we have an agreement. So unless you need the murder book back right away ..."

"At your earliest convenience will be fine."

"Got it. I take no joy in this, Detective." Okay, maybe a little joy.

"We don't see or talk to each other again after you return it."

"No problem. Just one more thing though. Gayle. From the diner. It's her, isn't it?"

Pronger replied by hanging up the phone.

"Yeah," Jeremy said as he pushed himself off the sofa. "It's Gayle."

CHAPTER THIRTEEN

Jeremy tapped his fingers on the dinette table. Beks was in bed and supposedly reading a book but most likely had Netflix turned down low. Maggie sat across from him with a small stack of photos, image side down.

"How'd you know?" she asked. "About Detective Pronger, I mean."

"Once I figured out he was lying about where he'd been, the rest was easy. The waitress was a little too friendly, you know? Put her hand on his back, and he didn't react."

"Maybe she wanted a big tip."

He arched his eyebrows. "I'm just going to leave that one alone."

Her lips turned up for a nanosecond, then she sighed heavily and rested her hand on the photos. "You ready?" she asked.

Jeremy half-nodded. He'd seen the rest of the murder book. All the details on the death of Holly, his wife, and Miranda, his unborn daughter. The official reports, the detectives' notes, the newspaper clippings. Everything was there and told him nothing he didn't already know. All that remained was the USB drive containing the 911 call, which he'd heard years earlier, and the crime scene photos of Holly's corpse.

Maggie kept her hand on top of the pile. "When Mom was killed, I was so angry because you wouldn't let me see her at the scene. But now, well, I'm grateful I don't have that memory. I picture her the way I want to remember her, not as a victim. I know you want to look at these, but you're making the right decision. If there's anything that will help in your investigation, I'll tell you, and then you can decide whether you need to see the photo. You trust me, right? I know what I'm looking for."

"You know I trust you." He forced a smile. "In my weaker moments, I think you're better at the job than I ever was."

She took a deep breath and brushed away a tear before turning over the first photo and holding it so he couldn't see it. "This is a shot of the crime scene from a distance. Looks like it was taken from where the PD thought the shooter stood. Holly is … Holly is on the ground behind a red SUV."

"She drove a black Ford Focus."

"I see it, not far from where she fell. There's a shopping cart close to her head, her purse is on her left shoulder, and a white bag is in her right hand. The cart has four boxes of diapers in the top. Underneath is a new car seat sitting on a brown cardboard box. I can't see any images or writing on the box, so not sure what's in there. The white sack in her hand is from a shop, but I can't make out the name." She swallowed hard and blinked several times. "Honey, there's too much blood on the bag for me to read the store's name."

He reached across the table for her hand. "It's okay. That was all in the report. There's three onesies, a pack of bibs, and some booties in there. The cardboard box has a crib in it. Hold on a sec." He grabbed a box of Kleenex off the kitchen counter, set it between them, and pulled two tissues. "We might need these."

Maggie dabbed at her eyes. "Should've bought a bigger box."

He smiled and patted her hand. "You're doing great, baby."

"The next photo is taken directly over Holly's body. There's, um, there's an obvious blood flow from her neck to under the SUV."

"The bullet nicked her carotid artery. The autopsy report said death came quickly."

Maggie ran her hand across her mouth. "Holly's eyes are closed. She's beautiful, Jeremy."

He nodded and clenched his jaw. Pain and sorrow flooded his chest. Holly's baby bump would be noticeable in the photo. Two lives taken with one bullet. He grabbed another tissue and wiped his eyes. Keep it together. Get through this.

"Want me to keep going?" Maggie asked.

His voice cracked. "Uh-huh."

She squeezed his hand. "Just a few more."

He listened as she described the remaining photos. Standard shots taken from every conceivable angle. Nothing there that would help catch the killer. If a suspect was ever detained, maybe something in the pictures would link him to the crime, but for now, they were merely a photographic documentary of a murder.

Maggie stood, moved behind him, and massaged his shoulders. "You okay?"

"I will be. Thanks for doing this."

"Your promise isn't over. You can never look at those photos. Not without talking to me first. Agreed?"

He looked up. Her red nose and swollen eyes added to the grief already flowing through him. "Agreed. I'm sorry to put you through this, Maggie."

She straightened. "No. Don't you dare apologize for letting me help you. You're not alone in this and never will be. Don't forget that. Now, enough of this for one night. I know a little girl who'd love a night-night kiss."

He stood and hugged her. "I couldn't do this without the two of you."

She buried her face in his shoulder. "I can't stand to see you hurting like this."

"It'll be okay. Really. I'd tell you not to worry about me, but we both know that's not gonna happen."

"Yeah, we do. Is there anything I can do to help?"

He tilted her head back and kissed her forehead. "You're doing it."

. . . .

Near midnight, four hours since they'd reviewed the photos, Jeremy sat alone in the kitchen staring at a half-eaten chicken salad sandwich and almost empty Diet Coke. Maggie went to bed two hours ago but made him promise to stay over. She'd thrown some blankets and pillows on the couch, turned on the NHL Network and muted the sound, and kissed him before turning in. Around eleven, he tiptoed into Beks' room, pulled the covers up higher—that girl tossed and turned like nobody's business— and brushed the wispy red hair off her face. He sat beside the bed a long time, dragging the side of his thumb gently across her cheek and watching her breathe. He wasn't a praying man, sometimes wasn't sure he was even a believer, but he asked God to protect the little girl. Keep her safe from all the things Jeremy had seen.

Going through the photos had been emotional. Draining. Revisiting the murder always hurt and always would. But time healed. What once was an open wound was now stitched and scarred, no different from the damage to his leg. Constantly there, continually reminding. A shrink might say he'd connected the two in his mind. Maybe he had. The trauma of his family's deaths and the mutilation caused by a grenade. Both occurring at the same time.

The doctors told him that if his leg took any more abuse, or if it formed another blood clot, there was a good chance they'd have to amputate. Not to worry though. They were doing wonderful things with prosthetics these days. The thing was, you couldn't amputate memories or the emotions that went with them. Maybe that was as it should be.

He finished the sandwich while thinking through the photos. Maggie's descriptions made it clear that none of them provided useful information. He didn't expect them to but had to make sure. With no bullet or shell casing ever found and no hard evidence recovered from the body, car, or home, there was nothing to go on without a motive. The Frederick PD listed it as an attempted robbery, with the thought being the shooter got scared and ran off before taking the purse.

But there was no gunpowder stippling, meaning the attacker had been at least a few feet away. Why not closer so they could maintain control? Why not just snatch Holly's purse and run? It didn't make sense, and the detectives' notes asked the same questions. There was also the possibility that the shooting was an accident. That someone's gun went off, maybe while they were getting in or out of their car, and they either didn't know they'd shot someone or panicked and fled. While highly unlikely, it had to be considered.

The other theory was that Holly wasn't the target. Either the shooter misidentified her or was aiming at someone else. To Jeremy, this made the most sense, but he couldn't prove it. No witness came forward. No anonymous tips. Nothing in the murder book pointed to even a hint of a suspect.

So far, it was the perfect crime, but one without a reason. Jeremy had seen his share of random deaths, but never without a motive. Serial killers murdered but did so for a purpose, be it because voices told them to or they enjoyed it, or Mommy was mean or any of a thousand reasons. But Holly's death didn't seem to fit. A lucky—or unlucky—shot from a distance. No other murders linked to this one. Nothing.

He'd heard the 911 call years ago and reread the transcript of it just this morning. The anonymous caller didn't do much besides report that she'd seen a body. The phone was a burner, a 7-11 Speak Out purchased forty-two days before the murder according to AT&T. Four people—a man, a woman, and two teenage girls—bought a phone on that day, and all had been identified. By the time detectives spoke to them, only the man still had the mobile he'd bought, and it wasn't a match for the caller. The other three claimed they'd tossed their cells after the minutes expired. None of the women were considered suspects.

The detectives tried to subpoena the records of the phones in hopes they could identify the 911 caller, but a judge refused their request, stating there wasn't sufficient evidence to warrant an invasion of privacy. There was nothing to indicate the 911 caller could shed any light on the murder then or now, but it was all Jeremy had left. If he could somehow figure out which of the women was the caller, he could tie off the last remaining thread.

He pulled the laptop over and shoved the USB drive into the slot, squeezed in earbuds, and opened the audio file.

A stoic female voice. "Nine one one. What's your emergency?"

"A woman's been shot. I think she's dead."

"Okay, ma'am. Where are you—"

"She's in the parking lot in front of that baby store over on East Thirteenth."

"I need you to—"

"By that Subway."

"Ma'am, can you tell me—"

click

"Ma'am? Ma'am?"

That was it. The caller was obviously upset, but whether that was because she saw the shooting or only saw the body was anyone's guess. Jeremy pulled the right earbud out, scratched as deep in his ear as he could, and put it back in. He hated those things. He listened to the tape again, this time with his eyes closed and a focus on any background noises. Nothing.

According to the police reports, none of the three women who were possible candidates for having the phone sounded anything like the caller. That didn't mean much since her adrenalin was obviously kicking in. Later, her speech would have been lower and less manic. Plus, she could've easily disguised her voice on the 911 call.

Maybe she just didn't want to get involved. Maybe she knew something but didn't know she did. Or maybe she knew everything. Only one way to find out. Jeremy was going to have to identify the caller.

It'd been seventeen years since the murder, so the cell records were most likely long gone. There was another way though. One that wasn't entirely legal. Wait, that wasn't accurate. It wasn't even partially legal. He'd need Maggie's okay to proceed—no more surprises—and he'd need some help to get it done. But if he could pull it off, he'd know who made the 911 call.

CHAPTER FOURTEEN

Shane aligned the edge of the binder clip to the top left corner of a stack of paper and laid the sheets beside his laptop. First things first. The computer finished booting, and he opened the spreadsheet. A database would be better suited to the task, but not so much that setting up the program was worth the effort.

He clicked in cell A28, then filled in the row with all the relevant details. First name, last name, date of death, location, comments, and a rating. On a scale of one to ten, Eddie Rodman's passing came in at an eight. The footprints left on the shed's wall mandated a two-point deduction.

Of the twenty-six names above Eddie, the lowest score was a four, and he'd done that twice, both years earlier. Those deaths caused quite a bit of anxiety, but such things were expected when one was standardizing their methods. In both cases, the weakness occurred in the planning stage. A failure to foresee a possible threat. The old business mantra was true: failing to plan is planning to fail. Since then, he'd increased the amount of time spent following his targets before the death date. The amplified surveillance proved its worth in higher scores and a lower error rate. If you can't measure it, you can't improve it.

He saved the spreadsheet and nudged the laptop to the side. When law enforcement eventually caught him, they'd appreciate the effort he put into maintaining proper records. Recognition and publicity weren't necessary, though they'd be nice when they came, but the widows needed to understand what he'd done for them. How he'd transformed himself and proven that abusers can choose to change.

Just ask Kimberly Westall. Back in college, she'd been his girlfriend. Things were never serious enough to discuss marriage, but they were exclusive. Not dating anyone else, or so he thought.

A night of watching football and drinking beer with his frat brothers changed everything. He'd gone to Kimberly's dorm room looking for some early morning companionship. When he got there, she wasn't alone. Too drunk to think clearly, he'd sagged to the floor and cried. She sent him back to the frat house and told him not to return until he was sober. They could talk about things then.

That afternoon, he'd returned to her dorm. Their argument escalated into a screaming match, and she told him to leave and not come back. Said things were over between them.

In his high school days, this was the part where he'd tell himself he blacked out and couldn't remember anything that happened afterward. That he'd never repeat the sins of his father. None of it was true, of course. He hit her once, his fist plowing into her upper left arm, staggering her backward.

She trembled, and her eyes widened. It was like one of those horror movies where the person is too afraid to even scream. They can't move, so they just stand there shaking and waiting for the inevitable.

Her fear sliced through him. The way she looked at him. Any semblance of affection gone, replaced by terror. Helplessness.

Just like Mom.

He could still feel the rage giving way to the remorse. The pounding in his ears fading as nausea swept through him. His fists opening as he wrapped his arms around himself.

He reached to hold her, tell her he was sorry, and it would never happen again, but she'd whimpered and shuffled back a step. He'd nodded, apologized, and told her he'd leave. She wouldn't have to worry about him again.

Back at the frat house, he'd contemplated suicide. Anything was better than becoming his father. Pills and alcohol would be easy enough. He had to make sure it was obviously self-inflicted though. As far as he knew, his life insurance policy didn't cover suicides. Dad had enough money already.

Dear old dad. There had to be a million more like him out there. To the outside world, he had it made. Great job, plenty of money, beautiful home. All of it true, but not the complete picture. Just because Dad had everything didn't mean his family did too. Whether caused by stress or alcohol or cocaine or whatever, he beat his wife. Not on a regular basis, but often enough, until the day she left him.

Left him. Right. Shane knew better.

That day, on the edge of his unmade bed in a wreck of a room in his frat house, he made his decision. He'd prove that people can change. No suicide. No more hurting women. Kimberly Westall wasn't the first girl he'd hit, but she would be the last. If he was to see fear in someone's eyes again, they would deserve it. He couldn't change their past, but he could eliminate their future.

He grabbed the stack of paper and removed the binder clip. Each of the twenty or so pages contained a photo and details on men charged with domestic violence. The particulars on their daily schedules, at least what he knew so far, were kept on his phone. Easier to update them there, plus always had them handy in case the urge struck.

Each of these men failed to foresee the threat headed their way. They hadn't done their due diligence, like a board of directors being blindsided in a hostile takeover.

Weak men.

He fanned the papers as if holding a poker hand.

Weak men who would soon be dead.

CHAPTER FIFTEEN

Jeremy rolled off the sofa around nine and shuffled to the shower. A vague memory of the girls kissing him goodbye hovered in the background. Something had been said about picking up Beks from school, but he had no idea who'd committed to do what. A phone call to Maggie was in order, but not until a cup of hot coffee sat in front of him.

Thirty minutes later, he felt nearly human. The shower removed the haziness, and the coffee awakened his innards. Hopes of a caffeine jolt disappeared decades ago when he'd grown immune to its effects. Go without a heavy dose though, and a headache was sure to appear.

He dialed Maggie, and she answered on the second ring. "Good mornin'," he said. "Busy?"

"Not too bad. Got a trainee assigned to me today, so she'll be my shadow for a while."

"Yeah? Met her yet?"

"Not until after lunch," she said. "You're picking up Rebecca today, right?"

Answers that question. "I am. You working late?"

"Not unless something comes up. My cases right now are all low-level. Good for training Tanessa, but not too exciting."

"Tanessa. That's her name?"

She chuckled. "Look at you, all mister detective and stuff. You've still got it."

His stomach fluttered, and he grinned. "Was there ever any doubt?"

"Nope. What's on your agenda today?"

"Well, that's up to you."

She paused. "Meaning what?"

"Meaning I need your okay to move forward. I want to try to find the

911 caller from Holly's murder."

"Sure, but why do you need my ... are you going to do something that will get you in trouble?"

"Probably not. I mean, I can't guarantee it won't, but there's a chance it might."

She sighed. "And you're not giving me the details because whatever you're planning is at least marginally illegal."

"If you want to know, I'll tell you."

"No, don't. Plausible deniability and all that. Assuming you get caught doing whatever it is I don't know about, what's the worst-case scenario? Are we talking jail time?"

"Maybe, but more likely community service or a fine. Nobody's going to get hurt, Maggie. No one, including me, will ever be in danger, and I promise it will have no effect on you, Beks, or your job."

"Fine. Do whatever you have to but be careful."

"Yes, ma'am."

"And don't forget to pick up Rebecca."

"I won't. Have fun with your trainee. Call if you're going to be late."

"Will do. Leave the weekend open. It's about time we started figuring out some of this marriage stuff."

His mouth was suddenly dry. "Uh, figure out what exactly?"

"Oh, not much. When and where we'll get married, deciding do we stay in an apartment or buy a home or what, switching over everything to one household, you know, little things."

He rubbed his forehead. "Sounds like fun."

She laughed. "Doesn't it though? Don't worry. I'll take care of most of it. All you need to do is stay out of jail. Think you can handle that?"

"I do."

"Nice choice of words. Keep practicing them."

. . . .

An hour later, Jeremy had the outline of a plan. Three women were potential candidates for the 911 caller. Once he found each of them, he'd phone and see if they would agree to talk. Several apps claimed they would do what he wanted and record the conversations, but the reviews all indicated varying degrees of success, and even when they did work, the quality could be questionable. He might only have one chance with each woman.

After installing the top candidate, he dialed the 800 number for his cable company's customer service. That would give him plenty of time to record the call without actually involving anyone else. Though Virginia had a one-person consent law for recordings, many states, including Maryland, required that all parties agree to being recorded. Depending on where the three women now lived, his actions could be illegal if discovered.

He went through four apps before finding one that worked to his satisfaction. Once the other party answered, all he had to do was shake his phone side-to-side to start the recording.

The first woman, Georgia Harding, née Mayer, was easy to locate. A quick Google search of her name provided links to a dozen companies that would, for a price, tell you anything and everything you wanted to know about her. All the information was most likely freely available elsewhere, but he didn't want to take the time to compile everything himself. Not when others had already done it for him. He paid his $10.95 and got a listing of every known detail about her.

Ms. Harding's details pointed to a normal life. There were no news reports, no obituary, and no jail records. The thirty-two-year-old woman now lived in Hagerstown, had been employed at the same job for nearly a decade, good credit, married four years ago to Julius Harding. That was it. Mundane from some people's perspective. Desired from his. He scanned the details again. No phone number. He'd have to go to her home and record her there.

The second woman, Christine Wolf, wasn't much different. He punched in his credit card info again, and her life was laid in front of him. Thirty-four years old, still lived in Frederick, was married, had two kids, and worked as a realtor. Three years back, the couple applied for and received a home improvement loan for forty thousand dollars, and all payments continued to be on-time. He jotted down the listed phone number. He'd give her a call later after he clarified what he was going to say.

Kayleigh Craig presented more of a challenge. His $10.95 got him very little information. Now fifty-one years old, the woman had been renting the house when Holly died. Five months later, when her lease expired, she moved to California. About as far away from Maryland as you could get. On the west coast, she'd had several menial jobs, then disappeared. Her records stopped over four years ago, and her Social Security number had not been used since.

Jeremy clasped his hands behind his head and leaned back. Could mean a lot of things. The most obvious was that she died, but no evidence of that. No obit. Of course, if she was a Jane Doe in a cemetery, there would be no record. She might also be using fake or stolen identification. For that matter, she could have been doing the same thing back when Holly died. Or maybe she'd gone to Mexico and decided to stay. A dozen other options were possible. Whatever the case, Kayleigh Craig was going to take some work to find.

He checked the clock. Time to call Christine Wolf. He reviewed her details one more time, then grabbed the phone, and after taking a few slow, deep breaths to steady himself, he dialed her number. On the third ring, he heard a click, like it was switching to voice mail. He pulled the mobile away from his ear and reached to disconnect the call.

"Hello?"

He nearly conked himself in the head when he shook his phone to start the recording. "Oh, hello there. Is this Christine Wolf?"

"Yes, or at least I was. That's my maiden name. Who is this?"

"Sorry. My name is Jeremy Winter. You don't know me but—"

"My number is on the government's do-not-call list. I don't care what you're selling. They can fine you for calling me. Now, please remove my number from—"

"Yes, ma'am. I mean, no, ma'am. I'm not selling anything. I'm looking into something that happened a long time ago, and I was hoping you'd be able to help me. There was a shooting in Frederick. A woman was murdered."

There was a pause before she responded. "Winter. You the husband?"

"Yes, ma'am. My wife was killed not long after 9/11."

"I'm sorry, but like I told the police back then, I don't know anything about it."

Keep her talking. The more on the recording, the better. "I understand. I was just hoping that after so much time had passed, you might feel freer to share information."

"Freer? Why? I don't have any trouble sleeping at night. My conscience is clear. I didn't know anything then, and I don't know anything now. I wish you the best, but I can't help."

"Sure. But I wonder if—"

click

He checked his phone to verify the recording had stopped, then played it back several times. Sounded clean. No static as far as he could tell. Should be good enough for what he had in mind.

After two more hours spent searching for a mobile number for Georgia Harding and any details he could find on Kayleigh Craig, he gave up. Tomorrow he'd drive to Hagerstown and look for Ms. Harding there. Once he had a recording of her voice, he'd move ahead with his plan. With luck, one of the two women would be the 911 caller. If not, the hunt for Kayleigh Craig would begin in earnest.

He peeked out the front window. An overcast sky, but nothing that looked like rain. Still an hour until he had to get Beks. Enough time to stop by his apartment, put on some sweats, and walk a few laps around the school's track. Shorts would be more comfortable, but his scars would be exposed. Too many stares and unasked awkward questions.

His mind, stomach, and mouth conspired to whisper a reminder that he'd need energy to exercise. Energy like the kind he could get from donuts or ice cream. He sucked in his belly, searched for any sign of his abs, sighed, and walked to his car.

CHAPTER SIXTEEN

Shane took one last look at the newspaper clipping before heading out the door. The grainy mugshot, typical of what the small-town papers printed, showed a man with a heavy face and bald head. He'd make a perfect jack-o'-lantern if he weren't the chief of police in a tiny South Carolina hamlet, some hundred and twenty miles away. Sterling Pickerill had been arrested on accusations of domestic violence several months ago, charges the district attorney dropped for lack of proof.

Shane shook his head. Wasn't a bruised wife and frantic 911 call enough evidence to at least take the case to the grand jury? Everybody knows what goes on in these little towns. The good ole boy network is alive and well, thank you very much. He should add the DA to the stack of future targets for the man's blatant culpability in Pickerill's freedom.

The list of potential victims grew regularly, sometimes exponentially. No way he'd ever get through all of them. Flexibility and prioritization, critical skills listed in almost every management article he read, served him well. He often sorted through his pile of candidates and reorganized them based on his thoughts that day. Plus, as in Brenda and Natalie's cases, he needed to be able to rearrange his schedule when more pressing targets jumped to the forefront.

Two weeks since the mechanic died, a long stretch without action. Every now and then it worked out that way as he planned and gathered intel. There'd been no indication foul play was suspected in Eddie's death. The local news stations gave a thirty-second spot to the man's gruesome demise, thirty seconds more than he deserved. Natalie had not been interviewed, but he knew the routine. She'd grieve—they always did—but she'd move on, hopefully to a man who respected her, though often they did not. For a while, Shane considered keeping tabs on the women in case they fell back into the trap of domestic abuse, but he'd opted against doing so, figuring he'd given them their shot at freedom. It was time for someone else to have their chance. Someone like the wife of Police Chief Sterling Pickerill.

Today's job had an extra element of danger. Shane was going to kill the man outright rather than try to make it look like an accident. On the earlier scouting trips, he'd failed to identify a suitable location frequented by Pickerill. And because the victim was a cop, the response would be immediate and overwhelming. The incident needed to occur as far from town as possible to give Shane time to get away. Based on his reconnaissance that shouldn't be an issue.

The bigger problem was he'd be driving a stolen car. He had taken the car last night after work, easy to do after watching a couple of how-to videos on YouTube. The new ride was a white 2004 Chevy Impala that had been parked beside dozens of other vehicles, each with a "For Sale" sign on the dash and facing the street in front of an empty K-Mart. The car had been sitting there as long as he could remember. Odds that the owner would check on his vehicle today were slim, but even if he did, Shane was ready.

He checked to make sure the Missouri tags, stolen a couple of days ago at a Cracker Barrel, were on the car, then headed south. It was a Saturday morning, and there was no hurry. Pickerill's routine hadn't varied over the last two weekends. Breakfast at the all-you-can-eat buffet, followed by a speed trap just inside the town limits on a back road. Shane had called the police station the previous Saturday and was told by the lone officer on duty that the chief didn't work on the weekends. Shane knew better. The man worked all right. He just worked for himself. He'd pulled over four vehicles for allegedly speeding, each time accepting cash in lieu of writing a ticket. Twice Shane witnessed the chief follow the speeder to an ATM to get the money. All the stopped cars had out-of-town plates. It was Mayberry gone bad. Cop killer had such an ugly connotation, but Pickerill had broken his oath to serve and protect. Not only to the public but to his own wife. He had to go.

This situation took far more planning than the others, and he'd discovered a joy for the preparation process. His BA in Business Management was paying off. He'd developed a modified SWOT Analysis to list the strengths, weaknesses, opportunities, and threats of his plan, then adjusted accordingly.

The strengths were easy. Shane would have surprise on his side and a sawed-off shotgun in his lap. The chief was a big man and sweated like a sinner in church. He always wore his short-sleeved uniform shirt, and its buttons worked overtime to contain his chest and stomach. If the man had a bulletproof vest, he didn't wear it; a fact verified when the sheriff pulled Shane over during last Saturday's planning trip. It had cost Shane a $200 fine—cash, of course, and certainly not reported—to get the information, a small price for such a valuable detail.

The weaknesses of his plan were troublesome, but he'd eliminated as many as possible. As he progressed in his duty to save women, he came to accept that he couldn't eliminate every potential problem. His shoe prints at the scene of Eddie's death were a prime example. You did what you had to do to get the job done. A two-point deduction on the spreadsheet, but necessary.

In this case, his plan had no backup. If something went wrong with the shotgun, he'd be captured. Purchased on a lark several years ago from a friend, the single-barreled weapon had been true, though it had done no more than shoot aluminum cans. Sure, he could've brought an extra gun, but the risk of purchasing one, stolen or not, was worse than the off-chance of the shotgun misfiring. Good cop or bad cop, law enforcement was going to go all out to catch whoever killed the man. The fewer people Shane interacted with, the better.

The stolen Impala constituted another weakness. He wasn't too concerned about getting caught on the way down, but after he'd done the job, the car would become a liability, especially if the cop had his dashcam turned on. Two containers of gasoline in the trunk and a previously identified remote location would solve that problem. It meant a nearly four-mile walk to a congested shopping area and an Uber back to Charlotte from there, but such was the price. The burnt vehicle would eventually be found and identified, but any evidence would be ashes in the wind.

He'd finalized the plan's opportunities last Saturday. The chief's desire to keep his activity hidden—though likely the locals knew all about the man's goings-on—would be his Achilles' heel. He chose an isolated area with no homes nearby and virtually no traffic. It was like fishing, and no doubt there were many Saturdays he didn't catch anything.

The threat came last. If Pickerill got suspicious for any reason and pulled his gun before getting to the car, Shane would have to shoot early and hope the cop didn't react in time. Otherwise, he risked being arrested with a shotgun in his lap, a prospect that did not sit well. No, the only successful outcome was a deceased police chief, no witnesses, and a happy widow. Anything else might lead to prison and unfulfilled promises.

. . . .

The drive took two and a half hours with no stops. As with his scouting trips, Shane left his cell phone turned on and at home. His paper map guided him the long way around the county. He planned the route so when Chief Pickerill stopped him, he'd be headed away from the town.

Nearly noon now, and the cop would be holed up in his fishing spot waiting for an out-of-town speeder. Shane set his cruise control ten miles over the limit, then slid the shotgun into his lap so the chief wouldn't see him reaching for something when he got pulled over. He'd fire from the low angle, and at this distance, there would be no doubt as to the outcome. The triple-aught buckshot pellets would rip the cop's chest, neck, and face apart. No coming back from that.

He wedged his knees under the steering wheel and kept his eyes on the road while opening the shotgun to confirm the weapon was loaded, then rested the butt of the stock against the Impala's center console, hoping the recoil wouldn't do much damage. Even if it did, better to break the armrest than his thigh.

His heart pounded in his ears, and he licked his lips. No other vehicles were in sight, and the chief would be parked about a minute ahead. If all went according to plan, he'd be on his way back to Charlotte in less than five minutes, and Mrs. Pickerill would be a free woman.

As he neared the target location, he identified another weakness to add to his SWOT Analysis. The chief already had someone pulled over when Shane spotted him.

The police car's flashing blue lights affirmed that the fishing had been good this morning. Now what? He was too close to stop or turn around, so he slowed as he neared. It was the chief all right. The big man stood beside the driver's window and stared at Shane's car as he passed.

He gave the cop a wide berth, the passenger side tires kicking up dust as they left the road. He looked away and scratched his cheek to hide his face as much as possible, then accelerated and watched in his rearview mirror as the chief turned his attention back to the cash at hand. Within seconds, the scene was out of view.

Shane continued for another couple of miles before pulling to the side of the road and stopping. Should he turn around and go back? Pickerill would surely be suspicious if he saw the same car again. Of course, there was always the chance he wouldn't make the connection. Was it worth the risk, or should he wait? He could move the man down the stack and revisit the situation in a few months. But a lot can change in that amount of time. There might never be an opportunity like this again.

Movement in the rearview caught his eye, and he glanced up. Flashing blue lights sped toward him. The decision had been made. The cop must have expanded his fishing hole.

Pickerill pulled behind him and stopped. Shane eased his finger onto the shotgun's trigger. The plan had gone completely awry, but he still had the strength and opportunity. Surprise and an unprotected wife-abuser.

The chief stepped out of his car, hitched his pants, and checked both ways down the road before walking toward Shane. He paused at the back of the Impala and tapped the trunk. "Going pretty fast when you nearly hit me back there. Missouri, huh?"

Liar. Shane pushed back in his seat, adding precious centimeters to the distance between himself and the upcoming shotgun blast. Earplugs. He should have gotten earplugs. "Yes, sir. Columbia area."

Pickerill nodded and moved toward the driver window. "Haven't I seen you be—"

The explosion blinded and deafened Shane. He coughed and squeezed his eyes open and shut several times until the haze cleared. The car reeked of gunpowder. The windshield was cracked, most likely a result of the shotgun hitting it after kicking off the destroyed center console. The weapon now lay in the floorboard in front of the passenger seat. As far as he could tell, he wasn't injured. He looked out his window.

The cop dropped straight down, and the reddish-gray material—liquid and solid—splattered across the road behind what remained of Pickerill's upper torso and head made it clear the man was dead. Shane clamped his jaws and swallowed the burning sensation in his throat.

He eased the car away from the body and set his cruise control for the speed limit. Wouldn't do to get stopped now. He lowered all four windows to try to get as much of the gunpowder smell out as he could. His ears still rang, though not loud enough to cover the pounding of his heart, and his eyebrows and nose hairs were singed. Adrenaline flowed through him, not so much from the thrill of meeting his objective as fear of not escaping.

He followed his planned exit route and passed no other vehicles. Within a few minutes, the tension eased from his shoulders, and he sank lower in his seat. The closer he got to major roads, the more traffic he saw. Now he was just another dirty car with a cracked windshield. A wave of panic hit him, and he angled his outside mirror down as far as it would go. No sign of blood or guts on the side of the Impala, at least none big enough to be recognized as such.

He made it to the interstate without seeing any emergency vehicles. After a few minutes, his heartbeat slowed, and his breathing returned to normal.

He moved his head in a circular motion to stretch his neck muscles. A productive Saturday, but an exhausting one. Still, it's like they say. Enjoy what you do, and you'll never work a day in your life.

And he did relish his work. The creativity and efficiency of bringing hope, salvation even, to those women who needed it most. He turned on the car radio and drummed his fingers on the steering wheel.

It used to bother him that he felt so little guilt at his job.

He grinned and turned up the volume.

His conscience never bothered him anymore. It couldn't. Not when he'd killed it too.

CHAPTER SEVENTEEN

Jeremy waited in his car and did his best to be inconspicuous. Not an easy task in the small residential neighborhood. Georgia Harding's house was half a block away down the narrow blacktop street. One- and two- story homes lined each side of the quiet road. There were no sidewalks, and the residents parked their cars in driveways and garages, meaning he stood out like a sore thumb.

The trees shading the houses had the barest hint of orange and yellow on their leaves. With fall less than a month away, the color outburst promised to be beautiful. He'd have to bring Maggie and Beks up this way to do some house hunting. A quiet middle-class neighborhood with good-sized yards would be ideal. Their refuge from the world.

First things first. Daydreaming about the future could wait. If all went well this morning, he'd take a big step forward in the investigation. He muted the radio as another one of the new so-called country songs came on. Rap and talk and pop mixed in with an electric guitar and a cowboy hat did not qualify as music. *Curmudgeon.*

He glanced in the mirror and shook his head, then shifted in the seat and squeezed his legs together. Another couple of minutes and he'd have to find a restroom. Shouldn't have had the third cup of coffee. Moments later, his patience was rewarded when a silver Jeep Cherokee turned into the Hardings' driveway. He started his car and idled to a stop in front of the home, then checked his phone to make sure the device was recording.

A woman came out of the vehicle with a bag of groceries in her hands and stared at him. Tall Caucasian, had to be close to five-ten, and thin with skintight black leggings and a too-large sweatshirt exposing one shoulder. Her oversize round sunglasses hid her eyes, but her rigid posture showed tension. Strangers must be rare in the neighborhood.

He slid out of the car and smiled. "Ms. Harding?"

"Yes?"

"My name is Jeremy Winter. I wonder if I could speak with you for a moment?"

"About what?"

He walked toward her, stopping when she took a step backward. Should've used the cane. Less threatening that way. "Ma'am, I'm investigating an incident that happened back in 2001. A murder in Frederick. A young woman was—"

She rubbed her neck and glanced up and down the street before speaking. "I'm sorry, but I don't know anything about a murder."

"Yes, I understand, but the police spoke to you back then, didn't they? About a cell phone that called 911?"

Her lips formed a thin line. "They did, and nothing's changed. I couldn't help them then, and I can't help you. Um, who are you? Police? Do you have ID?"

"No, ma'am." He cleared his throat. "That was my wife who was killed. She was pregnant."

Ms. Harding's expression remained stoic. "I'm sorry. I wish I could help, but since I had nothing to do with it, well, good luck with your investigation." She backed away a few more steps and then turned toward her porch.

"Please," Jeremy said. "Two minutes. That's all I need."

She looked at him over her shoulder. "That would be a waste of time. Now, I've got ice cream in this bag, and I don't want it to get soft. Have a nice day, Mr. Winter." She continued to stare while fumbling around in her purse.

Was she looking for her keys or mace or a gun? Jeremy smiled, nodded, and stepped backward. "Yes, ma'am. Thank you. If you do think of anything, would you mind—"

"I won't." She pulled a set of keys from her purse, glanced back again, then stepped inside her home and closed the door.

He stared at the curtains for a moment, wondering if she might peek out. She didn't. Once inside his car, he pulled the phone from his pocket and listened to the recording. The conversation sounded muffled like they were in a tunnel, but the words were clear. Whether it would be enough was beyond his ability to answer. If it wasn't, he'd have to come back.

Two women, two brief recordings. Not much to pin his hopes on, but a start. And if neither panned out, there was always the search for the third woman. Without question, one of the three had information he needed. A detail that would finally allow the search for the killer to move forward.

No justice, no peace. That's what people chanted at whatever they were angry about today. Holly and Miranda deserved their justice.

He cranked the engine and eased away from the Hardings' home. That was the problem with seeing all the things he'd seen, at war and in the Bureau. Justice often came. Peace rarely did.

CHAPTER EIGHTEEN

Jeremy scanned the website again. The FBI's Biometric Center of Excellence, or BCOE, had been around since the mid-2000s, and probably even helped in some of his own cases, but he had no contacts there. No one who owed him any favors. The people at the BCOE focused on using cutting-edge technology in the battle against crime. They specialized in things like recognizing and identifying a person's unique characteristics, everything from their face to their handwriting to the one he now sought, their voice.

He hoped to find someone who would compare his two phone recordings to the original 911 call. If they found a match, he could move forward. If they didn't, he'd continue his search for the third woman, Kayleigh Craig, and try again. And if her voice wasn't identified as the caller, the investigation was over. No choice. There was nowhere else to go. Nothing in the murder book hinted that the original investigation overlooked anything.

He stood, yawned, and grabbed a bottled water from the fridge. Despite his current status, he still had friends in the Bureau and CIA. Asking Maggie to run point for him was out of the question. Whoever did the tests would be, at minimum, risking their jobs. Combine that with the knowledge he had nothing to offer in return, and you ended up with a goose egg of options.

He downed half the bottle, its thin plastic crinkling as he drank. His stomach rumbled, and he debated eating a snack, but Maggie would be home soon. Better wait and see if we're nuking dinner or getting delivery or dining out.

Heavy footsteps echoed down the hallway, and he checked the table to make sure there was nothing out that Beks shouldn't see.

"Whatcha doin', Jeremy?"

He squatted and smiled at the seven-year-old. He missed the days when he was "Jewemy." "Getting some water. You've been awfully quiet back there. Did you get your homework done?"

"Yeah. I mean, yessir. Most of it, but I need some help with math."

"Yeah? Well, why don't you bring it up here and we'll—"

"I'll wait until Mommy gets home."

He chuckled and mussed her hair. "Good call."

He placed his hands on his knees and pushed himself up, grunting the whole way.

"You make that noise a lot," Beks said.

"I know. It's called getting old." He sat back down at the table.

"Can I help you work?"

"Oh, sweetie, that would be great, but I'm just about finished for the day. Your mom will be home soon. What do you want to do about dinner?"

She bit her bottom lip and tapped her finger on her chin. "Um, chicken and french fries."

"What a surprise."

She moved beside him and pointed at his laptop screen. "What's that?"

"One of the FBI's websites. This place does all the fancy stuff like identifying people just by their eyes or their voice."

"Is that what you're working on?"

"Kind of. I need to compare some, uh, audio files and find out if the same people are speaking on them."

"And that place is going to do it for you?"

"Maybe, but I don't know. I'm still trying to figure things out."

"Why don't you just do it yourself?"

"I wish I could, but it's way beyond my ability. I think the people might be disguising their voice, so I need something that will actually break the file down and look for similarities. Does that make sense?"

She squinted and puckered her lips. "Did you see if there's an app that will do it?"

He laughed. "No, honey. This is too difficult for an ..." Was it?

A quick search told him that yes, it was too difficult for an app, at least with current technology. There were gimmicky ones for entertainment and a few that claimed they worked but only if the exact same phrases were spoken, but nothing that came close to what he needed. He did find a link to something far more useful, however. The University of Minneapolis now had a program specializing in Media Forensics, which included voice recognition. Of course. Why wouldn't someone besides the government be working on these things? There's money to be made. Jeremy didn't know anyone at the school, but it should be way easier to talk them into doing the work than finding help at BCOE.

The front door unlocked, and Maggie stepped inside.

"Hey," Beks and Jeremy said in unison.

She dropped her purse on the sofa. "Don't everyone get too excited to see me."

Jeremy walked to her and gave her a kiss. "Welcome home."

She smiled. "That's better. What are you two doing?"

Beks squeezed her mother's waist. "I'm helping Jeremy with a problem."

Maggie arched her eyebrows and tilted her chin downward. "Oh? You're not working on math, are you?"

"No," he said. "But I don't understand how something as simple as one plus one can be turned into—"

Maggie held up her hand. "Stop. I don't want to hear this again."

He sighed and crossed his arms. "Fine."

"Oh, good grief," she said. "Are you pouting?"

"I don't pout."

"Uh-huh. So if you two aren't doing math, what are you working on?"

He straightened and grinned. "Like Beks said, solving a problem, and I think she's done it. I'll fill you in on the details later. For now, I say let's go grab dinner."

"I get to pick," the girl said. "Since I helped."

"Okay," Maggie said. "Anywhere but McDon—"

"McDonald's chicken nuggets! With french fries, apples, and Sprite."

Maggie frowned and sighed. "I was hoping for someplace a bit less, um, what's the word I'm looking for?"

Jeremy shrugged. "McDonaldy?"

Beks shook her head. "I don't like Burger King. Their chicken is yuck."

"Not there either," Maggie said. "I'm thinking I want a salad so why don't we go to—"

"McDonald's has salads," Jeremy said.

Maggie's voice deepened. "I'm fully aware of that. I want to go somewhere more, um, I don't know ..."

"Saladish?" Jeremy said.

Maggie snatched up her purse. "C'mon, Rebecca. McDonald's it is, but no fries. Yogurt instead." She glared at Jeremy. "And you owe me."

He closed his laptop and winked at her. "Oh, good grief. Are you pouting?"

CHAPTER NINETEEN

Jeremy's trip to Minneapolis was like any of the other thousand flights he'd taken over the years. Cramped, stale, and irritating. Even keeping his elbows tight at his sides, it was impossible to avoid touching—and being touched by—his seatmates. The concept of personal space didn't exist in planes. The friendly skies, indeed.

Twenty minutes until touchdown. He closed his eyes and focused on the sounds around him. The hiss of the cool ozony air being blasted down onto him. The idle chatter of the other passengers. Parents trying to hush their babies as the pressure changes hurt their ears. His breathing slowed, and he drifted into a state of semi-consciousness until the heavy thud of the landing gear being locked into place stirred him awake.

Once the wheels hit the runway, he fired off a quick text to Maggie to let her know he'd arrived. Forty-five minutes later, his Uber dropped him and his heavy overnight bag at the hotel. The plan was to only spend one night, but thunderstorms were in the forecast for Minnesota, and he didn't want to take any chances on being stuck without extra clothes. His appointment to meet with the director of the Media Forensics classes was first thing in the morning. If all went well, he'd be on his way home tomorrow afternoon with a promise from the professor to evaluate the audio files.

After a dinner of peanut butter crackers and a Diet Coke from the vending machines, he called Maggie, and they talked for a few minutes, but there wasn't much new to say since they last spoke. Her trainee, Tanessa Cousins, was doing well. The woman came to the Bureau from the Air Force where she'd been assigned to security at missile silos. Her demeanor was rough, no great shock considering her time in the military, but Maggie felt confident she'd make a fine agent.

Jeremy didn't know anything about the case the two were working, and, surprisingly, wasn't overly interested. As time passed, and that part of his life faded, he found he didn't miss it as much as he thought he would. Working on his own case might have something to do with that, but truthfully, he didn't think so. Once the investigation into Holly's death was behind him, he wanted something new. Something different where he didn't have to seek out the evil in people. After so many years though, such a thing might not even be possible.

....

Jeremy slept through the night, only getting up to use the bathroom once, an event that was becoming more common as he aged. The hotel's continental breakfast consisted of English muffins, French toast sticks, and slices of American cheese to put on … something. He opted for coffee and a bowl of frosted flakes without milk. Tony the Tiger says they're great, right? Maybe Beks should paint some tiger stripes on his cane. He might use it more if she did. It wouldn't change what it was, a stick to help him walk, but when people asked, he could tell them his daughter painted it. He grinned. Maggie insisted he refer to Beks as his daughter. None of that "step" nonsense. His chest swelled, and he took a deep breath. His daughter.

He'd already checked out in the hope he could go home today. If not, he'd need to rebook his flight and hotel. Certainly wouldn't be the first time that happened. His phone beeped, signaling that the Uber driver was there, and he refilled his coffee, tucked his cane under his arm, grabbed his overnight bag, and headed for the door.

The sun deceived the world into thinking it was warm outside. Temperatures had dropped into the mid-50s the previous night, unseasonably cool for early September, even in Minneapolis. The weather guy said something about a front coming through later that day and creating the chance for rain and storms. As long as the plane could take off, he didn't care.

He hobbled to the Uber, his left leg firing electric jolts and spasms with each step. Gonna be one of those days. The driver lowered the passenger window and asked if Jeremy needed help. He declined, set his cup on the car's top, and tossed his bag and cane inside, then retrieved his coffee and turned so his back was to the car. He kept his weight on the good leg, sat on the seat, scooted back, and pivoted both legs inside.

"Good to go," he said.

"Headed for the university, right?"

"Yep. College of Arts and Media, please."

The driver nodded and adjusted his rearview mirror. "You an artist?"

"No, not quite." He paused. "My daughter's the artist in our family."

"Yeah, how old is she?"

"Eight going on thirteen."

The man laughed. "I know what you mean. I've got two kids, boy and a girl, twelve and nine. They're a handful. First time in Minneapolis?"

Good question. Was it? He'd been so many places, but it was the killers he remembered, not the cities. "Yes."

"Great town, if you can take the winters. Planning to be here a while?"

"Uh, no. In and out. Trying to catch a flight later today if everything goes according to schedule." Which it rarely does.

"Don't blame you. Where's home?"

He settled back in his seat and sipped his coffee. "DC area."

The driver glanced in his mirror. "Yeah? You work for the government? You look a little familiar. Have I seen you somewhere?"

Now that the Cronfeld mess was behind him, his photo never popped up on the news, and those questions had thankfully become much less frequent. "No. I'm sort of between jobs."

"Tough times, man. Good luck to you."

The drive was just over thirty minutes, and Jeremy tipped the driver ten bucks when they arrived. He stepped into the crisp morning air and glanced at the structure. A rather generic sign confirmed he was in the right place. A garbage can stood vigil in front of the twenty-odd steps leading into the building. He hiked his overnight bag's strap higher on his shoulder and squeezed his cane before shuffling to the trash and tossing his coffee cup in.

He looked at the steps again, peeked over at the handicap ramp on the right, then moved straight ahead. His time in rehab after the Talbot incident taught him how to keep most of the weight off his leg. Let the cane do the work, they said.

Several students hurried past him as he climbed the steps, and one held the door for him as he reached the summit. He thanked her, and she smiled before hurrying off to class or breakfast or wherever. The director of the Media Forensics department had emailed him directions. Left at the first hallway, fourth entrance on the right. Jeremy found the room without trouble and stepped into a small sitting area. No one was in there, and the door beyond stood wide open.

He moved inside. "Hello?"

A voice from the office returned the greeting. "Come on back."

Professor Gisella Bridgford sat behind a desk cluttered with papers and computer equipment. At least fifteen years Jeremy's junior, she had the look of a woman who spent most of her time in a virtual world. Dark-rimmed glasses, hair pulled back in a ponytail, no makeup, and short fingernails. Computer nerd.

He smiled and offered his hand. "Good morning, Professor. Or do I call you Doctor?" The woman had two Ph.D's listed on the university's website, though by now she might have more.

She stood and leaned over the desk. "You call me Gisella. You're Mr. Winter, I assume?"

"I am. I appreciate you taking the time to meet with me."

"My pleasure. Sit, please. And excuse my appearance. I had a rather late night."

"Computer problems?"

She chuckled. "Foo Fighters were in town. A bunch of us went, and I didn't get home until around two this morning."

What's a foo fighter? "Sounds like fun."

"It was, but I'm paying for it this morning. If my boyfriend hadn't pushed me out of bed, I'd probably still be asleep. Getting too old for that kind of stuff."

Just wait. "Yes, well, I won't take up much of your time."

"You said something about wanting more details on our audio recognition programs, right? I can tell you it's a fluid process. The technology is still a bit behind where it needs to be, but I'll bet the NSA is years ahead of what we've got here. You want the layman's version?"

He chuckled. "Please, but don't be surprised if you have to explain that to me too."

"Sure. Basically, we teach students how to break down audio files into their individual pieces. Those are the building blocks. From there, we can manipulate that data, and by 'manipulate' I mean handle, not change, and do what we want with it. Our focus here is on training the students for opportunities in companies like Google, Amazon, or Apple, where the need to correctly identify human speech through technology is growing exponentially. Of course, the auto industry, law enforcement, and untold other career paths are also available. Still with me?"

He shifted forward in his seat. "I am. So, in my case, once you break down the files and have that data, you can just compare it to other samples to see if they match? Find out if it's the same person, I mean."

She shook her head. "Not that easy. Humans aren't robots. Not only do people pronounce words differently—picture a guy from Boston and a guy from Alabama having a conversation—an individual doesn't always speak at the same level, the same speed, the same enunciation, and so on. The variables are endless."

"But it can be done?"

"Comparing voice samples? Sure. We use algorithms to process the data, look for similarities, adjust for conditions, that kind of thing. What we do here would never stand up in court though. It's a lot of trial and error. We have the tools, and while they're fairly cutting edge for non-government issue, they're still primitive. That's why this department exists. We want our students to learn what's out there and come up with better ways of doing things."

He nodded. "I don't need anything that will hold up in court. I'm hoping for a result that can tell me, with a reasonable amount of accuracy, how likely it is that the speakers are the same. Can you do that?"

She shrugged. "I won't know until I've heard the samples. But don't get ahead of yourself. I'm not agreeing to anything until I gain a better understanding of what you're getting my department involved in. You're ex-FBI, aren't you? Why not have them do the work for you? Or better yet, the NSA. I guarantee you'll get a more accurate result."

He smiled. "You want the layman's version?"

She motioned for him to continue.

"The FBI and I parted on less than ideal terms. They're not likely to do any favors for me."

"Fair enough," she said. "Mr. Winter, do these audio files have anything to do with Colonel Ramsey Cronfeld or Senator Diane Morgans?"

"You've done your homework. No, I promise you they don't."

"In that case, why don't we begin by you giving me the details?"

"The tapes, uh, files are from an unsolved case. A murder. One file is the 911 call from the time of the crime, back in 2001. The other two are recent. I'm trying to compare them to see if either of the new ones are the 911 caller."

"Have all parties agreed to the recordings?"

He dabbed at his forehead. "The 911 call is public record. The other two … no. They didn't know I was recording. And before you ask, it was in Maryland, and they have a two-party consent law."

She leaned back. "So they're illegal."

"That's one way to look at it."

"You know another way?"

He sighed and shook his head. "No, I don't."

She stared at the ceiling for a few seconds. "Why is this so important to you? Is this like the one who got away? The cop, excuse me, FBI agent who retires but can't sleep because of this one case?"

He focused on a dark spot on the carpet in front of her desk. "Kind of. It was never my case though. She was my wife."

Her shoulders slumped. "I'm sorry."

"It's okay. Look, I don't want to get you in any trouble. All I can do is assure you I'll do everything I can to keep your department out of this. No paperwork, no reports, nothing. The police investigation was good, but there was no way to do a test like this back then. I just need to know, best guess or whatever, are either of the women likely to have made the call to 911? There's a third woman out there who I haven't found yet. I'm hoping I don't have to look."

"You're asking for a lot, Mr. Winter."

"I realize that."

She laid her glasses on the desk. "How long are you in town?"

"As long as you need me to be."

"Come back in two hours."

"So you'll do it?"

"I didn't say that. But I will ask three of my best students if they'd be willing to work on a project. No extra credit. Doesn't help or hurt their grade. And they do all the work on their own time. If they agree, I'll have them here in my office when you come back. You will then explain to them why this is so important to you."

"Of course, but if they've already agreed to do it, why do I—"

"Technology isolates people, Mr. Winter. I want my students to remember that. They need to put a face, in this case, *your face*, to their work. It doesn't mean the results or the effort will change, but I hope it means that my students *won't* change. Technology has to remain a tool, not an end-all. If not, we might as well be those robots."

Jeremy stood. Could not have been more wrong about her. "Thanks, Doc. I'll be back in two hours."

"Look forward to it."

He smiled and moved toward the door.

"Mr. Winter," she said, "the Foo Fighters are a rock band."

. . . .

Jeremy stood in Professor Bridgford's office and explained to three kids why he wanted to have the files analyzed. The trio looked like they were barely out of their teens, and he wondered how much of what he said sank in. The two boys and one girl sat quietly and asked no questions. When he finished, they told him they'd do their best and, depending on schedules and file quality and a lot of things he didn't understand, it could take anywhere from a day to a few weeks to get it done. He thanked them, and Ms. Bridgford said she'd be in touch. Ten minutes later, he was on his way to the airport and his flight home.

CHAPTER TWENTY

Shane took a break from completing employee evaluations and stared out at the customer service agents. Ten days since he'd killed the cop. A long time to go without helping another woman, but a necessary delay. Shooting a policeman brought a lot of attention to the area, an anticipated outcome.

It wasn't like he'd been slacking though. Surveillance and planning, the backbone of an effective operation, filled his free time. Several candidates' files were nearly completed, and soon he'd be ready to act. As of today, Roy McIntyre of McIntyre's Roofing and Paving, where their motto is "We've got you covered from top to bottom," sat atop the list. The man's habit of sending his workers home while he ended the day operating the big asphalt roller alone made the plan easy. Mrs. McIntyre would be liberated within the next couple of days.

A ripple of laughter arose from a far corner of the customer service room. His heart tweaked, and he sighed. Sometimes it bothered him that he spent so much time alone. There'd been a period when he wondered if he should get a few friends. But what was the point when they ignored those at the moment of their greatest need? Mom had plenty of friends, didn't she? Sure, she tried to hide the bruises, but they had to know. Had to. Besides, when he got too lonely, Buzz Lightyear always lent an ear, albeit a plastic one. But talking to Buzz came with risks. A hazard that grew as each day passed. The irony never escaped Shane.

All the planning and execution of his routines would ultimately give way to random chance. A decision by a toy whether it was time to finish what he'd started. If it was up to Shane, he knew which way things would go. But it wasn't his choice to make.

He stood and made a circuit around the employees, pausing here and there to chat. Management-by-walking-around, a favorite of his. Sometimes he'd listen to one of the customer service agents on a call and make suggestions or tell them they'd done well. His own boss sat in an office on another floor and was rarely seen except near holidays or if the execs were coming through soon on a tour.

Most of the small talk with his employees was inane, he had over a hundred personnel, after all, but they seemed to enjoy chatting. He spent a little extra time at Brenda's desk, making sure she was doing okay after the unfortunate death of her husband. Better every day, she said. It gave him a surge of satisfaction to know that her life had been improved because of him. Natalie was probably experiencing the same thing. He'd stopped by Chick-fil-A once to get a look at her, and she looked happy enough.

After thirty minutes of strolling among the workers, he returned to his shared office, settled back in his chair, and glanced at the next evaluation. A wave of whispers caught his attention, and he looked up. At the main entrance to the oversized room, a pair of uniformed policemen were talking to an employee.

Tension riveted his shoulders and legs. They couldn't be here for him. No way. Two patrolmen to arrest a cop killer? Uh-uh.

Unless they were keeping it low-key to minimize the danger to others. That would make sense.

But cops came here two or three times a year looking for someone, usually an employee who had a warrant or wasn't paying child support.

The officers nodded to the employee and headed toward Shane.

Should he run? He knew the building better than they did, but would other cops be waiting outside?

It still didn't make sense. Why here? Why not wait until he was in his car on the way home? Maybe they just wanted to ask some questions.

Didn't matter now. They were too close for him to do anything except wait.

Both officers stepped in front of him. The shorter of the two tucked his thumbs in his belt. "Are you Shane Kingston?"

He swallowed. "Yes. Can I help you?"

"I hope so. We're looking for Larry Kirkpatrick. Is he working tonight?"

The hair on Shane's neck settled back into place. "No, sorry. He actually transferred to first shift a couple of weeks ago."

"Typical," the taller cop said. "Thanks. We'll send someone by in the morning. Don't let him know we're coming, okay?"

"Not a problem, officer. Have a good evening."

He waited until they'd left the area to relax. Was paranoia becoming a problem? It was possible that killing the cop was a risk he shouldn't have taken, but try telling that to the man's wife. Taking extreme chances to save one woman meant risking the opportunity to rescue others on down the line. It was times like this he could use a friend to bounce his thoughts off. Buzz was good, but his feedback left much to be desired. It'd have to be a really close friend though. A person who understood and agreed with the importance of what Shane was doing. Wasn't very likely he'd ever stumble across someone like that.

He returned his attention to the stack of employee evaluations. Rote, monotonous work that served no purpose other than allowing his boss to check off a box somewhere. All employees would get the same petty raise regardless of what score he gave them or what notes he wrote. The same held true for the supervisors. His college degree had done nothing to further his career options. It had, however, done quite a bit to limit his disposable income.

He shook his head. A negative attitude wasn't going to help anyone. At times like this, it was best to get something on the calendar. An event he could look forward to.

He grabbed his pen and started on the next evaluation. On a scale of 1 to 10, with 10 being the best, rate the employee on …

Now there's a thought. Maybe he should take this process and apply it to the stack of possibilities at home. Come up with some sort of ranking system to determine who came next.

No. Mindless rules and procedures stifled growth. Flexibility was the key to being successful in business and in life and death. The ability to adapt to changing priorities was what kept a company, or an individual, at the top of their game.

He circled the 7 on the evaluation in front of him. Displays an aptitude for their assigned duties.

Aptitude. Was that what he had? It seemed so clinical. A "special talent" sounded better. Or a "gift." Either way, his success boiled down to a simple truth. He'd found his life's meaning in the deaths of others. Wait. More accurately, in the saving of women who were suffering. And he excelled at his job. On a scale of 1 to 10, he'd rate himself a 9. It would be foolish not to leave room for growth.

CHAPTER TWENTY-ONE

Jeremy taped another moving carton closed and labeled the box as kitchen dishes, though the contents were mostly plastic cups, mismatched plates, and loose tableware. The carton would probably never be opened. No wedding date had been set yet, but Maggie wasn't going to want to use his things. Might as well get ahead of the game and start packing.

His cell rang, and he moved the dish towels around until he found it. Professor Bridgford. Wow. Only two days since he came home from Minneapolis. His heart sped, and he fumbled to answer before the call went to voice mail.

"Hello?"

"Mr. Winter?"

Whew. "Yes. Hi. Sorry about that. I couldn't find my phone."

"I've got a couple of minutes before class. The team has the results if you're ready for them."

"That was fast."

"Yes, well, there wasn't much to work with."

Uh-oh. That doesn't sound good. "What did they find?"

"We analyzed all three audio files. Since the 911 call was the oldest, it's the most questionable. The quality isn't great, and it seems to be a recording of a recording if that makes sense."

"It does."

"Good. Anyway, even if the two other files were legally obtained, there's no way we'd go to court with them. We found nothing close to conclusive."

Hollowness flowed through his chest, and he sank onto a dinette chair. "So no luck, huh?"

"Luck has little to do with this type of analysis. Either the data's there, or it's not."

Might be time to start tracking the third woman. "Can you tell me if there's at least a chance that one of the women matches the 911 call?"

"I figured you'd ask. Normally we'd say that, in our opinion, neither of the two is a match. We base our results on probabilities that similarities in the audio files are population-specific."

He smiled. "Of course you do."

She chuckled. "Sorry. What I mean is that it's likely different people share commonalities in their speech, which may be due to upbringing, geography, whatever. That's why we need as much audio as we can get. Most of an individual's speech pattern is unique, and the more of it we can identify, the better chance we have of matching it to other samples."

"And you don't have enough audio from each person?"

"We don't and getting more won't help. The 911 call is simply too short. As I said before, if you can get the government involved, the NSA, FBI, someone like that, I'm sure they'd be able to give you a better indication."

"Not an option in my case, for obvious reasons."

"Sure, because we both know the government only deals in *legal* wiretaps and recordings, right?"

Ouch. Accurate, but ouch. "I didn't peg you for a cynic, Professor."

"A realist."

"I'm right there with you. Bottom-line it for me. On a scale of one to ten, chances that either of these women is the 911 caller."

"Christine Wolf, the woman you talked to on the phone, came in at under thirty percent match. Georgia Harding, the woman you spoke to in person, came in at just under sixty percent."

"Sixty percent? That's good, isn't it?"

"Not at all. We'd be laughed out of court with a result like that, especially with such a limited sample. It's not quite the same, but imagine saying there's a sixty percent chance a suspect's DNA matches what was found at a crime scene. No way a prosecutor would use that at a trial."

"So, if you were me, what would you do?"

"Sorry. We intentionally stay out of that side of the process. All we do is analyze the data. Our goal is a yes or no, nothing more."

"And I get a no."

"Mr. Winter, if I were you, I'd keep looking."

He thanked her and offered to treat the group to pizza the next time he stopped in Minneapolis. Finding Kayleigh Craig, the third woman, was going to be a challenge. Last heard from in California and no record of her for at least four years. He'd keep up the search online, but sooner or later, he'd have to travel. Not something he looked forward to.

There was another option. Sixty percent. Not enough, but better than going to California. He could bluff Georgia Harding. Tell her it was a sure thing and see how she reacted. He'd have to finesse things, or she'd flip out and get the cops involved, or worse, lawyers.

The question was whether to talk to Ms. Harding on the phone or in person. She hadn't answered his call last time, but maybe if he left her a voice mail saying he knew she was the 911 caller, she would … she would not say a word. He'd be worse off than he was now. No, he'd have to meet at her home again. Try to build some rapport to defuse any problems. Assure her again that she was not a suspect, and he had no desire to drag her into anything. All he wanted were the answers that only she could give.

Sixty percent. New math or old, those were terrible odds.

. . . .

Jeremy stood on Georgia Harding's porch waiting for someone to answer his knock. Her car wasn't here, but a different one was. Her husband maybe? The lock clicked, and the door swung open. A man, six-two, two-forty, bushy mustache, stared at him.

"Can I help you?"

"Yes, sir," Jeremy said. "I was hoping to speak to your wife if I could. Is she at home?"

The man crossed his arms. "Who are you, and what do you want?"

He handed him a torn piece of paper scribbled with his name and phone number. "My name is Jeremy Winter. I—"

"Georgia told me about you. You're the guy who accused her of—"

"I didn't accuse her of anything. I merely asked if she—"

"Interrupt me again, and this conversation is over."

Jeremy took half a step back and nodded. "My apologies."

"Georgia's not here, and even if she was, I wouldn't let her talk to you. She doesn't know anything about the killing that wasn't common knowledge."

Common knowledge? "Yes, sir, I understand. But she was aware of the murder back then?"

The man shrugged. "Lots of kids were."

"I see. Were you around then? Do you remember it?"

"Nope. Lived here in Hagerstown my whole life. I met Georgia when she moved here from Frederick a while back."

Jeremy nodded again. "Has she talked about the murder at all? Before I showed up, I mean?"

"Look, mister, this is sounding a lot like an interrogation. Georgia told you she can't help you. Don't ask her again. You try to call her or show up here again I'm calling the cops." He moved closer. "We on the same page here?"

Threatening me? Really? Jeremy tilted his head to the right and frowned. "The same page, Mr. Harding? We're not even in the same book. I don't think your wife is being entirely honest with me. Give her a message. I have solid evidence that she made the 911 call. *Solid evidence.* And if I find out she's involved in the murder somehow, it's going to be ugly."

"You can't possibly have—"

He squeezed his cane and leaned forward. "Don't interrupt me again. You have no idea what I have or don't have. Either she comes clean or she ends up as a star witness at the trial. The only question is whether she'll be testifying for the prosecution or trying to save her own skin. Tell her to make the call. I'll wait, but I won't wait long."

CHAPTER TWENTY-TWO

B eks sat curled in the recliner, her fingers dancing over the tablet's screen as she played some sort of musical spelling game. Maggie scrunched closer to Jeremy on the sofa and laid her head on his shoulder. He grinned and nuzzled his nose in her hair.

"Think she's spending too much time on that thing?" he asked.

"I don't mind as long as it's educational stuff, but yeah, we need to set guidelines."

"I'll leave that up to you. The last time I used a tablet I got chalk all over my fingers."

She pushed herself up and frowned. "I don't get it."

"Like they used in schools back in the 1800s or whenever. Tablets and chalk."

"Ohhhh … because you're old."

"Loses a lot when you have to explain it."

She patted his chest. "Uh-huh. An awful lot."

He twisted his finger in her hair. "Got to work on my Dad jokes. Good day at the office?"

"Mm-hmm. Tanessa's doing well. She reminds me of you. Her interpersonal skills need some work, but she gets the point across. I'm used to dealing with people like that." She laid her head back on his shoulder. "*Really* used to it."

"Har har. Got an interesting case?"

"Decent. Not too exciting though. Mostly financial stuff. I think that's where the Bureau wants Tanessa to end up. She's really good at finding trends and patterns in data."

"Analyst type, huh? How does she feel about that?"

"I don't know. Haven't asked."

He laid his cheek on her head. "Maybe you should."

"Maybe, but it's not like I can do anything about her assignment."

"No? You do her write-ups, don't you? It might be good to let her have a taste of other things. See how she likes them."

"No can do. I don't get to pick and choose what we're working on."

"Officially, you mean."

She doodled a circle on his chest. "You're not about to get me in trouble, are you?"

"You can always say no."

"I should've done that when you asked me to marry you."

He smiled and kissed the top of her head. "Sounds like revisionist history to me."

"We call it fake news now. Try to keep up."

"Will do. Anyway, I was thinking it might be helpful for Tanessa to get some real-world investigative experience."

"How considerate of you."

"That's the kind of guy I am. Can't help myself."

She sat upright and yawned. "And what exactly did you have in mind?"

"Something Georgia Harding's husband said bothers me. All the kids back then knew about the murder. Common knowledge, he said."

"So? It would've been big news in Frederick, right?"

"Yeah, but it was the way he said it. Not like they'd seen it on TV or anything. More like they all knew about it. Maybe a rumor floated around, or someone overheard something. Regardless, there's more there, and I don't think I'm going to get it from Georgia Harding."

Maggie nodded. "Background check? Identify Harding's known associates back then? Classmates, friends, that kind of thing? I can probably make that happen ... off the record. No talking to anyone or flashing our IDs around, but it would be good experience for Tanessa. Give me a chance to see how she operates, as long as she agrees to do it. I can't force her."

"Wouldn't want you to," he said. "But if she reminds you of me, you won't have to press her."

She sighed and shook her head. "I'll ask her tomorrow. Maybe we can meet for lunch or something. Your treat."

"Wouldn't have it any other way, but could you float me a loan? My next pension check doesn't come for a few days, and I'm a little light."

"Should've said no. 'Maggie, please marry me he said.' All I had to do was say no."

He grinned and shrugged. "Not the way I remember it, but either way, not too late to back out."

She stood and tapped a finger on her lips. "You're right. It's not too late. I could—"

He pulled her into his lap, and she cackled.

"C'mon, you guys," Beks said. "I'm studying over here."

. . . .

Jeremy searched the salad for more meat or cheese before giving up and placing the fork on his napkin. He ordered the dish to limit his calories and maintain a sense of refinement. Both considerations ebbed away as he watched Tanessa chow down on a chili burger and seasoned fries.

He liked the young African-American woman immediately. Chin up, strong eye contact, and a firm handshake. Good taste in food too.

Maggie patted his leg. "I told Tanessa you had something, uh, sensitive you wanted to discuss with all three of us."

The woman froze for a second, then cut her eyes back and forth between Maggie and Jeremy. "Is this where I say I'm flattered but …?"

Maggie's face beamed red. "What? No. Oh, I, uh …"

Jeremy arched his eyebrows, then laughed. "What she means is I have something work related I'd like to ask about."

Tanessa pointed a french fry at him. "Yeah, I knew that. Just messing with Mags."

Mags? "Well, okay then. I was talking to Mags last night and—"

Maggie shot a look at him, and he cleared his throat.

"As I was saying," he said, "Maggie and I were talking last night about a cold case I'm working on."

"Your wife and daughter, right? She's told me about it. I'm real sorry that happened."

"Thanks. Before I go any further, I want to make it clear that what I'm about to ask is entirely your choice. It has nothing to do with the Bureau or Maggie or anything official. Saying no won't have any effect on your job whatsoever."

Tanessa slid her plate toward the center of the table. "Eat some fries."

He shook his head. "Thank you, but I—"

"Jeremy," she said, "you've spent more time looking at my fries than at Mags. Eat some."

Maggie grinned. "I told you she was good."

"Well," he said, "if you insist." He took one and savored the crispy, peppery morsel. Tanessa gestured toward her plate, and he grabbed several fries and placed them on his napkin.

"So whaddya need us to do?"

"Run the background on a woman who may have more information on Holly's murder than she's telling. Based on her husband's reaction, I'm pretty sure she's the one who called 911, but so far, she's not talking. I want to track down other people she may have run around with back then."

"You talking high school yearbooks? That kind of thing? You don't need the FBI for that. Do it yourself online."

He glanced at Maggie, and she smiled. "Told ya."

Jeremy cleared his throat. "I was hoping you could shake the trees and see what falls out. Never know where something useful will show up."

Tanessa leaned forward. "Hard to shake trees when you're sitting in front of a computer. Yeah, we can do some digging, but what you need is a way to apply some pressure to the woman, right? Something to let her know you're serious. The easiest thing would be for me to stop by her place and flash some ID, but I expect Mags isn't going to allow that to happen."

"No," Maggie said, "I won't. This is not official Bureau business."

Tanessa nodded. "But using the FBI's resources to check into a citizen's background is. It's okay to do it as long as she doesn't *know* we're doing it. Got it. Sure, we'll see if we can find anything."

Jeremy faced Maggie and tilted his head. "I like her."

"This was a mistake," Maggie said. "Tanessa, I'm sorry I even—"

The young woman winked at Jeremy. "Just messin' with you, Mags. Be fun to do something that doesn't involve databases and spreadsheets for a change. Off the record, of course."

"I appreciate your help," Jeremy said. "If there's ever anything I can do in return ..."

"Get busy and marry this woman. If I have to look at one more homemade wedding decoration on Pinterest, I'll scream."

He grinned. "Can do. What's a pintrist?"

CHAPTER TWENTY-THREE

S hane rolled up the car window and switched on the air conditioner. Even from his position down the block and around the corner, the oily smell of hot asphalt hung heavy. A change of clothes waited in the trunk so he wouldn't reek when he went back to work, but the odor coated his body with a thin sheen of stink.

Roy McIntyre sat atop the faded yellow roller and steered it slowly back and forth over the length of the freshly paved driveway. The heavy cylinders on the front and back smoothed and compressed the asphalt into a flat surface. His path from the street to the garage followed a downhill slope with a sharp turn toward the bottom. Shane estimated that at the man's current pace, he'd be finished in about thirty minutes.

Yellow caution tape ran across the end of the driveway, with a couple of upside-down orange buckets acting as a secondary warning. No vehicles sat parked in front of the house, a good indication that the homeowners probably weren't there. If they arrived while Shane was doing his job, he'd scream for them to go inside and get some towels and bandages, then escape while they were preoccupied. If that didn't work, the scene itself should provide enough distraction. It's not every day you see a man after he's been flattened.

Flattened probably wasn't the right term, but it's all he could come up with. Smashed paper-thin like Judge Doom in *Who Framed Roger Rabbit?* But Roy wouldn't be peeling himself off the pavement. Once, back when Shane started driving, he accidentally ran over a squirrel. The animal ran across the street, got almost to the other side, then turned and darted directly into the path of his car. He braked and swerved, but a glance in the rearview confirmed his fear. When its tail twitched, Shane shuddered and knew what had to be done. He circled back and eased over the squirrel again, choking back bile as he imagined the scene playing out mere inches away under the car's tire.

After a last look around, he switched off the car, patted the fixed-blade knife strapped to his leg, and sauntered toward his objective. Newly purchased tennis shoes, a cheap pair from Walmart since they'd be trashed after one wear, squeezed his toes into a painful ball. A full size and a half too small, he'd opted for them in case he left a footprint anywhere. Sometimes good planning meant torturous walking.

Roy continued his slow, methodical movement up and down the driveway. The small wisps of steam off the asphalt had almost disappeared as the tarry substance cooled and hardened. Good. No footprints.

He angled from the sidewalk across the yard and stopped at the edge of the fresh asphalt. After a moment, he caught Roy's eye and waved to him. The man nodded but continued his work, backing up the hill toward the street. One more pass, maybe two, and he'd be finished.

Shane stood silently and watched as the roller completed its journey and began another trip down the drive. The machine moved along the far edge and squeezed the final section into a smooth surface. Roy looked at his watch and reversed the roller toward the street where his large pickup truck and trailer waited.

Shane hurried ahead of him, untied the caution tape, and nudged one of the buckets aside so Roy wouldn't have to stop. The man mouthed his thanks as he eased past and turned up the hill toward the trailer.

Shane paused to take a last peek at the area. No traffic. No one outside. Move quickly but cautiously. Don't be afraid to walk away if anything seems wrong.

He trotted toward the trailer and arrived as Roy dismounted and attached a winch cable from the back of the truck's cab to the roller, then twisted a knob on the machine. That would be the unload valve, a device that effectively acted as a clutch to allow both cylinders to roll freely. Amazing the things you could learn simply by downloading an owner's manual.

Things like the importance of performing this action on a smooth, level surface. Being certain the parking brake is set. Placing chocks on the downhill side of the rollers if necessary. Roy should've read the manual.

"Hey," Shane said. "I'm thinking about getting my driveway done too. How much you charge for something like that?"

The man shrugged. "Depends on a lot of things, like the shape it's in now and how much material we'll need. Best thing to do is call the office, and they'll set up someone to come out and give you an estimate."

"Will do. Got a card or something?"

Roy dug in his back jeans pocket and pulled one out. "Sorry, it's a little dirty."

"Sure. No problem." He walked toward the back of the roller. "I thought I … yep. You're leaking something. Hydraulic fluid, maybe?"

"Again? Third time this month." He sighed and strode behind the machine.

Shane moved closer and pointed toward the street. "A puddle of it right there. See it?"

Roy bent forward, the outline of his spine clearly visible against the filthy muscle shirt he wore. "I don't—"

The knife penetrated the full five and a half inches of its blade's length into Roy McIntyre, severing his spine and dropping the man instantly. Shane leaned over and retrieved the weapon. "You still with me, Roy?"

The man's eyes widened as he worked his mouth, but only a low wheezing sound came out. Might have punctured a lung too. No problem though, since identifying any damage on the body was about to go from routine to impossible.

Shane hurried to the trailer and pressed the button to release all tension on the cable holding the roller in place. It took a few seconds, but the big machine finally gave in to gravity and began its slow descent down the hill.

He scanned the area once more, jogged to his car, and watched long enough to confirm Roy McIntyre of McIntyre's Roofing and Paving would soon have his death spread, somewhat thinly perhaps, across every news station in a hundred-mile radius.

CHAPTER TWENTY-FOUR

Jeremy pressed the speaker button on his phone and laid the device on Maggie's dinette table. "Can you two hear me?"

"Yes," Tanessa said. "We hear you. Got something to take notes with?"

"Hold on." He rummaged through the junk drawer until he found a pen and scrap of paper. "Ready."

"Okay," Maggie said. "Here's what we learned. Georgia Harding grew up in Frederick, father unknown, mother in and out of jail on various charges, mostly drug-related. The girl lived with her grandparents and got average grades in school. She was sixteen when Holly was killed and—"

"Wait a sec," Jeremy said. He scratched the pen across the paper several times, leaving nothing but indentations. "This pen's out of ink. Why would you keep a pen that doesn't write?"

"Well," Maggie said, "I obviously didn't know it wouldn't write or I wouldn't have kept it, would I?"

"So you're telling me it ran out of ink at the exact moment you last stopped using it?"

Maggie sighed. "Really? This is what you want to talk about? I'm sure there's another one there somewhere. And you knew we were going to call. You should've been ready."

"I *am* ready. I just didn't know I would need to take notes. Give me a second." He shoved his chair back and checked the living room, eventually locating Beks' coloring stash. "Go slow. I'm writing in crayon."

"Is he always like this?" Tanessa asked.

"No," Maggie said. "Sometimes he's worse."

He grinned. "If you ladies are ready to continue ..."

"Yep," Tanessa said. "Georgia Harding was sixteen at the time. She does have a juvie record, but it's been expunged so I'm guessing mostly minor stuff. We can try to dig into it later if we need to. Her photo was in the paper when she was six. A shot of her at the state fair eating a foot-long hot dog. She's biting one end; a friend's biting the other. Looks staged."

Jeremy circled the *16* he'd written. "Were you able to get into her Facebook? I would try, but somehow I think she'd turn down a friend request."

"No need," Maggie said. "In those days everybody used AOL. Not exactly social media, right? Facebook didn't get going until a few years after Holly's death. But we—"

"It might be worth a look anyway," Jeremy said. "You never know what—"

"Does he always interrupt like that?" Tanessa asked. "Really, Mr. Winter, you should ... 'kay if I call you Jeremy? Great. Really, Jeremy, you should let Mags finish what she's saying before you barge into the conversation."

He smiled and doodled a frowny face on the paper. "Yes, ma'am."

"So no Facebook back then," Maggie said. "Even if there was, she's got her privacy settings pretty high, so we wouldn't be able to access anything relevant without some, um, extra work."

"And," Tanessa said, "since this is all off the record, we can't really do that. No sweat though. We found something better. Myspace."

"Your space?" Jeremy asked.

"Jer," Tanessa said, "I know you can't see me right now, but picture me rolling my eyes, 'kay? God forbid we should actually do a video chat or something. I don't have grandparents, but if I did, I imagine they'd have your technological prowess. You need to work with him, Mags. Get him up to speed."

Maggie laughed. "I've tried, but you can't teach an old dog and pony show. Jeremy, Myspace was the first big social media site. Facebook eventually overpowered them, but they're still around. Most people who had a Myspace account don't even remember it's still there, but it is. They didn't get going until a couple of years after Holly's death, but we took a look anyway. Georgia Harding has a profile on there with lots of photos and names. Several people show up a lot. Probably a clique she ran around with."

"Yep," Tanessa said. "They look like clones. The girls wearing low-rise jeans or cargo pants, suede boots, and crop tops. The guys all had on ripped jeans, trucker caps, and bleached blond hair. Not good looks. You ever dress like that, Jer? That's something I'd have to see."

"No," Maggie said. "No you wouldn't. It's hard enough to get rid of some of the memories this job gives you. No need to add more. You still with us, Jeremy?"

"I'm here. Glad you two are having such a good time. Really. But is there anything that might, you know, actually be helpful? Or was this all just a setup for your Abbott and Costello routine?"

Silence filled the next several seconds.

Jeremy shook his head. "You just looked at Maggie and shrugged, didn't you, Tanessa? Because you don't know who Abbott and Costello are."

Her throaty laugh was loud and spirit-lifting. "See, who needs a video chat?" she said. "Sharpen your crayon and get ready. I've got six names for you but start with the first one. He was her boyfriend back then. They look pretty cozy in a lot of the photos. If Georgia Harding said anything to anyone, it'd be this guy."

"Got it. Fire away."

"Listen," Maggie said. "We're out of the loop on this after we give you the names. You're on your own."

"Mm-hmm. No problem."

"'Kay," Tanessa said. "The guy you're looking for is named Shane Kingston, and yes, I have his phone number."

CHAPTER TWENTY-FIVE

"Hi there. You've reached Shane Kingston. Leave a message, and I'll return your call when I can."

Jeremy left his name, number, and a vague message about doing historical research in the Frederick area and how helpful it would be if the two of them spoke. He repeated his name and number before hanging up. Kingston might call. Might not. He'd give him a day before leaving another message. Any sooner might spook the guy.

His $10.95 investment in Kingston's data search paid off. The thirty-three-year-old lived in Charlotte, alone apparently, stayed current on all his bills, worked for a large collection agency, and graduated from college with a massive student loan debt. A clean arrest record and no outstanding warrants. His parents, William and Rachel, were now residents of Baltimore.

Jeremy squinted at the clock displayed at the bottom of his laptop screen. Still a couple of hours before he had to pick up Beks from school. Plenty of time to call the other names on the list. He'd wait to run the background checks until after he spoke to them. The next name was—

His heart jumped as the phone rang and vibrated on the table. Area code 704. Charlotte. "Hello?"

"Mr. Winter? This is Shane Kingston. I'm returning your call?"

Jeremy cursed himself for not having a pen ready. The crayon would have to do. "Yes, Mr. Kingston. Thanks for calling me back so quickly."

"Sure. What can I do for you?"

"I, uh, I'm looking into an event that occurred in Frederick not long after 9/11. A young woman was shot and killed."

"You a cop?"

"No, I'm not. To be upfront with you, I *am* a retired FBI agent;

however, that has nothing to do with my interest in this."

"No?"

A long pause followed. Jeremy dotted crayon on the paper. He wants to know why I'm looking into it. Could just be curious or could be that it matters for some reason. "She was my wife."

"Oh, man. Sorry. Yeah, I do sorta remember it happening, but nothing specific, you know? Been a long time. I have to ask though. Why are you calling me?"

"It has been a long time. Seventeen years to be exact. I called you because, well, I hoped you might know someone who could shed light on the murder. Georgia Harding. Her last name was Mayer back then. I'm calling some of her friends to see if maybe she said anything about the shooting. Don't get me wrong. Ms. Harding is not a suspect."

"Georgia? I haven't talked to her since high school. I mean, yeah, we hung out and stuff, and I guess you could say she was my girlfriend for a while, but if she knows anything, she didn't tell me. Why don't you just ask her?"

I did. "I've been trying to get in touch with her for a while but haven't had much luck. That's why I'm reaching out to others, to see if they remember her saying anything." *Reaching out.* When had he started using that phrase? Ugh.

"Huh. So what makes you think she's involved?"

Involved? "Um, new evidence has come to light. She's not a suspect." At least she wasn't until you said *involved.*

"I'm sorry, but I can't help you. Like I said, I haven't spoken to Georgia in forever, and as far as I recall, she never said anything to me about the murder."

"But you were aware of it, right? My wife's killing. Everyone knew about it?"

"Sure. Not much big news in Frederick in those days. Maybe it's the same way now. Look, I need to get back to work, so if there's nothing else …"

"Um, no. Thank you, Mr. Kingston." Jeremy hung up and studied the paper with its red-crayoned *16* and *involved.* Georgia Harding knew something. No question about it. Time to apply some pressure.

. . . .

Thirty-seven minutes. Jeremy drummed his fingers on the steering wheel. That's how long he'd waited thus far. Georgia Harding's Jeep Cherokee faced the opposite direction in the parking spot next to him. He planned to remain in his car so as to not be threatening. Just a simple chat to let her know that if she didn't speak to him soon, he'd be contacting others. Her friends, coworkers, pastor, whomever.

Assuming she ever came out of Hobby Lobby. He'd been in the store once with Maggie back in Virginia. The sign on the door said everything was always thirty percent off its regular price. He'd started to tell her that if something's always thirty percent off, why not just put the real price— she'd shushed him and hurried into the store's depths. After a few minutes, he'd found a bench near the front doors and waited next to another man. The two never spoke, but their shared plight bonded them. That day, he texted Maggie after thirty minutes and said the bench was getting hard. She replied and said maybe he'd be more comfortable waiting in the car.

Thirty-eight minutes. Janice had called an hour before to confirm she'd picked up Beks and the two of them would wait at Maggie's apartment. And if they didn't mind a late dinner, she would fix lasagna for everyone. Jeremy assured her he'd be fine with eating a bit later than usual.

Finally. Georgia Harding stepped out of the store and headed toward her Jeep, no shopping bag in hand. Forty-plus minutes of wandering Hobby Lobby. His own version of whatever methods they were using down in Guantanamo now.

She used her key fob to unlock the doors and stepped between their two vehicles. He cleared his throat and leaned toward the window. The sound and movement startled her, and she froze a few steps back.

"Hello, Ms. Harding," he said. "I'm sorry if I alarmed you."

She glared at him and opened her car door without speaking.

"Ma'am," he said, "I spoke to a few of your friends."

"What friends? Why?"

"From when you were in high school."

She slid into her car but left the door open. "Why would you do that? I told you. I don't know anything."

"Yes, you did say that, and I want to believe you, but things keep popping up that make me, um, curious. Certain words are being used when I ask about you and my wife's shooting. Words like *involved*."

"Involved? Who said that? I had nothing to do with it. Nothing."

He nodded. "And you'll testify to that?"

Wrinkles creased her forehead. "I'm not testifying to anything. None of this has anything to do with me."

"I'm afraid that's not how our system works. If summoned, you *will* testify or risk going to jail. Unless you're the accused, of course. Can't make you get on the stand then. You and your attorney will have to decide that."

Her voice ratcheted up a notch. "Accused of what? There's no evidence. Can't be, because I didn't do it."

"Ms. Harding, I've been investigating crimes for a very long time. Most of the people I've caught said the same thing." He shrugged. "There are a few who bragged about their, uh, actions. You're not the type though, are you? No, you want the past to stay buried. I do believe you know something about what happened that day, so I have to ask myself why you're hiding that knowledge. With my suspicious nature, well, I think you can see how—"

"What will it take to make this—you—go away?" she asked. "I didn't kill your wife."

"The truth. That's all it will take. Tell me whatever it is you're holding back. All of it. I promise you this: if you're not involved, had nothing to do with it, you'll never see me again. Lie to me or not tell me the whole story, I'll be your shadow until I get what I want. I'm not a bad guy, Ms. Harding. At least I don't think I am." He paused. "Then again, most of the people I've caught didn't think they were bad either."

Her shoulders sank, and all expression left her face. "Not here. Tomorrow morning before I go to work. Denny's on Dual Highway. Six thirty. My husband will be there too."

"Thank you. Please don't disappoint me by deciding not to show up."

"We'll be there."

She closed her door, and he watched as she drove away. Her husband would try to talk her out of it, but she'd be there, with or without him.

Jeremy waited for a few minutes before leaving. Didn't want Ms. Harding to think he was following her. He wasn't, of course. Not with lasagna waiting at home.

CHAPTER TWENTY-SIX

Jeremy stared vacantly into the steaming cup of coffee, the third since he'd arrived at Denny's. He normally woke between five and five-thirty each morning. No need for an alarm and didn't matter what time he went to bed. Today he'd woken earlier because the seventy-mile drive to Hagerstown would take well over an hour. That meant setting an alarm, which in turn meant waking up every thirty minutes to make sure he hadn't overslept. Arriving late might provide Georgia Harding with an excuse to skip out, and he wasn't going to let that happen.

His stomach roiled as last night's lasagna reminded him he shouldn't have gone back for seconds. Or thirds. Janice was an excellent cook, and since retiring as Director Bailey's admin, the widow had adopted Jeremy, Maggie, and Beks as her new family. She doted on each of them as a mother would, for better and worse.

"Doing okay?"

He squinted toward the waitress. "Hanging in there."

"Rough night, huh?"

The woman probably saw her share of early morning customers nursing heavy hangovers. "Not too bad," he said.

"You sure you don't want something to eat?"

"Um, some wheat toast? Dry, please."

She arched an eyebrow. "Not much to eat. You know, they say breakfast is the most important meal of the day."

He turned his attention back to his coffee. Really don't feel like chitchat this morning. "Yeah, they do say that."

"Be right back. I'll top off your coffee then too."

"Mm-hmm. Sounds great."

The waitress returned with more coffee and his toast, then turned and walked off without a word. He'd have to increase his tip. He shifted his gaze out the window as a vehicle parked near the entrance. Georgia Harding was here, and she was alone. Either her husband decided not to come, or he didn't—nope. The man pulled alongside his wife, and the two stepped out of their vehicles and hugged before coming inside.

Jeremy shook his phone to begin the recording process and placed it upside down on the table, then waved his hand to get their attention. Neither spoke as they slid into the booth across from him. The waitress came by, and Georgia ordered coffee and a bran muffin, while her husband opted for a large orange juice, ham-and-cheese omelet, and two pancakes.

"Breakfast is on me," Jeremy said. He extended his hand across the table to the husband. "I didn't catch your name when we met at your home."

The man ignored the gesture. "Julius Harding. And we're here against my better judgment."

"I understand," Jeremy said. "I hope we can resolve this and go our separate ways. That's what we all want."

Ms. Harding sipped her coffee and nodded. "Separate ways sounds good. Mr. Winter, I swear I'm going to tell you everything I know. It won't take long. I'll answer any questions you have, but after that, we're done. I will never repeat what I say this morning to anyone else. If questioned, I will deny ever saying it. If I am being recorded, I explicitly deny giving permission for that to occur. Those are my terms."

Jeremy slid his untouched toast to the side and rested his forearms on the table. "I can live with that."

She waited as the waitress placed their meals before them, topped off their drinks, and moved on to the next customer. Mr. Harding slathered butter on his pancakes, doused his omelet in pepper, and squeezed her hand. "Ready when you are, babe."

"I do know who killed your wife," she said. "I saw it happen, and I called 911." She brushed away a tear. "I can still see it. She shouldn't have died. I'm sorry I didn't do more to help her."

Jeremy licked his lips. Stay level. No emotion. "Nothing you could have done. I've seen the autopsy report. There's nothing anyone could have done."

Mr. Harding nodded once in appreciation.

"Thank you," she said. "Doesn't make it easier though, does it?"

"Take your time, honey," her husband said.

"I've held this in too long. I saw him, Mr. Winter. He wasn't trying to shoot *your* wife. He was trying to shoot his own."

What? "Who was he?" Jeremy asked.

"The man was William Kingston," she said. "His son, Shane, and I dated back in high school. His mother used to get beat up pretty regularly. He told me some of the things his dad did." She shuddered. "Bad stuff."

Jeremy took a drink of water and let the coolness work its way down. Maggie's ex got rough with her once. Once. Her anger, coupled with her FBI training, sent him to the hospital. She never pressed charges, but she did file divorce papers. There was something especially heinous about a man hitting a woman. "Tell me what you saw."

She wrapped her hands around the cup of coffee and stared into it.

Her husband rubbed his hand on her back. "You don't have to do this."

She glanced at him, then returned her gaze to the coffee. "I know." After several seconds of silence, she took a deep breath and looked up. "Rough time at school that day, you know? I wasn't exactly a model student, but I managed. Got a couple of tests back and failed them both. No big deal, right, except I was already in danger of having to repeat my sophomore year. That wasn't going to happen."

Jeremy didn't respond. Let her talk.

"Repeating a grade or dropping out. Either way, I lose. Not because of any future goals. I'm sixteen, okay? School meant nothing, but watching my friends move on? Seeing them leave me behind? Whisper and point? No thanks. Anyway, like I said, rough day. I wanted a beer, and I knew the guy at the market down the street could make that happen."

The waitress stopped by and refilled their coffee, then placed the check in the middle of the table. Jeremy slid the ticket to his side.

Ms. Harding sipped her coffee and blew into the cup, forcing the heat across her face. "I'm walking past the little strip mall, the one where your wife ... where it happened. The place is nearly deserted. I see this woman, your wife, pushing a shopping cart packed with baby stuff. Diapers, crib, things like that."

Jeremy closed his eyes and pictured the scene from the murder book. Everything there, just as she said. "Go on."

She dabbed at her nose with a napkin. "All of a sudden, I hear a bunch of yelling. Not friendly. More like rage. So I stop and try to figure out where it's coming from. Stay away, right? That's when I saw the Kingstons. Recognized them right away. There used to be this row of bushes along the edge of the parking lot, but by then half of them were dead. I hid behind one. Didn't want them to see me. To be honest, neither of them were real happy about me and Shane being together, so I figured why make things worse."

Jeremy nodded. "Did the Kingstons live far from there?"

"Uh-uh," she said. "Maybe a block and a half away? Nice neighborhood too. A lot nicer than mine was. So they're both not really running but walking extra fast. She looks scared, and he's screaming at her to stop and waving his hand around. I could tell he had something in it, but until I heard the shot …"

Jeremy exhaled slowly. Stay focused. "So you saw him fire the weapon?"

"More like I put two and two together. The noise and his hand jerked back and their reactions. I froze. Thought he'd killed his wife, but she took off running again. He, like, stared at his hand, the one with the gun in it, then turned around and ran back toward his house. That's when I saw your wife was on the ground. At first, I thought she was, you know, protecting herself, but then I saw the blood and …"

Her hand trembled, and her husband placed his on top. "It's okay, baby," he said glaring across the table. "I think that's enough, Mr. Winter."

Jeremy tilted his head back and focused on the ceiling. Sorrow tugged his heart into emptiness. His jaw ached and his vision blurred as tears pooled in his eyes. So Holly died because a domestic violence incident escalated to a gunshot. "Just a question or two. Please. Ms. Harding, why didn't you report any of this to the police?"

"You know why," she said. "Same reason no one else reports stuff. Didn't want my name mentioned, especially since I'd already had my share of run-ins with the cops. Some weed, shoplifting, nothing major but enough that we weren't on the best of terms, you know? Look, I'm sorry. I know I should've, but, well, I'm sorry. I wish I had. At the time, I thought calling 911 would be enough."

It wasn't. "Who else knows all this?"

"I did tell Shane what I saw. We talked about it a lot. He said things got better at home after that. More peaceful. I kept up with the news reports, and it looked like the cops didn't have anything. No suspects or evidence.

It would just be my word against his. And if I called it in anonymously, Mr. Kingston would think his wife reported him. I can't imagine what he'd have done to her."

Jeremy sighed and frowned. *I can.* "Did you ever tell anyone else what you saw?"

"No, only Shane, and he didn't seem surprised, like he expected it would come to that sooner or later."

Shane knows his father killed Holly. Why is he protecting him? "Did his father abuse him too?"

She shook her head. "Never laid a hand on him. Shane always thought that's why his mother stayed. So she could take the abuse instead of him. Mr. Kingston has a nasty mean streak. Nobody knows that except his family though. Everybody else thinks he's a decent guy."

"Did Mrs. Kingston ever go to the police about the abuse?"

"Not as far as I know. I asked Shane about it once, and he said she figured doing that would only make things worse. A couple of years after all this, he turned eighteen, and she finally left. Guess she thought he could take care of himself at that point."

Her husband draped his arm around her, and she scooted closer to him.

"One last question," Jeremy said. "When was the last time you communicated with Shane?"

"Not long before he went off to college," she said. "Why?"

"Just curious. I'm not going to say I agree with your decision not to tell the police what you saw, Ms. Harding. If you'd pointed them in the right direction, who knows what might have happened? But we can't change the past. Is there anything else you can remember that could help me?"

"No. Believe me, I've relived that day a million times. There's nothing else. I hope you can prove your case, Mr. Winter. That man deserves to pay for what he's done. Not just to your family, but to his own."

Jeremy smiled but clenched his fists under the table. "Thank you both. As I said, I'll do everything possible to leave you out of this. Hopefully, you'll never see or hear from me again. If you do think of something else, I assume you still have my number in your cell phone?"

"I do," she said.

He stood, nodded, and walked to the cash register. He paid for their meals and handed the waitress a twenty-dollar tip before hurrying to his car. Once inside, he gripped the steering wheel until his knuckles whitened. Finally, after so many years, he had what he needed.

A name.

CHAPTER TWENTY-SEVEN

Jeremy massaged the back of his neck and nibbled on a baby carrot. After driving to Haymarket and walking four laps around the school's track—two of them without his cane—he'd stopped by the grocery before returning to his apartment. His fridge and pantry remained nearly empty. No sense stocking up when he'd be moving out as soon as the wedding took place.

The date still hadn't been set, and Maggie agreed that having the wedding sooner rather than later was better, but not yet. She couldn't take off work until she finished training Tanessa, and he was preoccupied with his own investigation. Preoccupied. Sounded better than "obsessed and under the gun to resolve his past before the future arrived." Meanwhile, the small stack of moving boxes waited patiently in the living room.

He swallowed the last of the baby carrot. What a scam. Take the big ugly carrots, shave them down to a cute, smooth size, and jack up the price. Because, you know, ugly carrots taste worse than pretty carrots. He'd bought four bags.

After using his tongue to work a smashed tidbit from a back molar, he reread his notes. According to William Kingston's profile on LinkedIn, the man worked as the Chief Experience Officer (CXO) at the corporate offices of Dependable Guaranty Insurance in Baltimore. His primary responsibility was ensuring excellent interaction with customers at all levels of the organization. Jeremy grunted. Sounded like government-speak for "I make a lot of money doing a made-up job."

Kingston had divorced his wife, Rachel, thirteen years prior, citing abandonment. As near as Jeremy could tell, the timing matched Georgia Harding's statement that once Shane turned eighteen, his mother fled. If Kingston had remarried, there was no indication of it online. He lived in a gated community, and there were no records of any arrests or warrants. From an outsider's perspective, William Kingston was a generic white male, though better off than most. Nowhere near the one-percenter status, but nothing to complain about either. At least not yet.

Jeremy needed to meet with the man. Get a feel for how to proceed with the investigation. Georgia Harding gave him a starting point. That's all he'd ever needed.

He phoned the insurance company and was forwarded to Kingston's assistant. He asked to schedule an appointment, she asked why, he said it was a private matter, she said she needed more information, he said no she didn't, she said yes she did, he said tell him it's about something that happened a long time ago, she said she needed more details, he said Mr. Kingston would know, she said she doubted it and she'd call him back if her boss wanted to meet with him.

Jeremy made a mental note to tell the man that a CXO ought to provide a better customer experience to callers. Of course, he'd leave out the part that he wasn't actually a client. He stood and paced for a few minutes. How to deal with Kingston? A direct approach would shut him down. Revealing that a witness named the man as Holly's killer might shake him, but not for long. A subtler tactic was required. One that built a longer path to Kingston's guilt. If only he had another—

Idiot. Rachel was the key. Find her and get her to talk. After so many years away from her abusive ex, her fear may have dissipated. And she wouldn't need to see Kingston or speak to him. Not until charges had been filed. He grabbed a Diet Coke from the fridge and did a quick Google search for the woman.

An old newspaper article announcing William Kingston's upcoming wedding gave her maiden name as Rachel Lynn Anderson. He chased the usual trails and found her birthdate and prior addresses. No credit history, which meant everything had been in her husband's name. No criminal record either. And nothing since she'd fled fifteen years before.

Not surprising, really. It's only natural that someone in her situation would want to disappear in case her husband came looking. People dropped off the grid all the time. Maggie could run a far more detailed search on the woman's Social Security number but asking such favors didn't need to become a habit. Too much downside for her job and their relationship.

But a mother would want to keep in touch with her son, wouldn't she?

If anyone knew how to contact Rachel Anderson, it'd be Shane. And if he hadn't heard from her in all these years?

Well, that opened up another possibility.

William Kingston might have more than one murder to answer for.

CHAPTER TWENTY-EIGHT

Jeremy dialed Shane Kingston's number and left a message asking if he'd mind answering a couple more questions. The conversation would be tricky. According to Georgia, Shane knew all about his father's guilt in Holly's death. If that was true, confronting Shane with that fact would push him away. He was already protecting his father for whatever reason. He needed to step forward on his own and be willing to give a statement to law enforcement.

It was already mid-afternoon, and Jeremy needed to pick up Beks soon. William Kingston wasn't going to call. The man probably phoned his lawyer and got the same advice all attorneys give: nothing good ever comes from talking to anyone except your well-paid legal counsel.

Nothing to do but wait. If he was still with the Bureau, he could pull more search data on the wife-slash-mother. Dig into the husband-slash-father deeper. Possibly stumble across the one tidbit of information that started the trail of breadcrumbs leading to a conviction.

But he was no longer an agent. There were other ways to obtain information, of course. Private investigators always knew cops who'd get info for the right price. Hackers could finagle their way through cyberspace and learn anything you wanted to know. Could he even ask Detective Pronger to help? Yeah, he could, though that would probably be a dead end. But this was Jeremy's case. His last. When the time came, and if he needed them, he'd explore other options. But not yet.

His phone beeped, and he unlocked the screen. A voice mail? The thing never rang. How come sometimes it rings and sometimes it doesn't? "Technology's going to make your life easier," they said. Right. The wrong button got pushed in some app, and now some things make noise and others don't. He'd have Beks fix it later.

The message was short. "Mr. Winter? This is Shane Kingston returning your call. I'll be on break for another couple of minutes; otherwise, you can get me in the morning. Thanks."

Jeremy swore under his breath and punched the redial button. Answer the phone. Answer the phone. Answer the—

"Hey, Mr. Winter."

Jeremy exhaled. "Thanks for calling me back, Mr. Kingston."

"Shane, please."

"Sure. I'm following up on our previous conversation."

"About Georgia? You talk to her?"

"I did. Have you spoken with her recently?"

"Not in years. Before I went off to college, I think. Why? What did she say?"

"Dead-end street, I'm afraid. Listen, I do have a favor to ask if you don't mind. I'd like to speak with some of the adults who lived in the area at the time, but I'm running into a problem locating very many of them. Lots seemed to have moved on."

Shane chuckled. "Frederick's not exactly a boomtown. Kind of quiet. Like I said before, not a place I want to go back to."

"Really? Seems like a nice area."

"Guess it depends on what you're looking for."

"I suppose it does. Anyway, I thought you might be able to help me out and put me in touch with your parents. I promise not to take much of their time. Just a quick phone call to see if they heard any rumors about the murder. Then maybe I can get the names of some of their friends who lived nearby and go from there."

A long pause followed. "Yeah," Shane said. "I'm not sure I can help with that. My dad and I aren't exactly on speaking terms. He lives in Baltimore now, last I heard. You can look him up there."

"Oh, I'm sorry to hear that. What about your mother?"

"My, um, my mom left home a long time ago."

"Would it be all right if I called her? Do you have her number?"

"Yes. I mean, no. I have her number, but I can't give it to you. It's a privacy thing. She wants to be left alone."

"I certainly understand that. Do you talk to her often? Would you ask her if it'd be okay for me to speak with her for a few minutes?"

"Once or twice a month, but I don't think that's a good idea. She doesn't want to be bothered."

Jeremy squeezed his eyes shut to try and force back the headache coming his way. "Do you think you could at least ask her? It's important that I—"

click

Dropped the call. Or he hung up.

Jeremy redialed, and it went straight to voice mail. No ringing. He'd touched a nerve. Shane was determined to protect his mother's privacy. Good for him.

But bad for the investigation. He was stuck. Confronting William Kingston with an accusation of murder would go nowhere. Georgia Harding wasn't about to step forward and stand behind her allegation. Shane apparently wanted nothing to do with his past. And the only other person who could help, Rachel Anderson, didn't want to be found.

If a phone call didn't work, maybe an in-person meeting would. It was time to go to Charlotte.

CHAPTER TWENTY-NINE

After working out the details with Maggie and Janice the night before, Jeremy woke early and hit the road. The drive to Charlotte took just under six hours. Gone were the days of booking a flight and traveling on the Bureau's dollar. He could live comfortably on his pension as long as he kept spending under control. No extravagances like last-minute flights, a warm apartment, or three meals a day.

He pulled into the motel parking lot and smiled. With their joint income, he and Maggie would be fine. Neither were big spenders, but he did want to be able to do things when they felt like it. A decent home with a good-size yard … and the money to pay a landscaper to mow the lawn. Maybe some sort of media room with a huge TV for hockey games or those Hallmark movies Maggie had become addicted to. And long vacations with the family sounded great. All those things cost money though, which meant finding a new job once this investigation ended. Whatever that turned out to be, he was certain of one thing. No more bureaucracy at any level, local, state, or federal. No more rules or oversight or worrying about whose toes he might be stepping on. Enough was enough.

After checking in, he surveyed his room. Old, but comfortable and clean-looking. A blacklight would doubtless tell a different tale, but ignorance really is bliss in these situations. He'd seen far worse, though this was easily on the low end of places he'd slept in since Afghanistan. No way he'd let Maggie or Beks stay somewhere like this. Partly because of the faint musty odor, but mostly because of the safety issue. A door that opened to a parking lot. Small deadbolt and a worthless chain. The Glock would sleep on the bedside table tonight.

Barely noon. Still time to catch Shane Kingston before he left for his shift. The road trip gave Jeremy a chance to figure out how to handle the situation, and in the end, the best option seemed to be to simply knock on the man's door and introduce himself. If nothing else, they'd be face-to-face. Experience taught him it's a lot harder to say "no" in person than it is online or on the phone.

The journey to Shane's apartment took thirty minutes, ten of which were spent in the drive-thru lane at McDonald's. Apparently the McRib was back in town for a short visit, and customers didn't want to miss their chance. He passed on the opportunity and chose a grilled chicken wrap, no dressing. It was no McRib, but ... well, thank goodness it was no McRib.

The apartment complex was well-maintained, with lots of trees and open space to walk or play in. Jeremy pulled into a parking spot near the steps of Shane's building. He lived on the second floor, so cane or no cane? One option made the stairs easier and also gave an "I'm no threat" appearance. The other choice meant a slower trip up and down. Easy decision.

He slid from his car, gripped the cane, and moved toward the staircase. As he neared, a man, early thirties wearing khakis, dress shirt, and tie, took the steps down two at a time. Great.

Jeremy stopped and waited until the man reached the ground. "Hello there. You wouldn't be Shane Kingston by any chance, would you?"

"Yeah, I am. Can I help ... uh-uh. You're the guy on the phone. I've got to go. Late for work."

"A minute," Jeremy said. "That's all I need. Please."

"Nothing else to say. I don't know anything."

"So you've said. What about your mother though? Rachel Lynn Anderson, right?"

Shane's eyes narrowed. "You've done your homework. Doesn't make any difference. She doesn't want to talk to you."

"Then you did ask her?"

"Yeah, I called her. She said she was sorry, but she didn't know anything either. Now if you'll just—"

"When?"

"What?"

"When did you call her?" Jeremy asked. If he knew a time and date, then got his hands on Shane's phone records, it'd be a huge step toward finding the woman.

"None of your business, man. Why does it even matter?"

Maybe Shane isn't glued to his phone like most people his age. If there aren't a lot of calls and texts, it might not be difficult to isolate his mother's number. "Sorry," Jeremy said. "Old habits. Hey, how about I buy you breakfast tomorrow? Or lunch? You pick the time and restaurant? Give me a chance to make up for being such a pain."

"Um, I appreciate it, but no thanks. And please don't call me or come by my home again, okay? I've got nothing left to say." He strode toward his vehicle without another look, then backed out and lowered his window. "You can't stay around here. No loitering."

Jeremy nodded and waved but didn't move. "Got it."

"I'm serious. You have to leave."

"I heard you." He gestured at the cane. "Resting up for a minute."

"Sure, sure. You need some help?"

Awful eager to get me out of here. He walked to his car, exaggerating the limp each step of the way. "No, I'm good. Have a nice day."

When he pulled away from the building, Shane followed him until both were out of the complex. They turned opposite directions, and Jeremy watched as the man's car disappeared in the distance in the rearview. Whatever just happened at the apartments, it was obvious Shane didn't want him anywhere near his home.

An ex-FBI agent might think that was suspicious. Like maybe Shane Kingston had something to hide. Or, perhaps, *someone*.

No way he could head back to Virginia until he knew for sure. Some nighttime surveillance might tell him if Rachel Anderson lived with her son now. And if the stakeout accomplished nothing, so be it.

He'd broken into a police detective's car once. Granted, the vehicle had been unlocked, but still … an apartment couldn't be that much more difficult.

CHAPTER THIRTY

Jeremy returned to his motel to research picking door locks. It'd been years since he'd last had to do it, and even then he'd struggled. Something about the finesse and patience involved. Far easier to just kick in the door.

YouTube videos made the process look easy, though those guys were probably criminals or locksmiths. And if Shane secured the deadbolt, there'd be no chance. Still a few hours until dark, and if the stakeout paid off, no need to go inside. Any sign of movement in the apartment would provide enough incentive to continue. It wouldn't prove Rachel Anderson was there. Could be a girlfriend or roommate or whatever, but he'd at least have a reason to keep looking.

Only one thing left to do before heading out. He rubbed his palms on his pants legs as his heart palpitated. Time to get this over with. Maggie needed to know his plan. She'd be home by now, which meant any potential outbursts would be unrestrained. He braced himself and dialed her cell. She answered on the second ring.

"What's up?" she asked. "You talk to him yet?"

He shared the details of their encounter, focusing heavily on his suspicions about Shane's mother.

"Hold on," Maggie said. "Tanessa, got a sec? Great. I'm putting you on speakerphone, Jeremy."

"No," he said. "Don't put me—"

"Hey, Jer," Tanessa said. "How was the drive?"

"Fine," he said. "You guys having a girls' night or something?"

"We are," Maggie said. "Janice is here too."

"Hi, Jeremy," the older woman said. "Are you taking care of yourself? Rebecca is reading a story to me. One of those Harry Potter books. It's very good. Have you read them?"

He smiled. Janice always pretended her eyes were tired so Beks would read to her. "No, I haven't. Glad the whole gang's there. Maggie, can you, uh, pick up the phone?"

"Thanks, Jer," Tanessa said. "Don't trust me? Means a lot. Really. I'm gonna let you in on a little secret. Mags and I talk about everything. *Everything.* Long days, you know? But I get it. You want your privacy. No problem."

He ran the back of his hand across his forehead. "Tanessa, I didn't mean to offend you. I wanted—"

"I'm messin' with you, Jer. 'Kay? I swear. You need to loosen up. Now, what were we talking about?"

Maggie laughed. "I wanted her to hear what you told me about your run-in with Shane Kingston today. It'd be a good example for her of how people's actions are usually more important than their words. Rebecca, would you please go get ready for bed while we talk?"

"It's barely even dark outside," the girl said. "Why can't I stay?"

"Because I asked you to go get ready for bed," Maggie said. "Now go before—"

"Sweetheart," Janice said, "go on now. I'll be there in a minute, and we'll read some more. After some chocolate milk and cookies, of course, so wait to brush your teeth."

Jeremy sighed. "Is there anyone else around?"

"Nope," Tanessa said. "Just me, you, Mags and Janice. Oh, and your neighbors depending on how thin these walls are. Go for it."

"Don't mind me, dear," Janice said. "I'll tidy up the dishes then head to Rebecca's room."

"You don't have to do that," Maggie said. "Leave them, and I'll clean up later."

"Nonsense. A working *single* mother has her hands full enough. You hear me, Jeremy?"

"I hear you," he said. "Single mother. Subtle. Can we please get back to the reason I called?" He repeated the story, this time elaborating on the details. "I'm willing to bet," he said, "that Shane circled back to make sure I was gone. He's hiding something."

"Not necessarily," Maggie said. "Could be he wants to ... tell you what. Let's make this a learning exercise and get Tanessa's input first."

"Thought you'd never ask," she said. "Based on the information Jer gave us, I agree Shane seems shady." She paused. "Shane seems shady. Say that three times fast. Anyways, last I heard there was no law against acting suspicious. And the man's not suspected, much less charged with, any crimes, right?"

"Correct," Jeremy said.

"So let's think this through," Tanessa said. "You want to talk to his mother because she's the only other witness to Holly's murder."

He rolled his eyes. "You two really do talk about everything."

"Sorry," Maggie said. "I didn't figure you'd mind."

"I don't, but it would've been nice to have been asked first."

"So you don't care that I told her, but now you're mad because I didn't ask before doing something I knew you wouldn't care about?"

"That's not the point," Jeremy said. "All I'm saying is—"

"You sure you two aren't already married?" Tanessa asked. "As I was saying, it's important for you to talk to Shane's mother and see if she substantiates Georgia Harding's claims. But for whatever reason, the woman doesn't want to be found, and now you think you know where she's staying. That about sum it up?"

"Mostly," Maggie said. "We suspect that … what's the mother's name?"

"Rachel Lynn Anderson," Jeremy said, "assuming she switched back to her maiden name. I think she's afraid to come forward because of her ex. He apparently abused her pretty bad and pretty often."

"Never understood that," Tanessa said. "If you're scared of the dude, take the kid and leave. Call the cops. Do something. Anything's better than taking a beating."

"Think so?" Maggie asked. "You ever been in a bad relationship?"

"Plenty, but never one that got to that point. You?"

Jeremy closed his eyes. His heart sank, and he breathed deeply. The thought of someone harming Maggie or Beks brought pain and sorrow.

"Once," Maggie said. "My ex. I dealt with it. Individuals react differently though. Remember that. When—if—you go to a murder scene, don't put too much stock in how people are acting. Listen and watch, but when you lean toward someone as a suspect just because they didn't cry enough over a dead body, your investigation is already tainted."

"Fair enough," Tanessa said. "So what's the plan, Jer? Stake out the apartment and see if anyone else is there?"

"That's the idea," he said.

"You running his phone records too?"

"What?" Maggie asked. "He can't do that."

"I know *he* can't, but I thought maybe …"

"No," Jeremy said. "Absolutely not. No way are you two doing anything of the sort. We're clear on that, right?"

"Very," Maggie said. "Tanessa, you know we could get in a lot of trouble if we did that. Even lose our jobs. Shane Kingston is not under investigation by the FBI, and if he were, we'd need a warrant to get his records."

"I'm serious," Jeremy said. "This is not a wink-wink and look the other way moment. Do not get involved in this."

"Wasn't planning to," Tanessa said. "I just thought one of you might have contacts somewhere in government who owed you a favor. Let someone else get their hands dirty. And if you don't know anyone, I might have one or two—"

"You're not hearing me," Maggie said. "Rules and procedures are in place for a reason. Respect them. You're far too new to know when it's all right to … just follow the rules, okay?"

"All right to bend them," Tanessa said. "That's what you were going to say. Military's no different. You'll let me know, Mags? When I can bend the rules?"

Jeremy laughed. "Sounds like you've got your hands full, Maggie. Tanessa, if you hear nothing else I say, hear this: the fastest way to lose your job and possibly go to prison is to do the wrong thing at the wrong time. Do the wrong thing at the right time, or the right thing at the wrong time, maybe you've got a chance. Otherwise, uh-uh."

"Got it," Tanessa said. "Written in crayon in my mind. So that's a no-go on the phone records, at least for me and Mags."

"A definite no-go," he said. "I'll keep an eye on the apartment tonight. If there's movement, I'll knock on the door and see who answers. If no one comes, I'll maintain surveillance a few more days. They can't stay in there forever."

"And if there's no movement?" Tanessa asked.

Jeremy cleared his throat. "Pick up the phone, Maggie."

"Uh-uh. No, no, no. We're not having any of that," Tanessa said.

"Something you don't want me to hear which means it's illegal, 'kay? You best not put Mags in that situation, understand me? Go on and do whatever it is you're gonna do, but don't tell an FBI agent about it first. What's wrong with you?"

"Lots," Maggie said. "But we have a deal. When he's about to do something, um, *questionable*, he tells me about it. Learned that lesson the hard way."

Tanessa dropped her voice a notch. "So you give him approval to do these questionable things?"

"Bending the rules," Jeremy said. "Except the rules don't really apply to me anymore since I'm not an agent."

"No, but laws do. Let's get it out there for everyone, 'kay? B and E. Breaking and entering. That's what we're talking about, right? No movement in Kingston's apartment means you're going inside. It's what I'd do. If I wasn't an FBI agent, I mean."

"Jeremiah Bartholomew Winter," Maggie said, "tell me that's not happening."

The battle was over without a shot being fired. "That is not happening," he said.

She lowered her tone. "Are you planning *anything* illegal tonight?"

Not anymore. "No, ma'am."

"I'm serious about this. Do your stakeout, knock on the door, I don't care. But that's it. Clear?"

"Yes, ma'am."

Tanessa's baritone laugh squelched all other noise. "You should see her, Jer. Her face is as red as her hair. I wouldn't mess with her if I were you. I mean, I guarded nuclear missiles, and Mags is still the most dangerous thing I've seen. And she doesn't come with built-in safety measures."

"I know that look well," he said.

"I bet you do. I'll hang up now before I make things worse."

"Oh, wait," Tanessa said. "One more question. Bartholomew? Really?"

Jeremy shook his head. "Goodbye, ladies. Give Beks a kiss for me."

CHAPTER THIRTY-ONE

Jeremy angled himself so half his back was against the car door and his legs were stretched into the passenger space. Four hours of nothing. Shane left one light on in the apartment, and there'd been no sign of movement. If anyone was inside, they weren't being obvious.

He'd maintain his position in the complex's parking lot until Shane returned home and all lights were out. After that, back to the motel for some sleep. His belief that Rachel Anderson lived there had faded, which raised another question. Why was Shane so adamant about Jeremy leaving the area? It was possible the woman lived in a different apartment in the complex, but if she did, it wasn't under her own name.

And if Shane's mother didn't live with him, the phone records would be the only link to her. Another subject for another day. But suspicions die hard. If Rachel Anderson wasn't in the apartment, what was Shane hiding?

The chance that Jeremy would get a look inside tonight was slim, especially after the warning from Maggie. So another few hours of boredom, a bit of rest, and then move forward in the only way still open to him.

Ambushing the son had been fruitless. Nothing to do but try his luck with the father.

. . . .

Shane paced another lap around the customer service area. The Winter guy had gone, but what if he came back? It hadn't taken much research to uncover most of the man's life. His run-in with Ramsey Cronfeld led to hundreds of online stories. The flow of information petered out after Senator Morgans divorced the colonel, but Shane learned enough to be worried.

He dodged an employee coming back from the restroom and continued his loop. What were the odds? His worthless father accidentally killing the pregnant wife of an FBI agent who later became national news? At least Winter wasn't an agent anymore, though he surely had enough friends who'd help him with anything he wanted.

The man's visit created a grave dilemma. Normally Shane would sit and list the pros and cons of his options, but not this time. Too hard to be still. The easy answer was to turn Winter loose on Dad. Deflect all attention away from himself. But that produced a new problem. He wasn't sure how much his father knew—or suspected—about his own proclivities, and the man wouldn't hesitate to throw his son under the bus in an attempt to save himself.

He could always do nothing. Let Winter's investigation run its course. Ultimately it would point to Dad. He had, after all, killed the woman. No question about it. But how deep would the ex-agent dig before he found enough to satisfy himself? Too much rooting around was a very dangerous thing. A definite hazard on the SWOT analysis.

The key was to identify whether this constituted a crisis or a threat. Each was handled differently. Past high-profile incidents taught today's CEOs that a crisis should be confronted head-on. Get everything out there in the open. A threat, however, should be watched, but not at the cost of losing focus on day-to-day activity. Track the danger, see if it changes, and don't waste time worrying about it.

A threat. Jeremy Winter was no crisis. Not yet. Nothing had happened. As long as it remained that way, life would continue as normal. But if other things came to light, activities known only to him and Buzz Lightyear, the situation would dictate a more deliberate response.

One that left little doubt as to his resolve.

Little chance for redemption.

And little pieces of his target.

CHAPTER THIRTY-TWO

The surveillance provided nothing more than a sore back and aching legs. Shane Kingston returned to his apartment from work right on schedule and turned the lights off shortly thereafter. At two a.m., the stakeout ended, and Jeremy drove to the motel. One glance at the bed and he decided to head home to Haymarket.

The late September night had a briskness to it, so he cracked his windows for the drive. Hot coffee plus cold air did the job, though a few times he stopped to stretch his legs and work energy back into his body. His joints ached from fatigue, but he soldiered on in the knowledge nothing felt as good when you're exhausted as your own bed.

Shortly before nine o'clock, he texted Maggie to let her know he was home, showered to get the all-nighter grunge off, and collapsed into a deep sleep. The alarm woke him at noon, and he crawled out of bed, splashed water on his face, and dressed. His initial thought was some laps at the track might get his blood pumping, but that idea faded by the time he made his way to the living room.

He yawned, grabbed his laptop and a Diet Coke, and plopped onto the sofa. Google Maps didn't have a street-level view of William Kingston's home outside Baltimore, but it did show an overhead perspective. A guard shack was clearly visible at the gated entrance, but whether it was manned was an open question. If not, Jeremy could follow close on the tail of any vehicle as it entered. In all his years as an FBI agent, he'd never seen anyone stop after passing the gate to make certain it closed before another car came through.

The drive over would take less than two hours unless there was heavy traffic or an accident. He didn't know if Kingston was at work today or what time he left the office or even what kind of car he drove. A trip to the Dependable Guaranty Insurance headquarters for some on-site reconnaissance was required.

After he keyed in the address, the map realigned to a satellite photo of the building. A large parking garage sat next to the five-story office structure. Kingston would have an assigned spot, though it might be in a secure area. Only one way to find out.

He closed the computer and tilted his head back onto the sofa. The light blurred as his eyes demanded more rest. What possible difference would one or two more hours of sleep make? None, right? Everything could still be accomplished today. Just stretch out on the couch so he wouldn't get too comfortable and doze too long.

He kicked off his shoes, scooted down, and grimaced as a thin ray of sunshine beamed through the barely open curtains and pinpointed his face. Wonderful. He rolled off the sofa and shuffled to the window, pausing once to stretch. A wave of lightheadedness washed over him, and he waited for it to pass before …

He squinted at the floor. An envelope lay on the tile by the front door. It wasn't there when he arrived home this morning. Or was it? He shook his head to clear the cobwebs and shambled over, then grunted loudly as he knelt to grab the envelope.

No writing on the outside and it wasn't sealed. He removed the single sheet of paper from inside and studied the front and back for a moment. On one side were Shane Kingston's phone records for the prior two months, shrunk so they'd fit on the page. Couldn't be more than thirty calls total. On the back of the paper was a lone typed sentence. "No record of Rachel Lynn Anderson for the last 15 years."

An adrenaline rush chased off any tiredness. This information, if accurate—and why wouldn't it be?—could be the catalyst that ignited the investigation. Shane's phone calls should point to his mother, who apparently was now living off the grid or under an assumed identity.

A vein behind his ear twitched, and he squeezed his free hand into a fist. This is out of bounds. Maggie knows better than to risk getting involved. Trying to remain anonymous was ridiculous. If it ever came out that he had this information, it wouldn't take a genius to figure out where it came from.

Even worse, Tanessa may have done it. Her career with the Bureau would end before it started. She was too smart for this though. Even if she'd taken steps to ensure her anonymity, she'd know suspicion would fall on Maggie. If she wanted to prove her usefulness, this wasn't the way to do it.

He snatched his cell and dialed Maggie.

"Good afternoon, sleepyhead," she said. "Sleep well?"

"Tell me you didn't do this, Maggie."

"No idea what you're talking about."

He held the paper higher. "This envelope under my door. Did you have anything to do with it?"

"What? No. What envelope? What are you talking about?"

"Is Tanessa there? Ask her."

"Jeremy, you need to calm down and tell me what's going on."

He closed his eyes and breathed deeply through his nose twice. "Somebody slid an envelope under my door. Inside was a piece of paper with Shane Kingston's phone records and a note about Rachel Anderson."

Maggie was silent for a moment. "That didn't come from me. I promise."

"Good. Think Tanessa had anything to do with it?"

"She's not here, but I'll ask when she gets back. I can't imagine she does though. Too smart. Even if she could get the information without anyone tracing it to her, she knows I'd be livid about it. Not a good way to impress someone who's training you."

He gritted his teeth. "Who then? I didn't tell anyone else, and if you didn't either … Janice?"

"Oh, wow. You think? I mean, she *was* there when we talked. I've never known her to do something like that though. Would she even know how?"

"No, but who has more contacts at the Bureau than the Deputy Director's ex-admin? No telling how many favors she's done for agents over the years."

"You gonna call her?"

"I am. If she sent this, she could get in a lot of trouble."

"Want to hold off until after I talk to Tanessa?"

He shook his head. "We both know what happened here. Go ahead and ask her, but I'm calling Janice."

"Be nice to her, Jeremy. She's only trying to help."

"I understand that. I'm not going to threaten her, but I'm not going to thank her either. She needs to appreciate the possible consequences of getting caught."

"Uh-huh. So what's the note say about Rachel Anderson?"

He smiled. "I don't know if I should tell you. Without knowing how this information was obtained, I could be putting your—"

"What's the note say, Jeremy?"

"Nothing. I mean, it says there's no record of the woman for the last fifteen years."

"Hmm. Assumed identity or dead. Which is more likely?"

He wrinkled his forehead. "Shane talks to her regularly."

"So he says."

"Now who's paranoid? Easy enough to figure out since I've got the phone records. And if she *is* dead, our—my—prime suspect is an executive in Baltimore who's about to have his world rocked."

"Be careful, Jeremy. You're not law enforcement. Just a normal citizen. If there comes a point the police need to get involved, don't screw up their investigation by alerting Kingston he's a suspect."

"I'm not going to, but my priority is Holly. If something happened to Rachel Anderson, I'm sorry, but that's leverage that gets me to Holly's killer. The police can deal with the fallout later."

She paused. "Rachel Anderson is not leverage. Dead or alive, she's a woman who deserves the same respect as Holly."

"You know what I meant."

"Do I? Slow down. Widen your focus. What's one of the first things new agents are taught? Eliminating tunnel vision, whether it's in a shootout or investigating a case."

He paced and remained silent. He didn't have tunnel vision. He had a solid lead that needed to be followed up on immediately.

"You still there?" Maggie asked.

"Yes."

"Stop. Whatever it is you're doing, stop. Take a deep breath and hold it in for a ten-count, and let it out. Then do it two more times. I'll wait."

"Maggie, you don't—"

"Do it, Jeremy. Now."

He shook his head but closed his eyes and did as she asked. "Done," he said.

"Your heart rate slower or do we need to do it again?"

"No. I mean yes, but no, I don't need to do it again."

"You sure? You still sound a little testy."

His jaw began to throb. "Well, you just accused me of not caring about a woman's murder, so …"

"Possible murder. And was I wrong?"

He sank onto the sofa and rested his elbows on his knees. No, she wasn't wrong. "Tanessa's lucky to have you as her trainer."

"Yes," Maggie said. "Yes, she is. Now, go back to bed, hear me?"

"What? No way. I'm too hyped. I'm driving to Baltimore and—"

"Not today," she said. "Slow. Down. Take a nap, then pick up Rebecca from school. I'll call Janice and tell her you've got it covered. I'll invite her to dinner too so we can both have a chat with her about the letter. Will you do that for me?"

He nodded. "I can do that. It'd be good to spend a little time with Beks. Seems like it's been a while since we've goofed off together."

"Funny. She said the same thing last night."

His heart sank and puddles formed in his eyes. "Don't let me lose sight of her."

"Widen your focus, Jeremy. You don't need an investigation to see what's right in front of you."

CHAPTER THIRTY-THREE

Jeremy slept better than he had in ages. Exhaustion played a part in that, but his time with Beks lifted his spirits. Talking, teasing, reading, coloring, everything. They'd even tried to make Rice Krispie treats. Somehow a simple recipe consisting of only three ingredients turned into a block of food hard enough to function as a heat tile on the space shuttle. Neither minded.

Janice confirmed that yes, she left the envelope and no, she didn't care what Jeremy or Maggie thought. At her age, her choices were her own. If she asked people to do things for her and they agreed to do so, what difference did that make to others? Take the information and use it or toss it in the trash. As far as she was concerned, nothing would change.

He thanked her and said he'd watch what he said around her in the future. She told him to hush and eat more chicken casserole. All in all, a very good evening.

Today's tasks included reviewing the phone records and scoping out William Kingston's office and, if possible, the man's home. Jeremy's elevated mood defied staying in an empty apartment, so the Starbucks down the street served as his morning hangout. Burnt-tasting coffee or not, the buzz of sounds and motion made the work more pleasant.

Thirty-four calls to and from Shane's phone over a two-month period. Jeremy knew people who made that many in a day. He eliminated several of the numbers quickly. Shane's work, a pizza delivery place, and rogue telemarketers accounted for two-thirds. The rest were one-offs. A movie theater, other delivery restaurants, an Uber driver, his bank. Every single call identified. No friends. No texts.

If Shane did call his mother, either she worked for the pizza place, or he used a burner phone. If—when—he spoke to Shane again, it would be the main topic of conversation.

The records at least appeared to back up Shane's claims that he and his father weren't on speaking terms. That knowledge could prove to be useful. Their stories about Rachel Anderson might not mesh, which nearly always meant an opening in an investigation. Pit the two men against each other. See how their versions of events changed over time. And possibly force Shane into disclosing the whereabouts of his mother in order to protect himself.

And if he couldn't do that? Then chances were the woman was dead. William Kingston abused his wife regularly, according to Georgia Harding. Yes, that was hearsay since she got the information from Shane, but there was no reason to doubt it. The fact that the father and son were estranged added credibility. Was it that big a step from abuse to murder, especially when he'd already killed Holly?

Jeremy dropped his nearly full cup into the trash can and made a bathroom stop before beginning the drive over to Baltimore. He drummed his fingers on the steering wheel and turned the radio up, humming along with the country music song.

Man, last night was great. They'd have to make another go at Rice Krispie treats soon.

. . . .

Jeremy ran his palm along the plush maroon fabric of the Queen Anne chair. The velvety material darkened and lightened depending on which way he dragged his hand. And why did he know this was called a Queen Anne? He shook his head. Somewhere, sometime that tidbit of information entrenched itself in his brain. Had to be a crime scene, but which one?

The lobby of the Dependable Guaranty Insurance headquarters ranged between ornate and ostentatious. Its sparkly chandeliers, plethora of live plants surrounding a bubbling fountain, and fancy area rugs cried "look how rich we are!" Maybe the glitz instilled awe or confidence in others, but to Jeremy, all it meant was they either had too much money or no clue how to spend their dollars.

The giant wall clock, trimmed in shiny gold, of course, ticked another minute off. Thirty-six of them since he stopped at the counter and asked to see William Kingston. The receptionist had smiled, dialed a number, whispered, asked Jeremy to repeat his name, whispered again, then hung up. She asked if he'd like a drink while he waited. He declined, mostly out of fear he might spill it on the fancy furnishings, and took a seat.

The reconnaissance plan had evolved on the drive over from Haymarket. No point in coming this far without at least trying to talk to the man. As Maggie liked to say, kill two birds in the hand with one stone. And meeting Kingston at his office would give him a sense of security while also showing Jeremy's determination that sooner or later the two would speak.

"Mr. Winter?" The receptionist waved him over. "Mr. Kingston will see you now. If you'd please sign in and wear this visitor's identification?"

He scribbled his name and slapped the paper badge on his shirt.

"Thank you," she said. "The elevators are around the corner directly behind me. Mr. Kingston's office is on the fifth floor. Will you require assistance?"

Assistance? Oh. The cane. "No, I'm fine."

"Wonderful. Have a great day."

"Yeah. You too." He strode around the corner, intentionally putting extra weight on his bad leg. Bolts of pain jarred him from shin to hip, but he ignored them. The elevators matched the lobby, minus the chandeliers and fountain. No fingerprints on the golden metal panel surrounding the floor buttons. Someone must clean them after every trip.

The doors opened into another lobby area. Three receptionists, two women, and one man, worked behind a curved glass desk. Five heavy-looking wooden doors, evenly spaced and each with a gold nameplate, lined the wall in the back. Cut flowers and fresh fruit adorned a side table beside a cluster of chairs. A man sat there, stocky with short hair and a dark blue suit, shuffling through a magazine. Jeremy sighed. The guy might as well be wearing sunglasses and an earpiece. Kingston wanted security nearby.

One of the receptionists made eye contact. "Sir, you're here to see Mr. Kingston?"

"I am."

She stood and walked to the last door on the right. "This way, please."

He stepped through the door into a smaller waiting area where a young woman, Susan Kilwalski according to the nameplate, waited behind a desk. This place was like a maze, and the last time he navigated a maze, things didn't go too well.

"Susan, this is Mr. Winter. He's here to see Mr. Kingston."

The young woman smiled. "Of course." She stood, tapped on the door behind her, and opened it. "Mr. Kingston will see you now."

Jeremy nodded and moved into the room. William Kingston stood, walked around his oversized desk, and extended his hand. The man had one of those permanent tans like he only needed to be outside a few minutes a year to keep his color. He wore khakis, pressed to a sharp seam, and a white polo shirt with the company logo.

"Mr. Winter. A pleasure to finally meet you."

I'll bet. Jeremy's muscles tensed and he wrung his cane until his knuckles hurt. This was the man who'd, allegedly, murdered Holly and Miranda. "Same. Thanks for taking the time."

"Not at all." He waved toward a grouping of three thickly padded chairs near floor-to-ceiling windows. "Please, have a seat. May I offer you a beverage?"

"No thanks. I'm good."

He nodded. "Susan, that'll be all."

She backed out of the room and closed the door behind her. The two men made their way to the chairs and stared out the window for a moment. The parking garage filled most of the right side of the panorama, its upper deck barely a floor lower and nearly touching the building. To the left was a wooded area with walking trails, a pond, and large open spaces. Jeremy held his grin inside. Kingston was at the bottom of the pecking order. The farther left your office was, the less of the parking structure you saw. The CEO must have a magnificent view.

"How can I help you, Mr. Winter? I believe you said something about investigating an incident that occurred many years ago in Frederick? Are you law enforcement?"

Like you haven't done any background on me. Jeremy shook his head. "No, sir, I'm not. Used to be but retired from that life. I suppose you could say this investigation is more of a personal matter. My wife was killed shortly after 9/11, and her murder was never solved."

Kingston frowned, scooted forward in his chair, and clasped his hands. "I am so sorry."

Doubt it. You'll know real remorse soon enough. "Thank you. Do you remember anything about the crime?"

"Only in the vaguest sense. I do remember an unsolved murder—

gunshot I think?—but not any details. Those kinds of things didn't happen much in those days. May I ask, why me? You'd do better researching old newspapers or talking to the police than spending your time here."

"Yes, sir. I've done both of those. You'd be surprised what an experienced FBI agent can learn from old information."

Kingston tilted his head. "Perhaps I would."

No acknowledgment of the FBI remark. *He knows all about me.* "However," Jeremy said, "you can also learn a lot by talking to people who were around at the time. People who might have second- or third-hand knowledge or heard some rumors. Nothing that would ever hold up in court, of course, but enough to give direction. And once you know which way to head, well, it's only a matter of time."

Kingston scooted back in his chair. "Makes perfect sense, but again, Mr. Winter, how can I help? As I stated, I don't recall any specifics regarding your wife's death. And I don't believe you picked my name out of the phone book. Why are you here?"

Jeremy tapped a finger on the armrest. "Why do you *think* I'm here?"

The man's smile revealed straight, gleaming white teeth. "I already pay my therapist a great deal of money to repeat my questions back to me. Sorry, but I have a busy day ahead. If there's nothing else, you may—"

"Your wife. Ex-wife, to be precise."

Kingston's eyebrows squished together. "Rachel? What about her?"

"Have you spoken with her lately?"

"Not that it's any of your business, but I have a feeling you know quite well we don't speak. She left so I divorced her. End of story."

"Maybe," Jeremy said. "It's *why* she left that concerns me."

His mouth hung slightly open, and he shook his head. "I don't follow. Look, I'm not going to pretend Rachel and I had a great marriage, but that's all in the past. She went her way, and I went mine."

"You haven't spoken with her since then?"

"Not once. I believe my son keeps in touch with her, but I fear my relationship with him is damaged as well."

"I suppose watching you beat his mother all the time does that to a kid."

Kingston leapt out of the chair and glared. "I don't know what Shane told you, but … and what does any of this have to do with your wife's murder? We're done here. Please leave."

Jeremy pushed himself out of his seat and tapped his cane on the carpet, allowing time for the anger to peak. "I know things, Mr. Kingston. I just can't prove them yet. But I will, and soon. Call your son and get your stories straight because I'm going to rip it to shreds. I've waited a long time. What's a little more?"

Kingston moved behind his desk and pressed a button on the phone. The door opened, and his admin stood there wearing her perpetual smile. "Can I help you gentlemen?" she asked.

"No," Jeremy said. "We're just finishing up here. Please let the security officer up front know that your boss won't be needing him today."

By the time he made it to his car, both of Jeremy's legs throbbed. The anger jump-started an adrenaline rush which pulled energy from his extremities. He clamped his mouth closed and forced breaths through his nose to slow his heartbeat and calm his nerves.

The meeting went about like he'd expected. Kingston wasn't going to cave just because a stranger all but accused him of a crime. Why should he? With no evidence, nothing but hearsay and innuendo, no D.A. would even consider taking the case to a grand jury.

The trip to Baltimore served only to confirm Jeremy's thoughts. The key to proving Kingston's guilt lay with Rachel Anderson. She was the only person alive who could help convict Holly's murderer.

And if she wasn't alive? Then William Kingston killed her. That would be easy enough to prove once they found the body. Rachel Anderson's justice would come. Holly's killer would be in prison.

That would be enough.

Wouldn't it?

CHAPTER THIRTY-FOUR

The deli's line of customers stretched out the door, meaning the outside odor of vehicle exhaust mingled with the restaurant's strong sauerkraut smell. Jeremy dabbed at a spot of mustard on his shirt and leaned across the table to be heard over the constant honking from the street and yelling from the counter.

"Any questions so far?" he asked.

Maggie and Tanessa shook their heads.

"Good," he said. "So here's the problem. Shane says his mother is alive. I can't be certain, but it sure seemed like William Kingston thought the same thing. That gives me three scenarios. First, Rachel Anderson *is* alive, and Shane has a way to contact her. Second, she's alive and for whatever reason Shane is lying about speaking to her regularly. Third, she's dead, and once again Shane is fabricating the story."

Maggie dipped a potato chip in ranch dressing. "Only reason to lie about it is to protect someone. Her or himself. Who knows? The mother might be the witness you're looking for, but don't count all your eggs in one basket until they're hatched."

"Right," Jeremy said. "I think. But if Shane's lying to protect himself, what motive would he have for killing Holly? We know his father abused his mother. He has a violent streak. That makes him the likely candidate."

"Do we know that?" Tanessa asked. "Your whole case is built around one woman telling the truth. If Georgia Harding is lying, you've got everything wrong. For all we know, she's the one who shot Holly. Maybe she called 911 because she panicked or felt guilty."

"She's right," Maggie said. "It's not enough. Talk to some of the others they ran with. See if any of them back up her story about the abuse. A thing like that, plenty of whispers would be floating around."

Jeremy rubbed his palms on his cheeks. "I can do that, but even if everything I believe is wrong, there's still the issue of Rachel Anderson."

Tanessa yanked another napkin from the dispenser, handed it to Maggie, and pointed to Jeremy. "Clean him up, would you?"

Maggie laughed, dipped the napkin in her water, and scrubbed around Jeremy's lips. "Can't take him anywhere. But he is right. Even if all this has nothing to do with Holly, where's Rachel?"

Tanessa shrugged. "Maybe we should start inviting Janice to these meetings."

"Maybe," he said. "I suppose, at least from your perspectives, the question is at what point does Rachel become a matter of concern for law enforcement? No one's reported her missing, and there's no evidence of a crime."

"There's no evidence," Tanessa said, "because no one's looked for any."

"True," Maggie said, "but that means nothing. It's like that show that used to be on TV where those guys went looking for Bigfoot all the time. They said the fact that they never found the creature is proof it exists because it'd have to be smart enough to avoid humans if it wanted to survive."

"'Kay," Tanessa said, "I can't begin to wrap my head around that. All I'm saying is that if we had the slightest inclination something criminal occurred, we'd have a responsibility to act on the information. Report it to the local PD or at least take the time to look deeper ourselves."

"Maybe," Maggie said, "but we don't have the authority, not to mention the time, to hunt for possible evidence in a maybe crime."

Jeremy eased his plate toward the center of the table. "No, but I do. The answers we need are in Charlotte."

Maggie squished her mouth to the side. "I don't see Shane telling you anything. Why would he? Your best bet is to play up the father angle to him. Tell him his dad looks great, is doing well, beautiful house, yadda yadda yadda. Let him know, without saying it, there were no consequences for abusing his mother."

"Good thinking," Tanessa said. "Dad's living the high life while Mom's cowering somewhere. See how the kid reacts and go from there."

Jeremy stared at the table for a moment, then peered at the two women. "That's all well and good, but I need to get a look inside his apartment.

That's where the trail begins, whether it's a burner phone or postcards or emails."

Maggie bit her bottom lip. "So how are you going to convince him to invite you in?"

"Let's say," he said, "hypothetically, of course, I knock on the door and, for whatever reason, the door isn't latched completely and opens a little. I yell, but no one answers. Don't I, as a responsible citizen not to mention ex-law enforcement, have an obligation to ensure everyone inside is okay?"

"I'll do you one better," Maggie said. "Let's say, hypothetically, of course, I find out something like that happened. Wouldn't I, as your *maybe* future wife, have an obligation to tell you that of all the idiotic, moronic, reckless, stupid—"

"Whoa there," Tanessa said. "Put the thesaurus away, Mags. We'd all like to know whether Rachel Anderson is safe, right? It's how we arrive at the answer that seems to be creating issues. I feel like a bit of marriage counseling might help, 'kay? Do you, Bartholomew Winter, promise to do your best not to break any laws and if you do, not to get caught? And if you're stupid enough to get caught, do you promise to use whatever 'get out of jail free' cards you have lying around? Most of all, do you agree that *nothing* is as important as this woman sitting next to you? Her, not me."

Jeremy nodded. "I do. Beks too."

"Great. And do you, Maggie 'what-was-I-thinking' Keeley promise not to ask too many questions about what your future husband is up to, being fully aware that no man has the ability to stop doing idiotic things no matter how much you may wish otherwise? Do you agree that he takes these actions only because he feels they are needed, and if the shoe were on the other foot, you'd do the same?"

Maggie held up her index finger. "I'd like to add that—"

"It's a yes or no question," Tanessa said.

"Fine. I do, but—"

"Great. Glad we got that resolved. Jeremy, do something you can't get out of, and Mags will have to get in line behind me, understood?"

He rolled his eyes. "The confidence you two have in me is inspiring. I'm not going to do anything, um, *iffy* unless I'm certain it's the only way forward. The last thing I want to do is taint any evidence that may be needed later by the police."

Maggie sighed. "So we're going with a policy of don't ask, don't tell?"

"We are," he said. "And if I do find anything, we'll readdress the situation, okay?"

"You know I don't like this," Maggie said. "I'll be worried sick. Promise to call after you do whatever it is you're not going to do. Let me know you're safe."

"Of course," he said. "If it's all right, I'll head to Charlotte tomorrow. I need to pick up a few things today."

"Including Rebecca?" Maggie asked.

He grinned. "Of course. We're giving the Rice Krispie treats another go."

"Yeah? Stop by the store and grab another fire extinguisher on the way home."

CHAPTER THIRTY-FIVE

Jeremy watched Shane's apartment from a parking spot at the next building. He'd left Virginia shortly after four this morning, eager to get started. Once in town, he selected a motel closer to Shane's home and with décor nearer this century. The room was still nothing to brag about and likely hid the same bodily fluid stains all lodgings did, but the updated furnishings made it easier to pretend the place was spotless. As long as no bedbugs showed up, no problems.

He shifted his body a little left to position the sun back behind the visor. Shane would be heading to work soon, and with luck, he'd stop somewhere to eat first. That's when Jeremy would reintroduce himself. People tended not to react violently when surrounded by strangers in a public setting.

Right on cue, the man bounded down the staircase to his car and drove past without noticing him. A few minutes later, he pulled into a Wendy's and went inside. Jeremy parked a few spaces away and waited until Shane got his order and sat.

He entered the restaurant and paused to get his bearings. A few customers waited near the front to place their orders, and the dining area was about a quarter full. Shane sat alone on the opposite side of the building. Jeremy maneuvered so he'd approach from behind, walked past him, then pivoted and slid into the booth. "Hi. Got a minute?"

The brief look of confusion faded as Shane's lips formed a thin line. "No. Please let me eat in peace."

"No problem. Just wanted to follow up on a couple of things, if you don't mind."

He placed his cheeseburger back in the wrapper. "I'm out of here."

"I saw your dad," Jeremy said.

Shane froze for a second. "And?"

"He seems to be doing quite well for himself. Did you know he was a CXO now? Chief Experience Officer. You ever hear of such a thing? What's that even mean? I swear, they're just making stuff up now. Man's got it all. Big house, big office, big bank account. Must be nice, right?"

"Whatever. Got nothing to do with me."

"Yeah, I know that. He pretty much said the same thing about you."

Shane leaned back in the booth. "He doesn't know anything about me."

"Maybe not. He did say that your mom left so he divorced her, but he couldn't understand why she went away. Said he figured it had something to do with you. That you weren't the easiest kid to raise."

His jaw muscles tightened. "He knows why she left. I had nothing to do with it."

Jeremy shrugged. "The abuse, you mean? Never happened, according to your father. In fact, he said if you didn't stop spreading the rumor, he'd be forced to take legal action. Between you and me, I don't think he can do that. Besides, I tried to explain that I didn't hear it from you, but, well, things kinda got out of hand."

"Georgia told you, didn't she? Not like it was a big secret or anything."

"Mm-hmm. That's why your mom left, isn't it? Afraid of your dad? I can understand that. But here's the thing, I think there's more to the story. In fact, I *know* there's more to it. I need to talk to her, Shane. You're shielding her because you're a good son. But that doesn't change things. I'm going to find her with or without your help."

He scooped up his burger and stood. "Do it without me."

Jeremy nodded. "There is another option. Maybe you're not protecting your mother. Maybe you're protecting yourself."

"What is that supposed to mean?"

He hunched forward. "See, I get these suspicions. Can't help it. Too many years with the FBI, I guess. But these doubts, they build in me until they're all I can think about. I can't do anything until I clear them up. And right now, these suspicions are whispering in my ear. Know what they're saying? That Shane Kingston is hiding something."

Shane picked up his drink and took a sip. "Mr. Winter, do whatever you're gonna do, but I won't help you. My mom suffered enough. She deserves to be left alone." He dropped his burger on the table. "I lost my appetite."

Jeremy watched as the man got in his car and drove off. So much for playing the father against the son. Neither appeared to want anything to do with the other. He stood, gathered the trash from the table, and dropped it in the bin up front.

He scanned the menu and decided to eat later. More pressing matters demanded his attention. Something that couldn't wait. It was going to be a long night.

He needed a nap.

. . . .

Jeremy watched the YouTube video one last time. The salesman at the spy gadget store in Virginia assured him the lock picking gizmo was state of the art. For $250, it ought to be. The device consisted of a narrow silver tube holding the battery and an on-off button. On one end was a thin stainless-steel rod that vibrated when powered. According to the guy at the shop, all you had to do was insert a separate piece called a tensioner into the lock, then slide in the gadget's rod, turn it on, and presto. An unlocked door.

He'd demoed the device and let Jeremy operate it on a row of locks mounted along a door jamb. Once he got the hang of handling the tensioner, he could pick each lock in less than a minute. It wasn't going to open any safes but, assuming Shane's locks were typical of most homes, it should get the job done.

He slipped the tool into his pocket and drove to the apartment complex. Clouds obscured the stars, but any hope for a cloak of darkness was lost when he spotted the well-lit parking area. Rows of lights also lined each hallway. Security cameras were mounted near the roof on a few of the buildings, but none appeared to cover any zone beyond the staircases. Once in the hall, he'd be clear of observation unless a neighbor stepped outside.

He pulled into a spot near the steps, opted to leave the cane in his car, and strode toward the building with his head high and hands exposed. Just someone visiting a friend. The stairs elicited a series of low grunts, and beads of sweat formed on his forehead. Not nerves. Exertion. Right.

Shane's apartment was four doors down on the right on the second floor. The building seemed quiet, with low sounds from TVs being the only noise. As he approached his target, he fiddled with the device in his pocket. It was too large to disguise in his hand, so if someone questioned him, he should have a cover story. Problem was, what kind of tale would make sense in that situation? None he could come up with.

The plan was to pass Shane's door and scope out the rest of the hall before attempting to pick the lock. Make sure he didn't hear any talking that sounded like someone about to leave. At the last second, he ditched the strategy and veered toward the door. His heartbeat echoed in his ears, and he licked his lips. Most people don't lock the deadbolt unless they're home, so he went straight for the doorknob. He bent forward and jabbed the tensioner in the bottom of the keyhole, applied a slight amount of pressure, and slipped the gadget's rod inside. Within seconds, he turned the doorknob and straightened. *How are these things legal?*

After a quick glance in both directions, he took a deep breath, pulled on latex gloves, wiped the doorknob clean, and stepped inside Shane Kingston's apartment.

CHAPTER THIRTY-SIX

Jeremy eased the door closed and surveyed the apartment. A row of pendant lights illuminated a counter between the small kitchen and living area. He paused to gain his bearings and listen for any sound that could indicate a person or pet. Nothing.

He opened a stopwatch app on his phone and set the alarm for fifteen minutes. Shane wasn't due home for hours, but the risk grew with each second inside the apartment. A vein in his neck throbbed, and he spent the first minute slowing his breathing, then snapped photos of his surroundings. If he moved anything, he wanted to ensure he replaced it exactly where he found it.

The living space consisted of a wall-mounted TV, sofa, coffee table, and recliner. Everything in its place. Hard to believe a bachelor lives here. Other than an empty glass in the sink, the kitchen and eating areas emitted the same neat-freak vibe. If nothing else, Shane Kingston was no slob.

A hallway led to a pair of bedrooms and one full bath. Jeremy switched on the lights as he inspected each room. The bathroom was tidy with a faint odor of bleach. The medicine cabinet contained the usual allergy drugs, pain relievers, and cough syrups. No prescription meds. Any illicit products would be concealed within easy reach in the bedroom. He took a few photos and continued his work.

The walls of the hall were bare except for a thermostat. No posters or photos. In fact, everything he'd seen so far lacked any personalization. A shrink might have something to say about that. Maybe the guy just wanted to make sure he got his security deposit back.

The first bedroom appeared to be a home office, and Jeremy bypassed it. Any items that pointed to Rachel Anderson would be in Shane's room. His time would be best spent there.

The queen-sized bed filled a majority of the room. One side was shoved against the wall to save space. A digital clock, lamp, and remote control sat atop a wooden nightstand. Opposite the foot of the bed, a TV rested on a dresser that matched the rest of the furniture. A closet completed the room.

Jeremy searched the dresser first and found nothing helpful. All the clothes were perfectly folded, and the bottom two drawers were empty. He switched on his flashlight app and glanced under the bed, then lifted the top mattress and checked there. Again, nothing. The nightstand drawer consisted of various charging cables and little else. Next came the closet. The clothes hung neatly, several of them still in their dry-cleaning bags. Shoes were placed to the right and in the back left was a toy of some sort.

He eased to his knees and snapped a photo. Buzz Lightyear. Weird. Beks had gone through her *Toy Story* phase a few years back. Jeremy still got queasy at the thought of watching them. All good movies the first time around. Tolerable the second. By the third viewing, he wanted to scream. By the tenth, he would have confessed to kidnapping the Lindbergh baby to make it stop.

A door slammed, and he froze until he realized the sound came from another apartment. Four more minutes and it'd be time to go. This whole expedition had been an unnecessary risk based on what he'd seen so far.

He stood at the bedroom door. Everything was back in place. All drawers closed, no wrinkles on the bed, closet doors shut. If Shane hid something in there, it'd take another much longer visit to find it. This would all be easier if he had help. Someone to watch Shane and send an alert if he was on his way home.

Jeremy switched off the light and hurried to the office. With only a couple of minutes to go, photos would have to do. A desk, chair, empty shredder, and filing cabinet were the only furniture. The closet held nothing but a heavy winter coat. A laptop, its screen saver cycling through generic nature pictures, clicked and whirred on the desk. Could check it, but probably has a password. No time.

His phone sounded a low beep, and he shook his head. What difference would a few more minutes make? Almost done anyway.

No. Stick to the plan. He snapped a few quick photos and tugged on the top drawer of the file cabinet. Locked. For $250, he should get more than one use from his new toy. He squatted, picked the lock in seconds, and grinned. Kinda fun using that thing.

The top drawer was empty, as was the bottom. Almost. A small stack of paper nestled in one of those green hanging folders. He lifted the file and laid it on the desk. Inside were around two dozen pages held together with a binder clip in the top left corner. Each had a single photo of a man along with a screenshot of an internet article. And they'd all been charged with domestic abuse.

He removed the fastener, separated the pile into three stacks, and spread the first cluster out, being careful to keep each sheet slightly overlapped. After photographing, he repeated the process with the other two groups, then recombined everything and placed it back in the cabinet.

By the time he got to the car, the adrenaline from the evening's escapade had begun to fade. His mind still raced though. No sign of Rachel Anderson, but what was the deal with that file? Why did Shane have it? Hard not to jump to conclusions.

He'd watched his mother being abused, and now he had a list of locals that did the same thing to their wives? Jeremy sighed and drove away from the complex. No rash judgments. Get back to the motel, relax, and think this through logically. Do the research on the men before forming any theories.

As always, easier said than done.

What was Shane Kingston planning?

CHAPTER THIRTY-SEVEN

Jeremy stretched on the bed, then wedged another pillow behind his neck and pulled up the next name on the list. Twenty-two men in Shane's folder, but why? All were still alive and going about their daily business, as far as he could tell on the internet.

After arriving back at his motel hours before, he'd texted Maggie to let her know all was fine, and please call him first thing in the morning. Since then, he'd been reviewing the photos of the apartment and going through the names, all without discovering anything that led him closer to Rachel Anderson.

The phone rang promptly at eight, and he answered midway through the first ring. "Right on schedule," he said.

"What's going on?" Maggie asked. "You find something about his mother?"

"Not a thing. I didn't try to access his computer though. Not enough time. But I did find something else. I'm not sure what to make of it, and I don't know whether or not to tell you."

"Fruit of the poisonous tree?"

Illegally obtained evidence that could damage chances of a conviction, no matter how overwhelming the proof. "Yep."

"Tell me this … is anyone's life in imminent danger?"

Was it? For all he knew, Shane was doing nothing more than gathering names to send pamphlets to the abused women. Or maybe some sort of research project. Or even a twisted hobby. There were plenty of things this could be besides a hit list. Would there ever be a day he didn't jump to the worst-case scenario? "I don't know if anyone's in danger."

"Then keep it to yourself. You can do that, right?"

"No choice. I'll keep tabs on them and see if anything changes."

"Them?"

"Forget it." He yawned and blinked several times. "I used to go thirty-six, sometimes even forty-eight hours or longer without sleep. Now I can't make it all night without a nap first. Getting older bites."

"It's better than the alternative," she said.

He chuckled. "I suppose so. I'm considering calling Detective Pronger today. Ask him to look into Rachel Anderson's disappearance. What do you think?"

"Couldn't hurt. If you play it right, you might even get back in his good graces. You know, set him up to be the hero in the case by figuring out what happened to her."

"I don't think I've ever been in his good graces to begin with. And he can't be a hero unless Ms. Anderson's dead. Otherwise, all he's done is disturb a woman who's trying to live her life in anonymity."

"True," Maggie said, "but do you think she's alive? Nothing points that way. I mean, if Shane Kingston never said he talked to her regularly, I'd say to drop this. But where's the evidence he's spoken with his mother recently? Not in his phone records, that's for sure."

"There are other ways. Lack of evidence isn't evidence, remember? Shane's not going to talk to me again. Not without a good reason. If I can get Pronger to open an investigation, maybe that'll do it. Force Shane to put up or shut up."

"So you're coming home?"

He pulled all but one pillow from under his head. "Not yet. Hanging out here another day or two if it's all right with you. I'll call Janice and have her take care of getting Beks to and from school."

"We might as well let Janice move in. You're not going to, uh, repeat last night's exploits, are you?"

"No. Not unless I have to, and I promise you'll get notified early enough to yell at me before I go."

"Smart man," she said. "Let me know what Pronger says."

"Will do." He paused and scratched his cheek. "You know, that's not a bad idea. About Janice moving in, I mean. Not now, but once we have a house. Maybe get a mother-in-law suite or even a separate little cottage. What do you think?"

"Maybe. We'll talk, but for goodness' sake, don't say anything to her. It'll crush her if we mention it then decide not to do it."

He rolled his eyes. "Give me credit. Believe it or not, I do have *some* tact."

She laughed. "Prove it. Get Detective Pronger to open an investigation."

....

Jeremy's two-hour nap left him more tired than rested. The motel's thick curtains worked great at blocking light but did little to keep noises at bay. Car doors slamming, people talking, the ice machine sounding like it was preparing for liftoff. A warm shower only made things worse.

He dressed and drove to find a late breakfast with copious amounts of coffee. A quarter-mile down the road, Waffle House waved him over, and he limped inside, putting extra pressure on his cane.

Two other customers sat at the counter, but he otherwise had the place to himself. After mouthing *coffee* to the waitress and receiving a nod in return, he slid into a booth with his back to the sun. The warmth eased the aches in his shoulders. When all this was over, he'd take an extended break. Plenty of sleep and exercise.

Right. Good luck convincing anyone of that when he didn't believe it himself.

The waitress brought his coffee and took his order of two scrambled eggs and toast. She pushed the bacon, but he declined. Too fatty, plus he'd be tasting it all day. But mostly too fatty.

He scrolled through the contact list in his phone, found Pronger, and pushed the button. The voicemail needed to be upbeat and give a hint of—

"Detective Pronger."

He answered? Does he not check caller ID? "Uh, hello, Detective. This is Jeremy Winter. I hope you're doing well."

"I know who this is. What do you want?"

And a happy good morning to you too, sir! Jeremy sighed. Tact. "I apologize for calling. I know we didn't leave things ... that is to say, I could've handled myself better. I'm aware that I still have your, uh, property, and I'll get it back to you as soon as I can." No more need for the murder book anyway.

"I would appreciate that," Pronger said. "Is there anything else?"

"Actually, there is."

"And why doesn't that surprise me?"

Jeremy waited for the detective to answer himself, but the response didn't come. "I've got some information you might be interested in."

"Involving your wife's murder?"

"Indirectly, or at least I think so. A woman who may have firsthand knowledge of the crime seems to have disappeared."

"Uh-huh," Pronger said. "Someone who *might* know something *maybe* disappeared. Well, with hard facts like that, it's a wonder you haven't already solved the crime."

When is he supposed to use *his* tact? "Rachel Lynn Anderson. Wife, ex-wife now, of William Kingston."

"And?"

And get off your ... "No record of her in the last fifteen years and a history of domestic abuse before she went missing. Husband used to beat the woman regularly according to my info. I can't find her, and I think you understand that with my, um, *government contacts* I was able to run a very thorough search."

"Does that impress me? No, it doesn't. If you have a witness, let me speak with them myself."

Can't. Promised the Hardings. "Not yet. Look, sooner or later I'm going to find Rachel Anderson. I'm throwing you a bone here, Detective. I think the woman's dead, and if she is, I figure the first place to start looking would be her old home in Frederick. Yeah, it's been a long time, but there could still be something there. Maybe even her body."

Pronger chuckled. "And with all the details you've given me, getting a search warrant is going to be a piece of cake."

Forget this. "Listen. In two days I'll be back in town. When I get there, I'll do it all myself if you haven't. Think it through. The Kingstons don't live in the house anymore. Knock on the door, introduce yourself, and ask if you can take a look around. Surely you've done actual *detective* work before, haven't you?"

click

Jeremy sighed and slipped the phone back in his pocket. Second time that guy hung up on me.

The waitress brought his food, refilled his coffee, and dropped the check on the table before wandering off to chat with the cook. Jeremy poured pepper on the eggs and took a bite before motioning to the waitress.

"Everything okay?" she asked.

"I think I will have that bacon."

CHAPTER THIRTY-EIGHT

S hane slumped in the car seat and reviewed the plan one more time. Coming up with a way to kill Gary Camblin hadn't been easy. The man went from home to office, then eight hours later reversed the drive. He rarely ventured out, probably because his wife didn't work and did all the running around during the day.

Camblin had been on the radar for almost two years, ever since his mug shot showed up in the paper. As the most tenured member in the file and the most difficult, getting him off the list had become a unique challenge.

He shuddered. The meeting yesterday shook him more than he wanted to admit. Jeremy Winter was becoming a problem. The easiest solution was to give the man what he wanted, but that could open the door to other problems. Dad would do everything in his power to deflect the blame, and if the cops spent time looking into Shane, no telling what they may uncover. No, he'd give it another day or so. See if Winter made contact again.

Today was something different. Camblin's death would be a first for Shane. As a partner in a prestigious accounting firm, the man's arrest had been worthy of an article on the third page. Apparently, he lost his job because of the incident and now toiled away as a nine-to-fiver. It had to be depressing.

Very depressing.

The accountant stepped out the front door of his home and Shane scooted onto the rear floorboard of the Buick, his gloved finger poised on the pistol's trigger. If someone spotted him, he planned to run, but if things got really ugly, the gun was his escape plan. Shane's hoodie limited his peripheral vision, and he fought the urge to ease his head higher for a better view.

Camblin opened the car door, tossed his briefcase into the passenger seat, and scooted behind the steering wheel. He dropped his bottled water into the cup holder, started the vehicle, and turned to look out the rear window.

"Keep going," Shane said.

The accountant screamed. "What—who are you? What do you want? Money? I don't have any. Take the car."

"Who I am is the man behind you with a gun, and I'm telling you to drive. Do as I say, and I won't kill you."

"How do I know that? If you're going to kill me anyway, then—"

Shane pressed the pistol against the man's head. "Do you want to die?"

Camblin shook his head and backed out of the driveway. "Listen," he said. "I don't have anything. If this is a kidnapping, my wife would as soon let me die, I think."

And I wonder why that is? Maybe if you didn't beat her, she'd care a little more about what happened to you. Shane climbed off the floor and sat behind the driver. "No more talking. I'll give the directions, and you follow them. Any attempt to break any traffic laws or get the attention of someone will not go well for you. Got it?"

The man nodded.

"Great. We're going to get along just fine. And don't worry. This will be over soon enough. I have to be at work by two."

. . . .

The church parking lot was exactly three-point-seven miles from the man's home. Shane knew because he'd walked it early this morning after leaving his car a short distance away. The accountant's old office building was across the street, the outline of his name still visible on the brick wall if you knew what to look for, and Shane did. He'd have much preferred to do this over there, but the building had security cameras. The church didn't. The parking spaces near the accountant's former office filled quickly, and as the seconds turned into minutes, the steady stream of vehicles grew closer to them.

"Time's up," he said. "Make your decision. Pills or bullet?" He'd take the pills. It was the coward's way out.

Tear streams marked Camblin's face, and his nose glowed bright red.

"Can I leave a note?"

"I think your body will be note enough."

"Can't we talk about this? Work something—"

Shane placed the gun against the back of the man's head. "I wanted this to be a suicide. Easier for everyone that way. Doesn't make much difference though. The end result will be the same. Goodbye, Mr. Camblin."

"Wait! The pills. Give me the pills."

Shane dropped the unmarked container of fentanyl in the front seat. The powerful painkiller, easily purchased on the street, would do its job with no muss and no fuss. "Smart man. It'll be just like going to sleep. Take them all and do it now. No more stalling."

The man's hands shook as he emptied the pills into his palm, whimpered, and popped them into his mouth.

"Don't forget your water. Don't want to choke on them, do you?"

The accountant drank, then opened his mouth and stuck out his tongue. Shane smiled. "I trust you."

In less than a minute, the man's head flopped side to side as the drugs took effect. "Can you at least tell me why?"

"You ever hear that loaded question? Do you still beat your wife? See, no matter whether you answer yes or no, you're guilty."

Camblin struggled to keep his eyelids open. "Whaaa? She ... she ..." His chin dropped against his chest.

"She doesn't know about this, but I think she's suffered enough. Don't you?"

There was no response.

"Good, good. You sleep." He placed a finger on the man's carotid artery and waited until the pulse stopped. The parking lot across the street was nearing capacity. He eased the door open and squeezed out before gently closing it and squatting behind the vehicle.

Six minutes later, he was on his way back home for a nap before work. Birthday night tonight, right? Once a month, the employees got an extra thirty-minute break to celebrate everyone who turned a year older that month. May not sound like much, but it was a perk Shane had fought for. Upper management saw it as a waste of money, but the event, and others similar reduced turnover nearly ten percent.

He pulled into a Walmart and hustled inside to the bakery section. There'd be plenty enough to eat as it was, but Shane wanted to contribute.

He opted for a dozen cupcakes, chocolate with white icing. Overly sweet, no doubt, but so what?

He felt like celebrating.

CHAPTER THIRTY-NINE

Shane woke from his nap, showered, and fixed a ham and cheese sandwich before sitting at his computer to check email. He expected nothing but the usual junk and spam and was not disappointed. Nothing but the constant gloom and doom on the internet news either. Neither the local paper nor the TV stations had any mention of Gary Camblin. Again, not unexpected since the man may not have been found yet. And even if he was, suicides didn't make the news unless it was someone important. Poor Gary didn't fit the profile.

Shane opened the spreadsheet and scored himself a seven since he'd spent too much time in the church parking lot. Not really his fault because suicides were harder than accidents. Having to rely on a second party complicated things. Probably be a long time until he tried one again.

Regardless, after two long years, Gary Camblin was off the list. Time for him to hit the shredder. Shane unlocked the cabinet and removed the file. After Gary, twenty-one names remained. More were always being added, but thus far, none had dropped off without Shane's help. No deaths by natural causes, accidents, suicides, murders, whatever. Not unless he took care of it himself. More proof of the necessity of his actions.

He finished off the sandwich and slid the plate aside to give himself room. Gary was somewhere near the middle of the stack if he remembered—

The binder clip.

He always aligned it with the left edge. Not OCD, just neat.

The fastener was a good half-inch away from where it should be.

He glanced around the room. Nothing out of place. Tape still covered his laptop's webcam.

Maybe he put the clip on wrong yesterday. Got in a hurry or wasn't paying attention. It'd never happened before, but first time for everything.

He rubbed his chest, stood, and inspected the rest of the apartment. Everything was exactly as it should be. No sign of visitors. But the binder clip was wrong. And if someone *had* been in his home, he knew who it would be.

Jeremy Winter.

Shane sat on the edge of his bed. What could he do about it? Report a break-in? So what? Nothing was taken, and he had no proof. Even if he did, the last thing he needed was cops sniffing around. Not with—

Gary Camblin. If Winter knew about the file and connected Camblin's death, lots of questions would arise. Uncomfortable questions, but ones without evidence to back them up. He'd followed procedures. No witnesses. Battery removed from his phone. No fingerprints and little chance of any DNA.

He sighed and shook his head. The other twenty-one targets were now untouchable. Far too chancy that Winter would link the deaths to the file. The men would never know how close they'd come.

He'd leave Camblin's page in the file and come up with some sort of explanation for why he kept them. Not that anyone would ever ask since doing so would be a dead giveaway that they'd been in his apartment.

He had to play this perfectly. Winter's attention needed to be directed elsewhere. Once that was done and a sufficient amount of time passed, Shane could get back to work. For now, the priority was to remain calm and formulate a plan.

He punched the remote, pulled up the *Jerry Springer* reruns, and crawled into the closet. It'd been a while since he and Buzz spent any quality time together. That was the thing about the toy. Not much of a talker, but such a good listener. And the two of them shared a bond that couldn't be broken. They'd been through it all and survived. Maybe not without a broken wing and a scratch here and there, but they'd made it.

He pulled the closet door closed, breathed deeply, and curled into a fetal position with Buzz pressed firmly against his chest. Their talk lasted over twenty minutes, and when finished, Shane was soaked in sweat. But they had their plan.

He thanked Buzz and scooted him back to the corner, then dialed Jeremy Winter's number.

CHAPTER FORTY

Jeremy fidgeted as he waited for Shane to arrive. The Outback Steakhouse was almost deserted. Too late for the lunch crowd and too soon for the dinner rush. The waiter stopped by twice to top off his water and ask about an appetizer. Get the bloomin' onion, he said. You'll love it. True, Jeremy told him, but my heartburn won't.

The call an hour earlier could only mean one thing. Jeremy messed up. Somehow Shane knew he'd been in his apartment. Otherwise, why ask to meet? Certainly not for the free meal. The timing was far too coincidental.

Jeremy squeezed more lemon into his water. As soon as he'd hung up the phone, he called Janice. He promised this wouldn't be a regular occurrence and she should feel free to decline, but Janice laughed and said how much she enjoyed helping. Made her feel like all her time at the Bureau counted for something more than being an admin to the Deputy Director. The thought of the petite sixty-something-year-old woman acting as his informant ought to have been funny, and maybe would have been in a different situation, but not today. He needed leverage, and that meant finding out everything he could about Shane Kingston. Fast.

He was driving to the restaurant when she called back. Order the grilled chicken and vegetables, she said. Eat healthy. He said he'd try but did she have any information that might be helpful?

"No charges were filed," she'd said, "but there's a police report indicating a domestic abuse incident involving Shane Kingston."

Like father, like son. "Any indication why he wasn't arrested?"

"Apparently the victim, a girl named Kimberly Westall, didn't report it. Her roommate did. I do hope that's useful. And you shouldn't be talking on the phone while you're driving."

"Yes, ma'am."

"And don't fill up on bread."

He rubbed his stomach and stared at the untouched loaf before him. Movement toward the front of the restaurant caught his eye, and he glanced up. The waiter rounded the corner and pointed Jeremy's direction. Shane stepped from behind him, nodded, and walked over.

Jeremy stood and shook Shane's hand. "Not working today?" he asked.

"Took the day off. I've been having trouble sleeping, you know? Like I need to get something off my chest. That's why I called."

No mention of the break-in? Fine, let's play the game. "I hope we can help each other."

The waiter set a glass of water by Shane and stood there with his open pad and pen.

"I'll have a filet," Shane said. "The small one, cooked medium. Baked potato loaded and whatever the veggie of the day is."

"Sounds good," Jeremy said. "Same for me."

The waiter nodded and turned to leave.

"Hold on," Jeremy said. "Change mine to the grilled chicken and vegetables. No potato."

"Got it," the man said.

Jeremy waited until they were alone again. "Something to get off your chest, you said?"

"Yeah. I don't know anything about your wife's murder, but my mom, she, uh ..."

"That's why it's important I talk—"

"I believe my mother's dead, Mr. Winter."

Jeremy opened his eyes wide. He wasn't surprised Rachel Anderson was no longer alive, but he was shocked that Shane would tell him. "What? I don't understand. You said you spoke to her regularly."

"Lies, I'm afraid. I told them to protect someone." He shook his head and stared at the ceiling. "Like they deserve it."

His father. "Protect who?"

"Please don't play stupid with me, Mr. Winter."

He shrugged. "Fine. Your father. You wanted to shield him, which means you think he did something. Did he kill your mother?"

Shane shifted his focus to his hands and licked his lips. "The ending was inevitable. The fights, the screaming, the abuse, it was like a freight train barreling down the tracks. You can't turn it around. All it does is pick up speed until the crash. She wouldn't leave and he ... he ..."

"Take your time," Jeremy said.

Shane took a deep breath and sat upright. "I didn't see it happen. One day Mom wasn't there anymore. I got home from school, and no one was in the house, but it was obvious they'd had another fight. A big one."

"Obvious how?"

"Nothing like you'd see on TV. You know, trashed house, broken lamps, stuff like that. A torn poster in my room, plus a, um, collectible toy of mine was broken. The wooden round thing on the bannister at the top of the stairs was gone. Stuff like that. Nothing major but enough." He smiled. "Their fights used to be over quick. No damage except to Mom. She must have fought back this time."

Jeremy rested his elbows on the table and leaned forward. "And that's enough to make you think your mother's dead?"

"Pine-Sol."

What? "Excuse me?"

"Pine-Sol. I smelled it that day. My mom hated cleaning. Hated it with a passion. We had a maid that came once a week, and it wasn't her day. Somebody cleaned up something."

Jeremy intertwined his fingers and stared at them for a moment. "And you never saw her again?"

"Never. No call, no note, nothing."

"Did you ask where she was?"

"Dad said she left. Good riddance too. I think at first I wanted to believe him. Keep some hope that she might come back, you know? But over time I accepted the truth, or at least what I believe is the truth. All I wanted to do was get out of there. Just turned eighteen, about to graduate high school. Anywhere but Frederick and the farther, the better."

"So why not tell me the truth? Why protect him?"

It was Shane's turn to shrug. "It was easier than the thought of going through all that again. Nothing can bring my mom back. I moved on, but it's been eating away at me ever since you started asking about her."

You mean ever since I visited your apartment. "I appreciate you telling me all this, but you really should contact the police in Frederick. Let them know of your concerns. I can put you in touch with a detective there."

"No. This is as far as I go. Like I said, nothing's going to bring my mom back. I only wanted to make sure you didn't hold out hope she could help you."

"You don't want to see justice done?"

"He's my dad," Shane said. "Not all my memories are bad ones. If he's arrested and convicted of her death, fine. But it won't be because of me. I have no evidence that says he's done anything."

"You know I'll turn this information over to the police, right?"

"I assumed you would. Odd though, isn't it?" He tilted his head and arched his eyebrows. "How we pick and choose what we tell the cops and what we don't."

And there it was. "Not sure what you're referring to there?"

"Nothing," Shane said. "Just thinking out loud in case I'm being recorded. Not that I've said anything I regret."

"I'm not recording you." Why didn't I record him?

"No big deal either way. So you're going to tell the police? Fine by me. Let them know that if they call me, I won't have anything to say. They're on their own."

"Fair enough," Jeremy said. "They'll want to talk to your father first, then anyone who might substantiate your claims of abuse."

"Georgia can. Tell them to talk to her."

"Hearsay. You're the only one who witnessed the *alleged* activity."

Shane leaned back and smiled. "Is that part of the routine, Mr. Winter? Using words like 'alleged' to get me angry and cause me to slip up? It won't work because I'm telling the truth. My story won't change. That said, I believe you have other information from Georgia that would prove helpful?"

So he does know his father killed Holly. That's his plan. Use Georgia to go after his dad on Holly's death and in the process get him on Rachel Anderson's murder too. All without getting involved or subjecting himself to any scrutiny. Clever.

"Perhaps," Jeremy said, "if you could point me in a direction, off the record, of course, that might help us find your mother?"

"Off the record? Seriously? You're better than that, Mr. Winter. Anyway, you know what I know."

Not all of it. Not the story on the file in your apartment.

The waiter brought their food, and Shane apologized, said he had to leave, and asked if the meal could be boxed up.

"Sorry you can't stay," Jeremy said. "I feel like we were just getting started."

"Really? Huh. I feel like we were just finishing. Good luck, Mr. Winter. I hope you find what you're looking for."

The waiter handed a to-go box to Shane and retreated to the kitchen.

Jeremy stood and shook Shane's hand again. "Thank you. I'm guessing we won't be speaking soon?"

"Don't see the need. If that changes, I'll be sure to let you know."

Time to push. "I'll bet. Oh, one more thing. Does the name Kimberly Westall mean anything to you?"

He nodded slowly. "It means there are things in my past I'm not proud of. I'm sure you know the feeling."

"I guess it's true what they say. The apple doesn't fall far from the tree."

"Do you know the statistics, Mr. Winter? The number of sons who grow up to be abusers like their fathers?"

"No," Jeremy said. "Seems to me that's a cop-out though. People make their own decisions."

"You may be right, but surprisingly little research has been done that specifically tracks the children of spouse abusers. Sure, they grow up and have issues, but are they more inclined to hostility, and if so, is that genetic or environmental? I'm thinking about starting up my own little project. In fact, I've already begun gathering names of people I might speak with."

Nicely done. "Interesting enough, I guess. Wonder what Kimberly Westall would have to say about it?"

Shane smiled. "Ask her."

CHAPTER FORTY-ONE

nother day, another six-hour drive back to Haymarket. The meeting with Shane yesterday did little to clarify Jeremy's thoughts. He had called Maggie a hundred miles earlier and recapped everything, but no matter where the conversation went, it always returned to the same single truth.

William Kingston killed Holly while shooting at his then-wife, Rachel Lynn Anderson, based on the supposed eyewitness testimony of Georgia Harding.

Everything else, Rachel's disappearance, Shane's file, remained on the periphery. A lone unprovable theory. The call ended abruptly after Jeremy said he felt like a juggler who only had one ball. Maggie's infectious laughter caused him to pull to the side of the road. Now, an hour and a half later, he still had a bad case of the chuckles.

Today's agenda consisted of not much. Get home around noon, start the laundry, and figure out where to go next. Maggie said Janice was picking up Beks and taking her to buy some new shoes, then bringing pizza home for dinner.

He should call Pronger and find out if he'd paid a visit to the old Kingston home, but he knew the answer. The man might be a good detective, but his stubborn refusal to see things Jeremy's way was infuriating. He sighed and picked up the phone.

Pronger answered on the third ring. "Yes," he said. "I went by the home. No, I didn't learn anything."

A better detective than I thought. "Nothing, huh? Can't say I'm surprised, but I do appreciate you doing it. I really do. Did you get to spend much time there?"

"About as much as I needed. The homeowners were curious about what I was up to, but they didn't keep anything off-limits. I checked the closets, attic, backyard, all of it. Not that I expected to find a bloody ax or anything like that. And before you ask, I didn't walk around spraying luminol everywhere."

Jeremy laughed. "You know me well, Detective. Can't say as I blame you on the luminol though. Anyway, I appreciate you taking the time."

"If you decide to put me in touch with your witness, I might be able to justify a more thorough search of the place. Otherwise, I don't see it happening." He sighed. "I wish you'd let me in on whatever's going on. Believe it or not, I really do want to see your wife's murder solved."

"I know you do, and if things change to where I can share information, I will. Promise."

"No vigilante stuff, right?"

"Right. All straight up and legal." Mostly.

"I took some photos at the house. You want them? Nothing to see, but they'll give you the layout."

An olive branch? "Sure, I'd appreciate that. Send them to my phone, if you don't mind. I'll look at them when I get home."

"You got it. One more thing ..."

"I'll bring the murder book by first chance I get. Tomorrow maybe, but for sure soon."

The call ended, and Jeremy pulled off at the next exit to stretch his legs and top off with fuel. A gust of wind sent a shiver through him and shuffled trash and leaves through the gas station's parking lot. The farther north he went, the more colorful the trees became. With October right around the corner, the weather could decide at any moment that it was finished with warm temps and sunny skies. All the more reason for hockey season to get cranked up.

Late nights in front of the TV with Maggie sounded wonderful. They'd have to get a home with a natural gas fireplace. Turn off all the lights and watch the games together while Beks, and Janice maybe, slept soundly. Or, as long as the Caps weren't playing, whatever Christmas movie Hallmark happened to be showing that day. The program would decide which of them fell asleep first.

He walked a few laps inside the store, used the restroom and bought coffee, then resumed the drive home. Couldn't wait to see his girls tonight.

....

Jeremy, Maggie, Janice, Beks, and last-minute invitee, Tanessa, lounged in the living room with paper plates on their laps and pizza boxes on the coffee table. He'd texted Pronger's photos to Maggie, and they now cycled through on the TV courtesy of some gadget she had. Front yard, living space, kitchen, bedroom, bathroom, stairs, bedroom, bedroom, bathroom, attic, backyard. Rinse and repeat. Tanessa said she'd add the app to his phone later so he could stream pretty much anything from his cell to the TV, whatever that meant.

He stared at the last piece of cheese pizza. "You sure you don't want that, Beks?"

"You can have it. I'll have a pepperoni."

He reached for the open box. "Last chance."

The girl shrugged, dragged a slice of pepperoni pizza onto her plate, then proceeded to pull off each piece of meat and stack it to the side. "Now we both have cheese."

Tanessa pointed at the unwanted pepperoni. "Mind if I have those?" She ate them in a single bite. "Nothing better."

Maggie dropped her plate in an empty box and wiped her hands on a dish towel. "Finish up, Rebecca. You need to go to your room and get on that homework."

"I don't have much." She wrinkled her nose. "Why can't I do it in here?"

"Because I said so."

The girl frowned. "Because is not a reason."

Jeremy stifled a smile. "It's all the reason you're gonna get."

"But I don't want to go—"

"Come on, dear." Janice stood and took Beks' plate. "I'll go with you."

"You don't have to do that," Maggie said.

The older woman nodded. "I know, but honestly, I find her conversations more interesting. You three enjoy your chat."

When they'd made their way to Beks' room and closed the door, Jeremy gathered up the rest of the mess and carried it to the kitchen. "Anybody else want a beer?"

Both Maggie and Tanessa raised their hands.

He opened three bottles and took his same position on the sofa. "Any thoughts on where I go from here?"

Tanessa shook her head. "Me and Mags been bouncing this around all afternoon. What you think you know isn't close to what you can prove. Even if we got involved, officially I mean, we're dead in the water."

Maggie downed a couple of swallows of beer and wiped the back of her hand across her mouth. "Ladylike, right? Anyway, I agree with Tanessa. If you can't convince your only witness, Georgia Harding, to come forward, you've got no case. And even if she did talk to the police, what would change? Nothing I can see. No way you'll find evidence at the murder scene. Not after this long. And Detective Pronger already checked the house."

Jeremy waved at the pictures on the TV. "A cursory inspection."

"What was he supposed to do?" Tanessa asked. "Ransack the place? Looking for what exactly? If there was something obvious to be found, don't you think the homeowners would've stumbled across it a long time ago?"

"It wouldn't be obvious," he said.

Tanessa nodded. "I gotta tell you, Jer. That's a pretty weak rope you're pulling on. Find a reason to get a full-blown CSI team in there and maybe they turn up something. Otherwise ..."

"Otherwise we've got nothing," Maggie said. "Oh, and there is one other issue we haven't discussed. Whatever it was you found at Shane's apartment."

Jeremy arched his eyebrows. "Not relevant to Holly's case. At least I don't think so."

Tanessa leaned forward. "What's this now? You found something and didn't tell us? Mags, you knew about this?"

"I knew, but he can't tell me. Not without risking a potential conviction down the road."

"Uh-uh," Tanessa said. "None of that. No secrets, right?"

Jeremy flicked a drop of condensation off the bottom of his bottle. "I never agreed to that. What I found is a totally separate issue. I'm watching, and if it does become something that requires the involvement of law enforcement, I'll make it happen."

Tanessa flopped back against her chair. "Be that way."

"So what's left?" Maggie asked. "You can try to talk to William Kingston again. Let him know you saw his son and hint that Shane gave some credible statements implicating his father. See how he reacts to that."

"Worth a shot," Jeremy said, "but I doubt I'll make it past the lobby.

Even so, I'll, uh ..." The photo on the screen. The backyard. The picture faded and the next one appeared.

"Can you pause that thing? Run it back?"

Maggie picked up the remote. "Strangely enough, yes. You press the pause button, then the rewind button."

"There," Jeremy said. "The backyard."

"Wooden fence," Tanessa said. "And trees and a swing set. A lot nicer than what I grew up with, but nothing special."

"The trees are old, right? Too much shade for the grass to grow. That's why there are these huge patches of bare ground everywhere."

"So?" Maggie said.

Jeremy pointed at a spot along the fence near the back corner. "So why is grass growing here when there's nothing else around it?"

Tanessa squinted at the TV. "You don't think ..."

"I do," he said. "I'm calling Pronger. He needs to get his hands on a cadaver dog."

CHAPTER FORTY-TWO

Jeremy shifted from his right leg to his left and back again, then cupped his hands and blew into them. Should've brought some gloves.

A pall hung over the home's backyard, and all attention was riveted on an area about ten-feet square near the house. There, two CSI techs, each dressed head-to-toe in a white papery-plastic suit, were on their knees sifting through the dirt in an area surrounding a three-foot deep hole.

Detective Pronger handed him a cup of coffee. "Better to be lucky than smart, right?"

Jeremy debated his response. Did Pronger mean that as an insult? It had been three days since he'd phoned the detective about his suspicions. After a bit of prodding, Pronger agreed to contact the Maryland State Police and inquire as to the possibility of their cadaver dog coming to Frederick. They said they could do it, but with such a weak reason the trip had to be coded as a training exercise. Pronger assured them the local PD would cover all expenses.

Yesterday, the team arrived with their brown-and-white springer spaniel. At the pre-search briefing, the visiting cops laughed and informed Jeremy he'd read too many novels. Human corpses don't work well as fertilizer and whatever nutrients a body may share with the soil could never last more than two or three years. But they were here, the dog needed training, the homeowners were okay with it, and Pronger was paying, so why not do the search?

Within twenty minutes, the spaniel signaled a hit seventy-five feet from where Jeremy thought the body would be. Not a hundred percent conclusive, the trainer said, but if I were you, I'd get a shovel. The homeowners checked into a hotel, and a local cop was stationed on-site until a few hours earlier when a forensics team from Baltimore arrived.

The skeletal remains were already on the way to a lab while the two CSI techs searched for possible evidence.

Jeremy took a sip of the coffee. "Thanks. And yeah. Lucky or smart. I'll take either." The two watched in silence for a few moments. "They confirm it was a female yet?"

"Uh-uh," Pronger said. "We bypassed the local guys and sent the remains to Baltimore. Their coroner and a forensics scientist from the university will do the autopsy, but we both know who was in that hole."

"Think Kingston knows we found her yet?"

"Which one? Shane or William?" The detective tilted his head toward the fence around the yard. "Two or three news crews out there. Word will get out soon enough. I'm heading to Baltimore later this morning to talk to the father. He knows I'm coming, so I reckon he's already got a lawyer lined up. I don't expect to learn anything. Until we have a positive ID on the remains, not much chance of applying any pressure. Still, a body buried at your old house is going to make anyone nervous."

One of the white-suited CSI techs raised an object, inspected it, and dropped it into an evidence bag. At least the tenth time they'd done that. Experience taught Jeremy that most, if not all, of the items would be nothing more than assorted trash. You could randomly choose any spot in any yard or park, and if you dug long enough, you'd find something in proximity. A cigarette butt, pull-tab from an old soda can, Civil War bullet, something.

"What about Shane?" Jeremy asked. "You going to drive down to talk to him?"

"As soon as I can. I thought about having the Charlotte PD arrange an interview and doing it remotely, but nothing replaces face-to-face."

"Agreed." Pronger needed to know of Jeremy's suspicions. "Listen, Detective, I have some information. I trust the source, but I can't verify the details. My problem is that if I tell you, I'm afraid it will skew your investigation into Rachel Anderson's death."

The detective cut his eyes toward Jeremy, then resumed staring at the CSI techs. "Plenty of cases get solved because of rumors, but I've yet to see anyone convicted because of gossip. Anything you tell me is going to be hearsay, right? All that means is I have to find facts to back up your story. Do I wish I could speak to your witness directly? Of course. In the meantime, I'll take what I can get."

Jeremy held the warm coffee cup against each cheek before continuing. "I think that—"

"You think William Kingston killed your wife. I figured that out a while back. Wasn't hard. You suddenly focus on them while investigating a murder? There could only be one reason. What I don't know is what Rachel Anderson has to do with your wife's death."

"I don't give you enough credit, Detective."

"And I give you too much."

Jeremy laughed, held his cup toward Pronger, and the two men tapped their coffees together.

"So," the detective said, "what's your theory on Kingston's motive? Why kill your wife?"

"He was shooting at *his* wife, missed Rachel and hit Holly. It's that simple."

Pronger frowned and shook his head. "I hope you don't mind my asking, but does that make it better or worse?"

"Worse. Or better. Probably neither."

"And if he tried to kill his wife once, not hard to imagine he'd try again. I can't promise you we'll get him. Not for your wife's murder. But if he killed Rachel Anderson, he's done. I *will* prove it."

Jeremy blinked several times and nodded. "I told myself that would be good enough."

"Sounds like you're not—"

A commotion erupted behind them, and they spun around. The double gate on the fence was open, and a uniformed cop tugged a stranger back toward the front yard. "You can't go back there!"

Pronger took another sip of coffee. "That who I think it is?"

"Yeah. That's William Kingston."

CHAPTER FORTY-THREE

Jeremy hurried behind Pronger as the detective strode toward Kingston. The officer maintained his grip on the man's arm. "Sorry," the cop said. "Tried to stop him out front. I'll get him out of here."

"It's all right," Pronger said. "I'll take it from here."

The officer shrugged and retreated to the warmth of his squad car.

Jeremy started to speak but held back. His blood boiled at the sight of Kingston. The man was no better than any of the other killers now rotting on death row or buried where no one came to visit. Best let Pronger take charge. His scene, his investigation. If he wanted Jeremy's involvement, he'd ask for it. And if he didn't ask for it, no problem. One way or another, Jeremy would most certainly be involved when the time came to bring whatever brand of justice was needed.

The detective stood with his body between Kingston and the CSI techs, blocking as much of the view as possible. "Can I help you with something, sir?"

Kingston sidestepped him and moved toward the newly opened grave. Before Jeremy could react, Pronger had the man's arm twisted behind his back. Kingston doubled over as the detective applied upward pressure.

"You made me drop my coffee," Pronger said. "Did I like doing that? No, I didn't."

Kingston waved his free arm. "Okay, okay. Let me go. I'm sorry. It's just that … I heard … is it true?"

Pronger spun him around and guided him back to the gate. "Try that again, and you're going to jail, understand? Good. Now, let's start over. Who are you, and why are you here?"

"My name is William Kingston, and I used to live here. I got a call from a policeman who—"

"A detective, not a policeman. That was me. I thought we were meeting later?"

The man ran his hand under his nose and pressed his palms into his puffy red eyes. "Is it Rachel? My wife?"

Pronger glanced at Jeremy before answering. "Far too soon to know. Why would you assume it's your wife?"

"Ex-wife," Kingston said. "I filed for divorce after she left."

"Uh-huh. And when did she leave?"

"Um, fifteen years ago. I came home from work one day, and she was gone."

The detective nodded. "Did you report her missing?"

"What?" The man squished his eyebrows together. "No. We were going through a rough patch, and I assumed she'd, uh, she'd found a place to stay until things settled down."

"Settled down how?"

"You know what it's like when married couples fight. Sometimes the best thing to do is get apart for a while. Let the emotions fade."

"Sure," Pronger said. "I know all about it." He lowered his voice. "Me and my wife, we don't fight often, but when we do, whew. Better watch out, right?"

Jeremy used his coffee cup to block a small grin. He'd never been effective at building rapport with suspects. Not like the detective. Of course, if Pronger's wife knew everything that Jeremy knew ...

"Uh, I guess," Kingston said. "Can I see her?"

See her? What does he think there is to see? The man's putting on quite a show. Believable even, unless you consider his grief could stem from her body being found and not from her death.

"No," Pronger said. "I'm sorry, but that's not possible. Besides, like you said, it's been *fifteen years*. Think about that."

Kingston covered his mouth with his hand and nodded. The detective guided the man to the front yard. "You know Mr. Winter, right? How about we all talk inside my car where it's warmer, okay?" He glanced at Jeremy. "I believe you know which vehicle is mine?"

He can't let it go. Not that I would either. Jeremy half-smiled and slid into the back seat next to Kingston. The detective sat up front, started the car, and turned on the heat.

"Now then," Pronger said, "I was saying how much I understand the need to cool off when things get out of hand. My wife, man, I thought she was going to kill me when she found out I'd been cheating on her. Had to get out of there for a while." His voice faded. "Truth be told, I'm still out of there."

Jeremy's chest ached, and he made eye contact with the detective in the rearview mirror. If the man was lying, he deserved an Oscar.

"We weren't cheating on each other," Kingston said. "At least as far as I know."

"That's good," Pronger said. "Got to keep the trust, right? So, if you don't mind me asking, why'd she leave?"

"The usual stuff I suppose. Money was tight, and we fought a lot about that. Too much stress."

The detective nodded. "I hear it all the time. Did the fights ever get physical?"

Kingston's lips narrowed, and he sat back. "You're treating me like a suspect."

"Not at all," Pronger said. "I'm just trying to figure out how a body ended up in your backyard. And Mr. Winter here tells me you're one of those guys who likes to, well, I guess there's no delicate way to put this, you hit her, didn't you? A lot."

The man straightened and peered at Pronger. "Absolutely not, and that's the last question I'm answering without my attorney present."

"Smart," the detective said. "Get a lawyer. Exercise your rights. That's what I'd do, especially if I had a son who couldn't wait to get on the stand and testify how Daddy used to hit Mommy. The jury's gonna eat that up. You'll need a good attorney."

Kingston pulled on the door handle repeatedly. "I'd like to leave now."

Pronger grinned. "I'm sure you would. What do you think, Jeremy? Should I haul him in for questioning—with his lawyer present, of course— or should I let him go?"

Jeremy? Are we on a first-name basis now? "Let him go. I know where he lives. Where he works. Where he goes. If you need him, I can find him." He scooted closer to the man. "And if *I* need him, well, that'll just be between us, won't it, Mr. Kingston?"

"Fair enough," Pronger said. He stepped out of the vehicle and opened the rear door. Kingston pulled a phone from his pocket and hurried to his car while the detective settled back behind the steering wheel.

"That went well," Jeremy said.

"As well as could be expected. You buying his act?"

Good question. As bad as he wanted to believe in Kingston's guilt, there was a niggling doubt. "Oh, he abused his wife. I'm certain of that. Killing her is a different thing though, isn't it? Can't judge anything by people's reactions, but ... I don't know. Glad *I* don't have to figure it out."

"If word leaks that he abused his wife, true or not, he'll be convicted before he even gets arrested. Neither of us wants that." Pronger stared at Jeremy and frowned. *"Do we?"*

"Easy there, chief. The ball's in your court now. I'll keep my mouth shut. If anything leaks to the press, I swear it won't be from me or mine. But I suggest you get ahead of the abuse issue. Wouldn't surprise me if Shane took it on himself to put that info out there."

"Payback for Kingston killing his mother?"

"Maybe." Jeremy glanced away. "Hey, it's none of my business, but that stuff about ..."

"My wife?" Pronger sighed, and his shoulders sank. "I told her. Broke it off with Gayle at the diner not long after we met there. The worst choice I ever made. The affair, I mean."

"I'm sorry."

"Thanks. I'll survive. May not want to, at least for a while, but I will."

Jeremy nodded. Should he pat Pronger on the back or something? "You ever need to grab a beer sometime, you know, talk about it ..."

The detective smiled. "Wow. Never pictured you for one of those touchy-feely types. I won't pass up a free beer, but it better be in front of a big-screen TV with the Caps on."

"You got it. Listen, I'm going to get out of here. I know you don't have to, but—"

"Yeah, yeah, yeah. I'll keep you in the loop."

The men shook hands.

"And," Jeremy said, "I'll do the same if I come across something that might link with your investigation. Best of luck, Detective."

"Harley."

"Harley." Jeremy frowned and wrinkled his forehead. "Nope, can't do it. No offense. Detective or Pronger."

Pronger smiled. "Good call."

Jeremy hustled back to his car, grimacing as the weather shot darts of ice into his leg, cranked the engine, and stamped his feet while waiting for the heat to kick on. He plugged his cell into the charger and checked the battery level. Barely over thirty percent. Beks needed to figure out what kept draining the power, and "your phone is too old" was not the correct answer.

The green light in the top corner blinked slowly, and he checked his notifications. A new voice mail. Call from an unknown number over an hour ago. Nope. Never heard it ring. Didn't vibrate either. Stupid thing was useless.

He hit the speaker button and retrieved the message.

"Mr. Winter?"

Tanessa? Why was she calling him? Was Maggie okay?

"Mr. Winter, call me as soon as you get this. We have a problem. One of those men, the ones on Shane's list, one of them is dead."

CHAPTER FORTY-FOUR

Jeremy's heart raced as he dialed Tanessa's number. Who was dead, and how did she know about the list? Did this mean Shane was—

"Took you long enough," Tanessa said. "The purpose of a cell phone is to be easily reachable. You're not."

He rubbed his forehead. "How did you get my number? Does Maggie know you're calling?"

"One, I'm an FBI agent, remember? Two, no, she doesn't."

"Um, I'm a little uncomfortable with … wait, how do you know about Shane's list? I didn't even tell Maggie."

"FBI agent. Ring a bell? You gave me your cell the other night to put an app on it. Ding ding ding ding!"

A twinge of heat flushed his face. "You went through my phone?"

"What was I supposed to do? You wouldn't tell us your big secret, and I figured if it was important enough for you to worry about getting us involved, then it was important enough that we *needed* to be involved."

"That makes no sense."

"It makes perfect sense. But I didn't want to make you mad, so I didn't tell Maggie. She can still claim plausible deniability."

His head flopped back against the seat. "Wonderful. You didn't want to make me angry. How do you think Maggie's going to react when she learns you're talking to me behind her back?"

"Mm-mmm-mmm. You make it sound dirty, Jer. Tell you what. I'm going to give you a name, 'kay? Gary Camblin. He's the dude who died in Charlotte. Suicide, apparently. I've done nothing with it. No investigation, no phone calls, nothing. You can choose where to go from here. Tell Maggie or not; it's your decision."

"Not anymore, it's not. I see another option though. *You* tell Maggie what you did. Let her decide how to handle things."

"Nah, she likes me too much."

He gripped the steering wheel and took a heavy breath. "Tanessa, I swear I'll—"

"Y'all slay me." She laughed and the background noise intensified. "You're on speaker, Jer. Mags, get over here! Hang on, she's coming. And no, no one else is around."

"What's going on?" Maggie asked.

"Better pull up a chair," Tanessa said. "We might be here for a minute."

Half an hour later, they came to an agreement. Tanessa would, off the record, of course, continue to monitor the remaining names on Shane's list. Maggie would, also off the record, of course, make inquiries into Gary Camblin's death. Jeremy would, without regard to being on or off any record, drive back to Charlotte immediately and do whatever it took to learn whether Shane was involved in the man's death.

....

The sun hung low in the sky by the time Jeremy neared Charlotte. Much more of this, and he might as well get a month-to-month furnished apartment.

Pronger texted earlier to let him know the preliminary autopsy results confirmed the remains were female and cause of death was still officially undetermined, though the final report would most likely indicate homicide by gunshot due to a shattered rib.

Gunshot. The same way Holly died. Jeremy phoned and left a voice mail thanking him for the info and letting him know he was headed to Charlotte to look into something. As expected, that prompted a return call a few minutes later. Jeremy explained that, for the detective's own benefit, he couldn't give any details. Fruit of the poisonous tree. But not to worry. He wouldn't talk to Shane until Pronger had a shot at him first.

Was Harley happy about the situation? No, he wasn't, but he said he'd drive down the next day. Maybe they could meet for lunch. Jeremy agreed and said the meal was his treat. The detective used several expletives to confirm his expectation that if anyone should be buying his meals, it was Jeremy.

By the time he checked into the motel, the last shades of orange sky had given way to darkness. A stop at the local Whole Foods cost him time and money for apples, bananas, and carrots. Baby carrots. The hope was that the price of the food would be enough to outweigh his craving for something more desirable. He gave it a day until he'd be buying the huge cinnamon roll from the vending machine.

After getting a "nothing new" update from Maggie, he opened his laptop and looked for anything he could find on Gary Camblin. The man's obituary was listed on the local paper's website, as well as a funeral home's. No details regarding cause of death were given, not unusual for an obit, especially when suicide was involved. The burial unfortunately took place yesterday. Jeremy would've loved to hang around the edges and see if Shane showed up.

Other than the original article regarding Camblin's domestic abuse charge—the same one as in Shane's file—nothing else was found. The man's old accounting firm made no mention of why Camblin left, only that they'd changed the name of their business. As near as he could tell from public records, no jail time had ever been assigned. Community service along with anger management classes, probably.

Camblin lost everything, enough to cause any man to at least contemplate a way out. But he deserved it, didn't he? The rules are simple. You don't abuse your wife. Doesn't matter how mad you are at her or your boss or the guy who took your parking spot at Target. How frustrated you are that your life didn't turn out like you thought it should. How much alcohol or drugs you became addicted to. Abuse, physical or emotional, was weakness.

But sometimes anger turned to rage in a flash, and things happen that can never be undone. He shook his head and closed the laptop.

He knew all about rage. How it could take over and, even when you wanted to stop, you couldn't. His heart sank. He'd never forget what Maggie told him one day out of the blue.

They'd been at her apartment. Nothing out of the ordinary going on. She went down the hall to use the restroom, and he went to the kitchen to get a bite. When she returned, she was staring at her fingernails like she was deciding whether or not to repaint and didn't notice he was no longer on the sofa.

He tapped her on the back. "You awake?"

The look in her eyes when she spun around was more than fear. It was terror.

He reached to touch her, and she leaned away, began crying, then buried her face in his chest.

"Honey, what is it?" he asked.

She couldn't answer through the sobs. He wrapped his arms around her and shhh-shhh-shhh'd and it's-okay'd in her ear for what seemed like an eternity.

Finally, she pulled back and took a deep breath. "It doesn't happen often," she said. "And it's not your fault. But sometimes, I don't know, my mind thinks … one time. He hit me one time. That's all, and I never gave him another chance. But my mind can't let go. I don't know that it ever will."

He wiped his thumb under her eyes. "Listen to me, Maggie. I will *never* hit you. I swear. You and Beks, you know what I'd do to protect you. Anything."

She nodded and tried to smile. "I know that, Jeremy. I trust you more than anyone I've ever met. But there's the tiniest sliver buried deep inside reminding me my ex said the same thing."

He'd gone home and wept that night. The pain and sorrow burrowed inside him and took up permanent residence. His beautiful Maggie had been afraid. Of him.

He cried because her ex-husband took something she could never get back.

Because of the fear in her eyes for the briefest of seconds.

And because nothing he could ever do would make her whole again.

CHAPTER FORTY-FIVE

L unch with Pronger was casual and informative. The detective received an email stating that there'd been nothing suspicious in the Kingstons' old home. No Luminol hits. But a .44 Magnum Colt Anaconda was registered to William Kingston when his wife disappeared, and when Holly was killed, but the weapon had been reported stolen several years back.

"A revolver," Jeremy said. "That explains there was no shell casing when Holly was shot."

"Uh-huh," Pronger said. "Bit of a stretch, don't you think? No casing equals William Kingston must be guilty?"

"One more piece of the puzzle. The witness never mentioned the shooter picking up anything, so a revolver make sense."

"So does a crow seeing a shiny thing and carrying it off to its nest. But a bird doesn't fit your theory, does it?"

No, it doesn't. But tunnel vision wasn't such a bad thing when your destination waited at the end of the passageway. Jeremy changed the subject and hinted it would be wonderful if he could view the detective's interview with Shane as it happened. Pronger said that 'wonderful' for Jeremy was not the same thing as 'wonderful' for himself ... but he'd make it happen. This time.

The men arrived at the Charlotte PD shortly before the scheduled interrogation time of noon. After signing them in, a local detective escorted Jeremy to a room where he could observe on a monitor. Shane was already there, checking his phone and looking bored.

Pronger stepped into the interview room, introduced himself, and sat across the table from Shane. "I appreciate you coming in today. First off, let me say how sorry I am about your mother."

"Did they confirm it was her?" He sniffled and blinked rapidly. His red, watery eyes were surrounded by dark, puffy circles.

"Not yet, but we're confident they will soon. I only have a few questions, and then I'll let you go."

Shane placed both hands on the table. "Do I need a lawyer?"

Pronger shrugged. "You're not under arrest and are free to leave at any time. An attorney is up to you, but I'm certain you want to help solve your mother's murder, don't you?"

"How do you know it was a murder?"

"Mainly because her death was never reported and someone buried her in your backyard. Doesn't that seem, um, suspicious to you?"

"Of course it does." Shane tapped his finger on the table. "I thought you had more though. You know, a knife or weapon or something."

The detective rubbed his chin. "We have several items from the scene we're reviewing. Mr. Kingston, how do you think your mother ended up there?"

"You know how. My father killed her, and she let him. They'd had their mostly one-sided fights for years. It was only a matter of time."

Pronger scribbled a note. "What did they fight about?"

"What *didn't* they fight about? My dad liked to drink, right? For all I know, he still does." He shook his head. "Or he's in AA and completely rehabbed. Don't know, don't care. All I remember is he got to where he'd stop at the bar on the way home almost every day."

"And you believe the alcohol led to the abuse?"

"Man, how am I supposed to know? I was a kid."

The detective flipped back a few pages in his pad. "You were, let's see, here we go, you were eighteen years old when your mother disappeared. Hardly a kid."

"Whatever. All I know is when the fights would start I'd make myself scarce, okay?"

"Was that because you were afraid?"

Shane sighed and tilted his head back. "Yeah, maybe. Scared, worried, anxious, you name it. Not a great environment to grow up in."

"I wouldn't think so. Did you ever see your father with a weapon? A knife or a gun?"

"Uh-uh. But like I said, I didn't hang around for the play-by-play."

"Sure. Did your mother ever initiate the fights? Did she ever retaliate?"

"Not that I remember." He scratched the back of his hand. "Don't get the wrong idea. It's not like this was an everyday thing. Two or three times a month maybe. But even when they weren't fighting, the tension was there. Like you were just waiting for him to boil over."

"Must've been rough, huh?"

Shane paused. "You learn to deal with it."

"Tell me, did your father ever get abusive toward you?"

"Uh-uh. Guess he had his standards. Don't hit a kid or something."

"A real hero, huh?"

"Don't try to bond with me," Shane said. "That's not going to happen. Look, I've got to get ready for work. Can I go now?"

Pronger motioned toward the door. "Like I said, you're free to go anytime you want, but I'm almost done. Just another question or two. You say that you believe your father killed your mother. Did you see the incident happen?"

"No, but as far as I could tell all of her clothes were still there. Her purse was gone though."

"What about her car?"

"Gone. A couple of days later Dad said one of his friends saw it at the Amtrak station and he had it towed back to the house."

"Uh-huh. How did your father react when your mother disappeared? What did he say to you about her being gone?"

"I'd say he was calmer," Shane said. "He told me they'd agreed it was better for them to separate."

"Didn't you wonder why she didn't tell you this herself? Or at least say goodbye?"

"Sure I did, but I wanted to believe it was true. No more fighting and yelling."

Pronger wrote another note. "I can understand that. What would you say your relationship is with your father now?"

"Nonexistent."

"That strikes me as a bit odd."

"It wouldn't if you'd grown up in the home I did."

"No, I get that part." The detective drummed his pen on the table. "So why protect him? Why lie about talking to your mother regularly?"

Shane glanced at the camera mounted high in the corner. "Been talking to Winter, I guess. Whatever. First, I had my doubts about my mom leaving, but that's all. No proof. And just because my dad and I don't speak doesn't mean there's not something there. Like I told Winter, not all my memories are bad ones. I wanted to believe she was alive. That Dad told the truth, and we can all go our own ways and live happily ever after."

"Help me understand this. You protected your father, who you knew abused your mother because you were afraid if anyone started looking into her disappearance, what? They'd find out she was dead? Or she was living the high life in Aruba?"

He turned his palms upward. "I don't know, man. I figured leave well enough alone, I guess. Nothing can change the past. I'd rather believe she's alive than know she's dead."

"Not sure I follow your thinking there, but okay. One more question and we can wrap this up. Earlier you said your mother …" He ran his pen along the pad from top to bottom. "Here we go. 'My father killed her, and she let him.' What did you mean by that? 'She let him.'"

Shane's face wrinkled in anger, and he stood, pushed his chair under the table, and left the room without responding.

Pronger rocked back in his seat and turned toward the camera. "Did this case become a lot more interesting? It sure did."

CHAPTER FORTY-SIX

"Heading back so soon?" Jeremy asked. "You just got here."

"There's no point hanging around," Pronger said. "Until we get more information, I don't see either Kingston being willing to talk."

"What's your gut telling you? Shane, William, or someone else?"

"Oh, it's definitely William. Unless it's Shane. If you play the odds, bet on the ex-husband. I can't see a motive for Shane killing his own mother. If nothing else, she served as a barrier between him and his father's abuse."

"But …"

The detective sighed. "But there's something about the kid. Did you catch what he said in there? About his mother letting his father kill her? What's that supposed to mean?"

"Who knows?" He lowered his voice. "And you only have half the story on him."

Pronger held up his hand. "Uh-uh. Don't tell me."

Jeremy chuckled. "Wasn't going to. Before you go, any chance I can get a look at the photos taken at the crime scene?"

The detective pulled a USB drive from his pocket and handed it over. "You're too predictable, Winter. And you didn't get that from me. It'll cost you a pair of Caps tickets, and none of those nosebleed seats either. And you're buying the beers."

Pronger had to know what this would look like if anyone ever questioned it. Gratuities in exchange for confidential police information. That's not what this was though. The detective wanted off-the-books help. He was bending the rules hoping for a break in the case. Jeremy grinned. Guess I'm starting to rub off on him. Not sure that's a good thing.

"Deal," Jeremy said. "Drive safe."

"Okay, Dad." Pronger rolled his eyes. "Want me to text you when I get home too?"

"Nah. If it's after eight-thirty, I'll be asleep."

. . . .

The pictures on the USB drive showed little that Jeremy hadn't seen in person. He focused on the images of the twelve evidence bags, each containing one item collected by the CSI techs. As he expected, most of the gathered articles appeared to be the usual things you'd find anywhere. An old cigarette butt, two pennies, pieces of wire, rusted metal from who knows what, and the like.

A single image stood out. A piece of plastic, roughly a couple of inches square, one side jagged and broken. Largely colored in faded purple, the item also had a tiny section of red-and-white stripes and a green oblong bump along one edge.

The plastic had been found directly under the remains. If you looked close enough at the earlier photos, the ones with the complete skeleton still in the ground, you could see the item extending from under a rib. The colors indicated it most likely came from a toy of some sort.

Not unusual since plastic lasted forever and toys were a staple of every backyard. When he was a kid, those little green army men fought their share of battles in his own yard. Many lost their lives to brick grenades or cigarette lighter flamethrowers. If he went back there and dug, chances are he'd find a melted arm or broken leg.

But this toy was unique. Not because of its rarity. A gazillion of them had been sold since the movies came out. Those films that Beks watched over and over. This toy was nothing special except for the fact the last time Jeremy saw Buzz Lightyear was in the bottom of Shane Kingston's closet.

. . . .

"I don't understand what difference it would make," Maggie said. "Even if the piece found at the scene matches the one in Shane's closet, so what? That doesn't prove anything other than he had the toy at the time of his mother's death."

"Agreed," Jeremy said, "but it's one more insight we have into him. Why is the toy important enough that he'd keep it all this time?"

"First off, what you're really asking is 'how can we use that knowledge against him?' And second, 'is gaining that information worth the risk?' I'm a long way from being convinced."

"It's not just that." He rubbed the back of his neck. "I need to see if the file has changed. Is Gary Camblin still there? Have others been added or removed?"

"Can we agree that, in all likelihood, Shane's file has absolutely nothing to do with Holly's murder?"

"Yes, but can we also agree that whatever he's up to is suspicious enough to warrant further investigation, especially considering Camblin's death?"

"Suicide," she said. "That's what the autopsy will say. No bruising around the mouth and no indication he was forced to swallow the drugs. No other fingerprints on the water or pill bottles."

"An awfully big coincidence, don't you think?"

"Not really. When you look at the guy's life and the problems he'd been through, especially since they're self-inflicted, I imagine there are others who would have made the same decision."

"But how many of those others have the details of their domestic abuse locked away in the file cabinet of the son of a man who abused his wife to the point of death?" He paused to take a breath. "Assuming Shane didn't kill his mother, that is, and if he did, maybe that makes the file even worse. Like some sort of penance."

"Granted, and if another one on the list kills himself, *then* I'll say you might be onto something worth taking a risk for." She hesitated. "Don't say it. No, I'm not suggesting you let someone die to prove your point. It's just that ..."

"I didn't get caught last time, Maggie."

"By the grace of God," she said. "But Shane knows you were in there. He's probably changed the locks and put cameras in his apartment by now."

"So if I can't get in, no harm no foul, right? And if I do, I'll wear a mask. I won't get caught. Three minutes in and out. Compare the toy to the piece in the photo and check the file. That's it."

"I still don't like it."

"Neither do I, but I don't see any other way forward."

"Two minutes. From the time you open the door until you close it on your way out, no more than two minutes. And no identifiable clothing.

Everything you wear goes in a dumpster after you finish. Shoes, pants, shirt, and mask."

He laughed. "I thought you were going to tell me to burn them."

"Do you have a place you can do that?"

A grin spread across his face. "No. I left my 55-gallon drum at home. I've got this, Maggie. Don't worry. I'll call when I'm done."

CHAPTER FORTY-SEVEN

Jeremy tugged one side of the ski mask lower so he could see better. His forehead, neck, and nose itched like crazy. How do people wear these things? He'd been in Shane's apartment for fifteen, maybe twenty seconds. Either the lock hadn't been changed or at least not upgraded, since picking it took no longer than the last time.

He hurried to the closet first. Buzz was still there, though it appeared he had been moved. Jeremy gently pressed the red button on the toy's chest to extend the wings. A muted click sounded as the extensions popped into place. Most of the right wing was gone, and Jeremy snapped three quick photos before shoving Buzz's appendages back into their secured positions.

Everything in the living room and kitchen looked unchanged. The file cabinet was locked but yielded to his gadget nearly instantly. The pages remained in the same spot, and he eased them from their resting place.

He left the binder clip in place—was that what alerted Shane?—and scanned the papers. He'd studied the pictures from last time enough to recognize that nothing had changed. Every man, including Gary Camblin, was in the same position. No one new had joined the collection.

No big surprise. Shane knew Jeremy had visited his apartment. He'd have to assume the file was no longer a secret. The last thing he'd do was make any changes to it, especially if he had anything to do with Camblin's death.

Jeremy slid the pages into the hanging folder, locked the cabinet, and left the apartment. Two minutes and twenty-three seconds. Not bad for an old guy without his cane.

. . . .

"No," Jeremy said, "the dumpster was at a *different* apartment complex several miles away. It was nearly full, and I shoved the stuff halfway down. No one's going to find it, but I'm considering having my arms amputated right below the elbow. I don't know what was in that garbage, and I can't get the smell off."

Maggie laughed. "You're not cut out for a life of crime."

"Meh. Hopefully, that's the last of my, uh, adventures. Worth it though. No question that the plastic piece from Rachel Anderson's grave matches the toy in Shane's closet. CSI would have to confirm it, but the photos are clear enough as far as I'm concerned."

"Again, that proves nothing. You could … hold on. Rebecca, you're supposed to be in bed. What? Yes. Fine, but make it quick."

"Hey, Jeremy," the girl said. "What's up?"

He smiled. "Not much. What's up with you?"

"I'm not sleepy, but Mom says I have to go to bed. Where are you?"

"North Carolina, sweetie. Do you know where that is?"

An exaggerated sigh came through the phone. "Duh. We studied states like two years ago. When are you coming home?"

"As soon as I can. When I get there—"

"Miss Janice bought me some new shoes. Wanna see them?"

"I sure do. When I get—"

"I said my socks bother me so she said wear them inside out so now that's what I do."

"That sounds like a—"

"Mom says I'm too spoiled. I don't think so. Do you think I'm too spoiled?"

"Well, if your Mom says—"

"I told her nuh-uh. That's right, isn't it? Because she's always … Mom, I'm not finished talking."

"And you never will be," Maggie said. "Off to bed. Not another peep."

Jeremy cleared his throat. "I didn't get to tell her goodnight."

"I swear. You two are gonna … here, Rebecca."

"Night, Beks," he said. "I love you, sweetheart."

"Night, Jeremy. Love you too. Mom says I'll never finish talking. Do you think that's—hey!" Her voice faded. "It's not polite to grab things."

"In the bed," Maggie said. "Now." She waited a few seconds before continuing. "Okay, what were we talking about?"

"Buzz Lightyear."

"Right. You've got a match, which is good, I suppose, but means nothing. And the files?"

He frowned. "Nothing's changed, and Camblin's still in there."

"Of course he is, but even if he wasn't, what difference would it make? Shane would simply say he pulled Camblin's page out because he saw his obit in the paper."

"None of this sits right with me. There has to be a way to prove William and Shane Kingston are both guilty of, of something."

"Wow," she said. "That doesn't sound harassing and nonspecific at all."

"You know what I mean."

"You're frustrated. Back away for a while and clear your head. You've waited this long, don't get in a hurry now. Do it right."

"And if I can't prove that William Kingston killed Holly? What then? How do I live with knowing her killer is a free man?"

"I really wish we could have this conversation in person," she said. "Any chance of you coming home tomorrow morning? I could leave work early, and we'd have the whole afternoon to figure things out."

"Not like anything's happening down here. Yeah, I'll head back in the morning. But if worse comes to worst, I have to know, Maggie. I'm sure William Kingston murdered her, and if he's not at least convicted of Rachel Anderson's death, what then? I always said I'd do the best I could to find Holly's killer, and if I couldn't, so be it. But knowing who did it and still not getting justice? That's a whole different ballgame."

"One you're willing to risk everything for?"

"You know the answer to that. No, I won't jeopardize our family. I have no intention of spending the rest of my life in prison. But if there are alternatives, I need to find them."

"*Legal* alternatives?"

Great question.

But not one he could answer yet.

CHAPTER FORTY-EIGHT

Jeremy's drive home passed in a blur. His thoughts centered on the dilemma threatening to consume him. What if there was no way to prove who killed Holly? A call to Pronger earlier confirmed no new leads came from the crime scene or autopsy. No bullet had been found, but with such a powerful revolver, that was not unexpected. The projectile would have passed through her body without losing much momentum.

The two men spoke briefly and agreed that the detective was going to talk to the DA, not to get a warrant, but to ask what the chances were of getting one if Shane testified that his father routinely abused his mother.

Jeremy didn't hold out much hope. Strong circumstantial cases resulted in convictions all the time, but this case was far from that level, even if Shane did testify. And William Kingston didn't act like a man consumed with guilt. The possibility of getting a confession from him was nonexistent. Not without leverage.

Or something he feared worse than prison.

Like pain.

A person can come up with a lot of creative thoughts when they're alone in a car for six hours.

Maggie's vehicle was already there when he got to her apartment. Hopefully, she had a better plan, because the farther he'd driven, the darker the ideas. He hugged and kissed her, then waited while she scrubbed a spot of her lipstick off his mouth.

"How was your trip?" she asked.

"Long drive. Any problem getting off early?"

"Not really. Our cases are mostly routine. Tanessa's knocking them out this afternoon. I'm recommending she move on to something more intricate so she doesn't get bored."

"Intricate as in …?"

She kicked off her shoes and sank onto the couch. "As in something that requires interaction with living people. Spreadsheets and databases get old fast, no matter how good you are at them. She's definitely an extrovert too. Between her at work and Rebecca at home, ugh. My ears are exhausted by the time I crawl into bed."

"So did you broach my situation with her?"

"Tanessa?"

"No, Beks." He smiled and sat beside her. "Of course Tanessa."

"We might have chatted."

"I hope you two came up with something that doesn't involve rope and a sock full of quarters."

She angled herself to get a better look at his face. "A sock full of quarters? For what?"

"So you don't hurt your hands hitting someone. You've never heard of that?"

"Uh, no. Is it like a tube sock or one that goes halfway up your shin or what?"

He raised his eyebrows. "Does it matter?"

"I guess not. It seems like you'd get more momentum with a tube sock though. Fill it about a third of the way and—"

"Got it. Did you two ladies come up with anything?"

She nodded. "We did, but let's get back to the rope and quarters. You're not being serious?"

Not really, but sorta. "No. I can't afford that. I'd have to use pennies."

"Not funny. You're kidding around, right?"

"Yes. Besides, I left my last pair of socks in a dumpster in Charlotte."

She chuckled and elbowed his side. "Idiot. Anyway, Tanessa and I formulated a plan that might help. I'm not sure it will prove anything, but at least it should keep you out of jail for a while."

"Great." He slapped his hands on his knees. "What do I need to do?"

"Nothing except wait."

"For what? We already said nothing's going to—"

"You need to wait for *us* to do something. When we're finished, I'll let you know, and we can talk again. Until then, you bide your time."

He shook his head. "No. I told you both; I'm not going to let you do anything that could affect your jobs."

"Ahhh." She tapped her chin. "Because you getting arrested doesn't affect my job?"

"Not if we're not married, it doesn't."

"Yeah, that's another thing. I'm tired of that plan. What are you doing this weekend?"

"Come on, Maggie. That's not fair."

"Fair to you or me?" She squished her mouth to the side. "And you've tossed that word around a lot lately. 'Fair.' Last time I checked, 'fair' implies that the risk or reward is the same for all parties, and the way I see it, getting married is like an insurance policy that you won't do anything too stupid."

She had a point. He'd already taken risks that would impact her job if they'd been married and he'd been caught.

"Fine," he said. "When we get married, it won't be because you feel pressured into it, but I'll wait for your go-ahead on the investigation. Under one condition though. You tell me what you've got planned."

"You think I feel pressured into marrying you?"

"I meant the timing of it; that's all." He grinned. "But yeah, there's probably some pressure on you to get me off the market before someone else snatches me up."

"Oh, honey. I hate to break it to you, but you were put in the clearance section a long time ago."

He crossed his arms. "At least you didn't say 'damaged and dented.'"

"Only because I didn't think of it, and don't get all fake-pouty on me. You want to hear our idea or not?"

"I do, but not if—"

"Great. Unless something big breaks in Rachel Anderson's investigation, which doesn't seem likely at this point, you're not going to prove who killed her. The working assumption, one I believe is valid, is her death came at the hands of a Kingston. Sure, it could've been an accident, but doubtful. People don't typically bury their family in the backyard without a good reason. You with me?"

He nodded for her to continue.

"By extension, if we don't have the leverage of a murder charge in Rachel's case, we have no pressure to apply on William to confess to hers or Holly's deaths, or on Shane to testify against his father."

"I still say it's as likely Shane killed her."

She shrugged. "Doesn't matter as far as our plan is concerned. He's the target. We leak information to Pronger. Tell him that Shane has the toy matching an item from the crime scene. Whether Buzz Lightyear is relevant to the murder or not, it puts questions in Shane's mind about the direction of the investigation. If the detective plays things right, it may be enough for the son to roll on the father."

"Two problems," Jeremy said. "First, if there's a leak, it comes from me. You and Tanessa have to maintain plausible deniability. Second, even if Pronger uses the information, Shane will know where it came from. Totally inadmissible in court, and worse, could taint everything."

"Give Pronger some credit." She stretched her legs onto the coffee table. "He's smart enough to handle the situation."

He kicked off his shoes and placed his legs next to hers. "Let me make sure I understand this. I bide my time while Pronger shows some pictures to Shane in the hopes the kid breaks down? Don't get me wrong. I appreciate your help, but do you really think this is going to work?"

"Of course not, but it buys us time." She wiggled her toes and pointed her feet toward his socks. "You got a pretty good size hole there."

"It's from the quarters."

"Har har." She shifted so she could rest her legs on top of his. "You really think Shane killed Gary Camblin?"

"I'm not a hundred percent convinced of it, but I am leaning heavily in that direction. Why?"

"Because Tanessa and I are about to tear Shane Kingston's life apart."

CHAPTER FORTY-NINE

"What exactly does that mean?" Jeremy asked. "'Tear his life apart.'"

Maggie lifted his arm and dropped it around her shoulders. "Let's say Shane did have something to do with Camblin's death. Why? What's his motive? Obviously it's the domestic abuse, right? I mean, the file confirms that much, so it's either a guilt thing or a vigilante thing."

"Guilt because he is, or at least was, an abuser himself, or vigilante because he saw firsthand what that life is like."

"Right," she said, "but it really makes no difference because either way, he's killed someone. At the risk of sounding like mister-sees-a-serial-killer-everywhere-he-looks, would he only do it once? The Camblin scene was spotless. If it *was* a murder, it was well planned and executed."

He rubbed his hand along her arm from shoulder to elbow. "And any prior victims would've been identified by him using the same methods. News reports, arrest records, whatever."

"Mmm hmm. Thing is, suicides are pretty common. Number ten cause of death in the US. Did you know that? Far above homicides. And three-fourths of those suicides are men. Common enough that investigators might not look too closely."

"Still, staging a self-inflicted death is a hard way to cover your tracks."

She nodded. "The slightest indication that something's not right can lead to a full-blown homicide investigation. Regardless, Tanessa's going to check the suicides of males in a hundred-mile radius around Charlotte for the last five years to see if any of them were ever charged with domestic abuse."

"You don't sound hopeful." He wiggled his big toe until it stuck out the hole in his sock. "Darn it."

214 / WINTER'S FURY

"Your Dad jokes need serious work."

"Sorry. I'll try to make amends. Get it? A*mends*?"

She wiped the back of her hand across her lips. "Is it too late to get out of this marriage thing?"

"No returns on clearance items."

She laughed and twisted her index finger into his side. "I wouldn't have to fake your suicide. No jury would convict me if I told them your jokes. Cruel and unusual punishment."

He squeezed her shoulder. "You want to tell yourself my jokes aren't funny, go ahead, but we both know the truth."

"Wow. Talk about living in your own world. Anyway, as I was saying before your big toe popped onto the scene, Tanessa's going to work the suicide angle. I don't expect that will take long, so we'll move on to accidental deaths when she's finished. Far more plausible, I think."

How hard would staging an accident be? You'd have to do it in a way that seemed logical and didn't raise any suspicions. Something like a cut brake line on a car wouldn't work unless the vehicle also burned completely. And each incident would have to appear totally random. What worked in one death couldn't be used in another. Not without raising eyebrows. But if you only had to do it once, maybe twice …

"If Shane's staging accidents," he said, "chances of finding evidence are slim. The police wouldn't keep anything once they determined foul play wasn't involved."

"That's where I come in. We'll fall back on phone records and build a case around that. We confirm his cell is pinging off towers near the scene of two or three accidents to confirm our theory."

"Good start," he said, "but it won't be enough."

"No, it won't." She bit her bottom lip. "But it might be enough to take to the local PD and see if they'll put surveillance on him."

He took a deep breath. "No way you two are doing that. Too many questions will be asked. When we get to that point, I'll handle it."

"*If* we get there, we could do it anonymously."

"You know that won't work," he said. "First thing the cops would do is talk to Shane, and he's smart enough to figure out what's going on. He'd lie low for a while, then probably pack up and move across the country to start over. It's what I'd do."

"Me too." She pressed the back of her head against his arm. "But if nothing else, the phone records will tell us whether something's there. If we can't connect his cell to any prior deaths, chances are we're wrong."

"We're not wrong."

"We'll see," she said. "If we're right, we monitor local news sources for other men who fit the profile. He can't use his current list thanks to you, so he has to start over. I expect there'd be a somewhat lengthy delay before he acts again. Whenever that may be, it's critical the PD has surveillance in place."

He nodded. "I like everything about the plan except for you two's involvement. What happens if you're caught?"

"A slap on the wrist and a note in our files."

"You wish. Can I make a suggestion? Do the work here. Have Tanessa stop by when she needs to do anything involved with the investigation."

She glanced at him. "So if we're caught, we claim innocence, and you say you did it? Leaving our notebooks unsecured isn't much better than—"

"Than a questionable—and that's putting this nicely—investigation into an American citizen? Uh-uh. I take the fall if it comes. That's the deal."

"I can live with that." She pushed herself off the couch. "I'm going to put on sweats and then call Tanessa to make sure we're all on the same page."

"Okay. Oh, the Caps are in town tomorrow night. I thought—"

Her shoulders drooped. "I appreciate it, honey, but can't we watch the game on TV instead?"

"Um, we could, but ..." He grinned. "Actually, I was going to call Pronger and see if he wanted to go. If you're okay with that, I mean."

She planted one hand on her hip and tilted her head. "Does Jeremy have a new friend? I didn't need the word *new* there, did I? And of course I'm okay with it. Anything to keep me from having to go."

"Hockey's a whole different game in person. You'd love it."

"Mm-hmm. Maybe one day. I assume you have an ulterior motive for taking him?"

Would he invite Pronger even if he didn't want the detective to talk to Shane again? Yeah, he probably would. "I do. He's got kids, and I need to get a new batch of Dad jokes."

CHAPTER FIFTY

Jeremy lay in bed staring at the ceiling. The hockey game went into overtime, with the Caps losing with less than a minute left. It was nearly one-thirty in the morning before he made it home, doubled up on antacids, and fell into bed. The nachos, popcorn, and beer sang a song of bad decisions.

Sometime during the game's first period, Pronger mentioned that Rachel Anderson's body had been released, and Shane Kingston claimed the remains. The funeral would be in two days, and no, he didn't know if her ex-husband would be attending.

Jeremy commented that there was a possibility Shane could identify one of the items found near Rachel Anderson's remains. When the detective shrugged, Jeremy clarified that Shane may or may not still possess an object relevant to the found item. Pronger said he'd try to set up an interview in Frederick after the funeral. Oh, and the DA said unless Shane witnessed his father kill his mother and would testify to that fact, the abuse angle wasn't enough to warrant a grand jury for William. The Caps then scored a short-handed goal, bringing both men to their feet and an end to the conversation.

．．．．．．．

Maggie and Tanessa had worked over at Maggie's place the previous evening in spite of Jeremy's objections. He'd argued that if anyone ever dug into their research on Shane, it wouldn't be hard to figure out Jeremy had been at a hockey game and couldn't have accessed their laptops during that time. They'd outvoted him two to one, though when it became a democracy, he couldn't say.

He forced himself out of the bed and decided to skip the coffee. After last night, his stomach already grumbled and begged for simple, solid food. Toast. No butter or jelly. Just warm crunchy bread. Used to be a night like that wouldn't affect him. Used to be.

He texted Maggie to let her know he was awake, and she called immediately. Good news or bad?

"How was the game?" she asked.

"Caps lost."

"Yes, I saw that, but did you have a good time?"

"Up until the point they lost."

She blew a long breath into the phone. "Wanna call me back when you can be civil?"

He scrubbed his face with his free hand. "No, sorry. I'm good. Did you guys learn anything last night?"

"Janice came over, and Tanessa ended up sleeping on the sofa. Kind of a girls' night thing, I suppose."

"Mm-hmm. Fun. You paint each other's toenails and have a pillow fight?"

"Ooh. Close. We reviewed suicide autopsies for anything unusual. Not Janice. She and Rebecca stayed in the living room while we were in the kitchen."

He rethought his coffee decision and switched on the brewer. "Find anything?"

"Eh, a couple might be worth another look, but only if we don't have any luck with our other project. Is Detective Pronger going to talk to Shane?"

"He's going to try, but I doubt Shane is going to hang around after the funeral. I got the distinct impression after their last interview that he was done talking. And what other project?"

"Accidents, remember? Tanessa's pulling the data on all accidents in a fifty-mile radius of Charlotte in the last two years. If we broaden the scope any further, she'll be overwhelmed. Once she's built her database, she'll weed out any that involve multiple fatalities or witnesses."

"Good thinking." The coffeepot's gurgling matched his stomach's. "It's not out of the realm of possibility that Shane would be okay with collateral fatalities, but I doubt it. His targets are very specific. And once Tanessa has the data, what? You'll get the phone records and try to match them to the scenes?"

"Uh-huh. That's the plan. I've got a good feeling about this too. We're going to find something."

"I hope so. You thought about how you're going to get the cell data?"

"Thought about it, yes. Figured it out, no. I'm waiting until Tanessa gets her info together. If we spot a reasonable pattern of guys who could be ID'd as domestic abusers via local media, I'll be more confident about going through official channels. Otherwise, there's the Janice option."

"Official channels? Are you considering getting a subpoena for Shane's phone records? How are you going to sell that without, you know ..."

"I'll worry about that later, but I'm not going to get us in any trouble. We can make up some story about running algorithms on mortalities in Southern cities and blah, blah, blah. If I go to Bailey with it, he'll authorize the subpoena just so he doesn't have to hear more."

Jeremy laughed. "Tanessa give you a time frame?"

"Three or four days. Her priority has to be her assigned tasks, and right now she's analyzing data on some questionable financial activity at a port on the Eastern seaboard."

"Huh. Who'd have thought there'd be illegal goings-on occurring on the docks?"

"Your sarcasm is duly noted," she said.

He poured half a cup of coffee, sniffed the milk in the refrigerator, thought better of it, and drank the java black. "It's down to the phone records then."

"Yep."

"I don't like having all our chickens in one basket."

"Nope."

She's sure toned it down all of a sudden. "Is someone standing there?" he asked.

"Uh-huh."

"Well then, Agent Keeley. I suggest you quit wasting taxpayer dollars and get to work. Think you can do that?"

"Absolutely."

"Call me later, okay? I love you."

"Okay."

He grinned. "That's it? I tell you I love you, and all you can say is okay?"

"Thank you for calling, sir. I assure you I'll do *everything* possible to ensure your complete satisfaction. Have a good day."

He hung up the phone, cleared his throat, poured the coffee down the sink, and shuffled toward a cold shower.

CHAPTER FIFTY-ONE

S hane scanned the sympathy card one last time before tossing it into the trash. Most of his employees signed it, and several included a short note along the lines of 'thinking of you' or 'thoughts and prayers.' A few had hugged him after asking permission to do so.

He didn't want to go to the funeral. Not if his father was going to be there. But what choice did he have? Claiming Mom's remains had been the right thing to do. Better Shane control the situation than his father, and since Mom had no other relatives, there was a chance she'd end up wherever they buried the poor people.

He'd been searching online for funeral homes when an email came through from Dad, or more likely his admin. A small service was already planned and paid for, and if Shane had any problems with it or wanted anything changed, please respond as soon as possible. No phone call of course. They had nothing to say to each other. His anger at his father's presumptuousness faded as Shane accepted the relief that came from not having to plan—or pay—for the event.

Today was a travel day. The burial would take place tomorrow in Frederick, probably to keep Mom at a safe distance from Dad.

He tossed a suitcase in the car and settled in behind the wheel. I wonder if I'll cry? If not, should I? The cops will be there, hanging around the perimeter, snapping photos to see if anyone suspicious showed up. Anyone besides the Kingstons, that is. The detective already left a message about meeting, which wasn't going to happen. And Winter would be at the graveside too.

A few old friends might attend. Another reason not to go. They'd promise to keep in touch. Maybe even send a friend request on Facebook. But the past should remain in his memory. Any reminders weren't welcome.

There would be one good thing about going to Maryland. The trip would allow him to finalize his plans. His boss approved him for a full week of bereavement leave, three days unpaid. Plenty of time to scope out Dad's neighborhood. His travel routes to and from work.

When and where he was most vulnerable.

. . . .

Shane stood beside the grave, his head bowed. What a miserable day for a funeral. First day of October, sunny skies, warm breeze, leaves of all colors dangling from the trees. The weather didn't fit his mood.

His father stood a few feet away with a woman who had to be close to Shane's age. No sign of bruises on her, but she did have on those big dark sunglasses that hid half her face. A scattering of other people showed up, mostly friends of his mother, but Georgia Mayer was there with her husband, along with a few other acquaintances from high school. Each of their faces was dutifully sad and, as expected, several wanted to keep in touch. Not Georgia though. She stood off to the side and remained silent, doubtless aware that he knew of her conversation with Winter.

Her lot in life had improved since they'd last seen each other. She looked healthier. Happier. Of course, knowing how much his parents disliked her back then, she might be here to celebrate and remember the things that could have been.

He wanted to talk to her, maybe even give her a hug—odd to feel such a desire after so long—but it was enough that she was here. She shouldn't fret over her talk with Winter though. In a way, it was she who'd started the process that led to his mother's body being discovered. And now maybe Winter could get what he wanted, a murder conviction on William Kingston, and leave Shane alone. He glanced over his shoulder.

Detective Pronger and Jeremy Winter watched from the road where the cars were parked. Wonder if they'd have the courtesy to let him mourn in peace? Probably not.

He turned his face toward the breeze. After a moment, he sighed and stared at the ground again. No puffy, watery eyes or drippy nose. He glanced at his father. The man sniffed, and his girlfriend wrapped her arm around his waist. He's much better at this than I am.

The priest, or pastor, or whoever he was made a few more generic comments, then went down the line shaking hands. Shane wondered if he should fold up a twenty and slip it to him but decided not to. Dad arranged this whole sham. Let him cover the bill.

A few minutes later, the few people present wandered away and left Shane to himself. Pronger and Winter waited patiently, as did a couple of guys who stood at a discreet distance with shovels.

Last chance. Shane laid his hand on the coffin and took a deep breath.

I'm sorry, Mom. But you knew this would happen.

I told you to leave. That I could take care of myself.

You never understood. Staying was worse than leaving.

The fights were bad. Your crying was worse.

What do you think that did to me? Having to listen to your pain and knowing I couldn't do anything about it?

You should have left. Ended it.

Saved all of us from what we became.

CHAPTER FIFTY-TWO

"I'm afraid it's bad news," Maggie said.

Jeremy sighed and rubbed his forehead. Another in a list of roadblocks today. Shane refused to speak after the funeral. So did his father. Pronger had to put the Rachel Anderson case on the back burner, right next to Holly, until and unless something new came along. The bright spot of the day occurred when Maggie phoned and said she and Tanessa were coming to his apartment after work to discuss what they'd found so far.

"Let's have it," he said.

Tanessa slid a piece of paper across the dinette table. "The suicide angle is going nowhere, so I moved on to accidental deaths. Those are the names I came up with after filtering out anything that didn't seem to fit Shane's profile. Each of these men died alone in an accident and had some sort of media report regarding a charge of domestic abuse."

He scanned the list. "Fourteen names in the last two years? That seems like a lot, doesn't it?"

"We thought so too," Maggie said.

"I don't understand. Why is this bad news? Now we get the phone records and compare them to these names and dates. If we can place Shane at any of these locations, or even better, several of them, we've got the beginnings of a strong case."

The women exchanged a glance.

"You did it," Tanessa said. "You tell him."

"Fine." Maggie straightened in her chair. "I, uh, well, I kind of, skirted … is that the right word? Skirted? Anyway, I already got Shane's records."

Jeremy narrowed his eyes and placed his forearms on the table. "What did you do?"

"Nothing, really. I mean, I, uh, may have accidentally mentioned to Director Bailey that I needed to subpoena the cell records."

What? "How do you 'accidentally' tell the Director you need a subpoena?"

Tanessa laughed. "Settle in, Jer. This is good."

Maggie shot her a look, then folded her hands in her lap. "I might have been confused. We were investigating this case, right? The one concerning the ports along the coast. You know, lots of money going in and out, and we couldn't understand why."

"I remember," Jeremy said. "What's that got to do with Shane?"

"Nothing." Her forehead crinkled. "But Bailey doesn't know that."

Jeremy blinked several times and ran his hand through his hair. "You falsified a subpoena?"

"I made a mistake. Got my names crossed."

"Uh-huh." He glared at Tanessa. "And you let her do it?"

"I didn't know anything about it." She grinned and looked at Maggie. "That sounded sincere enough, right?"

He stood and paced around the table to burn off the nervous energy. "You thought through the implications, didn't you? Not just to your jobs and potential criminal charges, but to the case? Any defense attorney will rip the data to shreds by claiming it was illegally obtained. And why now? We agreed to go to Bailey if we had enough cause; otherwise, we could work through Janice."

"The Director would never approve a subpoena with what we had," Maggie said. "And I'm not willing to put Janice or her source at risk either. We knew this was a gamble but figured if we learned anything, we could maneuver a way out of it. Maybe once we ID'd the accidents where Shane may have played a part, dig deeper and find something in the files that substantiated the possibility. Then leak it to the Charlotte PD."

"This is unbelievable," he said. "You two went too far."

Maggie's face turned beet red. "*We* went too far? Are you kidding me? Am I supposed to twiddle my thumbs while you're doing B and E's in Charlotte?"

He held up his hand. "Not the same thing, and you know it."

"How is it not the same thing, Jeremy?" Maggie stood and crossed her arms. "You took a risk, and I took a risk."

He gripped the back of a chair. "Because you work for the FBI. If you get caught, they'll—"

"You two about done?" Tanessa asked. "Sheesh. You're doing this all wrong. Save the arguments until *after* you get married. Besides, it's not like any of this matters."

Huh? "Why doesn't it matter?" Jeremy asked.

Maggie pulled the chair back and sat again. "Because I told you it was bad news. There's no match."

His mouth opened, and he shook his head. "That can't be right. We need to check again."

"We checked three times already," Maggie said. "There's no link between Shane's phone records and the accident scenes. Camblin's suicide either."

There *has* to be. "We have to find another way then. That's all."

"We'd be glad to," Tanessa said, "but if there's another way, we can't find it. We're out of options here."

He sank into his chair. This is how it ends. Over 200,000 unsolved murders in the US, and Holly and Rachel Anderson just became permanent members of that growing assembly.

Except these homicides had been solved. Their problem wasn't who did it, but how to prove it and get justice.

Perhaps it was time to bypass the 'prove it' part of the equation.

CHAPTER FIFTY-THREE

———————————————

S hane returned from Baltimore three days early. Why not? There was nothing else to be done. When the time came, he and Buzz knew where they'd go. One last flight for the toy. To infinity and beyond.

This morning, he was on the way to check on the storage shed. It'd been months since his last visit, and events seemed to be accelerating. He wanted to ensure everything was still in place and ready to go on a moment's notice. Plus, with the extra time off work, he could finalize plans for his next target. Charlie Selowosky's mug shot had appeared in the paper a few days before, right above the words "charged with domestic abuse." Two other men's photos were there too, and Shane had eeny-meeny-miny-moe'd to make his selection.

The carefully compiled list of men in the file cabinet was now off-limits. Jeremy Winter made things difficult, and Shane was forced to revise his procedures to accommodate the new threat. If he continued to document his plans, his opponents might discover them and act. That was a risk he couldn't afford to take if he wanted to maintain a viable process.

But the long drive home from the funeral gave him time to reflect on the situation. He'd always known there'd be an end. That one day he'd be arrested and convicted and his chance to help others taken away. But that day used to seem so far off.

Was it time?

Mom was finally taken care of. Properly buried and free of the false shame of an abuse victim.

Dad was in a position where he couldn't afford for his past to come to light. A few well-placed phone calls, innuendos left on voice mails to the CEO and the press, about his father's abuse leading to murder, and the man's life would become unbearable. He wouldn't kill himself though.

Not man enough. Shane would have to take care of that.

So was it time? Handle Charlie Selowosky and move on to the end game?

He shook his head. Would he be thinking this if Jeremy Winter hadn't started poking around? No, but underestimating your opponent could be fatal.

Shane couldn't afford to disregard the danger posed by Winter, but he could adapt his own methods and see how long before his activity bankrupted his freedom. That's what good leaders do. Step out and take the actions that lead to positive change, no matter the peril.

He grinned as he slowed at the gated entrance to the endless rows of storage sheds. Maybe one day they'd do a case study on him.

．．．．．．．

Jeremy stared blankly at the kitchen countertop. He'd been up for three hours and hadn't made it to the shower yet. Last night's discussion drained any energy and willpower he might've gained from the little sleep he got. No way forward on Holly's or Rachel's deaths.

The hollow space between his ribs and spine would take time to fill. There'd come a day when he accepted the situation, but never a day when he didn't mourn it. William Kingston would go on living as a free man in spite of his actions. Jeremy could do something about that, but not without ruining his family's future. If not for Maggie and Beks, a different outcome was probable.

Maggie phoned earlier to check on him. His tone said it all, and she offered words of encouragement. He struggled—successfully—to sound better than he felt, but she knew. Three texts so far, each saying "I love you!!!" She'd spelled everything out. No emoticons or abbreviations. She knew.

He focused on the backs of his hands as they rested on the kitchen counter. Wrinkled, achy, and tired. Just like the rest of him.

He closed his eyes and breathed deeply. When had he become this person? The man who accepts what he shouldn't? Who grumbles and mopes and spends more time worrying than working?

Maggie and Beks were everything to him.

Everything.

They deserved a better husband and father. Not a different one, but a better one.

He squeezed his fists and opened his eyes. No more.

He'd protect his family. Spend every possible moment with them. Do nothing to jeopardize their future together.

But William Kingston would pay for his crimes, as would his son.

Legally if possible.

And if not?

Payment came in many forms.

CHAPTER FIFTY-FOUR

Jeremy, Maggie, and Tanessa sat in a booth at their local pizza restaurant, ordered, and waited until the waiter dropped off their drinks. Thirty minutes earlier, Maggie had come by his apartment expecting to find him lounging on the couch, unshowered and depressed. Instead, he'd been on his way out the door, unsure of where he was headed but determined to move things forward in his investigation.

"All right," Jeremy said. "Now are you gonna tell me what this is about?"

Maggie held up three fingers. "First of all, we've got three names we're monitoring around Charlotte. Three men whose arrest record for domestic abuse showed up in the news there. If anything happens to one of them …"

"We'll know our theory is right. There's got to be a better way though. Shouldn't we warn them or something?"

"Warn them how? 'Oh, by the way, don't have any accidents that might kill you?' I don't see that being very effective."

He scratched behind his ear. "I can go back there and surveil him."

"For how long? We have no idea when, or even if, he's planning to attack one of the men. And since he knows we're watching him, would he take that chance?"

"No. Not unless he wants to be caught." He drummed his fingers on the table. "But Pronger's got the Rachel Anderson case, so it makes more sense for me to be in North Carolina than here."

"We'll see," Maggie said. "Anyway, you said something a while back. 'Lack of evidence isn't evidence.' Remember that?"

"Not specifically."

"Well, you did." She licked her lips and leaned forward. "But what if it is?"

"What if it is what?"

"What if a lack of evidence *is* evidence?"

He glanced between the two women. "I'm assuming you're going to explain?"

Tanessa nodded. "What do you know about how cell phones work?"

"I assume you mean for location identification purposes? They ping off a tower, and the phone company has a record of that. If you know where the tower is, you know the cell is within that range."

She took a sip of her drink. "Mostly true. But if a bunch of people make phone calls at the same time, the tower might become congested, which means the company's algorithms start routing calls to other towers."

He shrugged. "The chances of that happening on every one of Shane Kingston's calls can't be good."

"They're not. But let's think about that for a minute. Shane's not stupid, right? If he's committing crimes, especially if they're planned to the detail we believe they are, would he take his phone with him?"

"Probably not. But when you listed the suspicious accidents, the records we saw definitely showed Shane had his cell with him on those dates. I guess he could be giving it to someone and telling them to drive around all day, but who? There's no indication he's close enough to anyone to ask for that kind of help."

"Agreed." She scooted her drink aside and rested her arms on the table. "So we know two things. First, he has his phone with him on the days in question. And second, the cell records show he wasn't anywhere close to the scenes of the accidents. But how does that info mesh with our conviction that Shane's involved?"

"It doesn't, except to prove we're wrong."

"Think outside the Pandora's box," Maggie said. "Assume our suppositions *are* true. He has the phone with him when he commits the murders."

"Fine." He shifted in his seat. "Knowing what we know, the only way that can be true is if he turns the phone off before he kills and then back on again afterward. He'd have to do it far enough away that there's no danger of him hitting off the wrong cell tower."

She pointed her fork at him. "Exactly. And if that's true ...?"

"What? You can't prove he's doing that, and even if you could, I'm not sure it would accomplish much. Certainly not enough to convict him of anything."

"But it might be enough to raise questions and get the local PD started on an investigation. From there, who knows?"

"Possibly," he said. "But the problem remains. You can't prove he's turning his phone off, killing someone, then turning it back on again."

"No, I can't." She smiled and tapped her fork on his hand. "But Tanessa can."

CHAPTER FIFTY-FIVE

Jeremy cycled through the TV channels again, pausing a nanosecond on each to confirm there was nothing he wanted to see. This was his third round through the rotation since he figured that at any given moment three-fourths of the stations would be showing commercials. Checking the on-screen guide would've been easier, but also faster. Time moved too slowly as it was.

Beks was supposed to be doing homework back in her room, but the lack of whining meant she'd veered off to other things. Her tablet or Netflix probably. He'd give it another minute or two before venturing down the hall to check.

Maggie called almost two hours ago to say she'd be working a little late, but that she and Tanessa would be there as soon as they could, and they had some news about the investigation. He phoned back fifteen minutes later and was told in explicit terms by Tanessa that all he was doing was slowing them down and not to call again or she'd, well, she'd take appropriate action when she saw him. Jeremy had no doubt she could make good on her threat.

He wandered toward Beks' room and peeked around the corner. She was sprawled on her bed with a book, oblivious to his presence. He smiled and backed away. Homework or not, he wasn't going to interrupt her while she read.

"We're home," Tanessa said. "Miss us?"

He stepped into the living room, hugged and kissed Maggie, and extended his hand toward Tanessa.

"C'mon now, Jer." She clinched him in a bear hug, with an extra tight squeeze right before she released him. "I think we've moved beyond a handshake, 'kay? And I wanted to make sure you knew I could take you if I had to."

He grinned and shrugged. "I hope I never have to find out. So you two found something?"

Tanessa arched her eyebrows. "No messing around, huh? Straight to the point."

Maggie rubbed his arm. "I'll go say hi to Beks, and then we can get started. You fix us some dinner?"

"Um, yes. Leftover pizza. You want it heated or cold?"

"Cold beer, hot pizza," Tanessa said. "Or cold beer, cold pizza. Doesn't matter as long as the beer's cold. That's not an option, 'kay?"

By the time Maggie returned, the food and drinks were spread on the coffee table. She grabbed a paper plate and slice of pizza and settled next to Jeremy on the sofa. "Okay," she said. "What do you want to talk about?"

He glanced between the two women. "The FBI teaching torture methods now? Shane Kingston's phone records. What did you find?"

"Still not enough to prove anything in court," Tanessa said, "but enough to say something's not right. I ran through everything again and compared the dates and times on his phone records to the fourteen accidents we found. No change there. Shane's cell didn't bounce off any of the towers at any of the scenes at the proper times, but we already knew that, right?"

Jeremy nodded for her to continue.

"So, assuming Shane staged the accidents, there's a pattern. Every time one of these fourteen men died, his phone wasn't anywhere near them. Granted, neither were a gazillion other people's cells, but hey, it's a pattern. And when it comes to data analysis, patterns are everything. So I thought there had to be a way to use that information. Turns out there was." She took a drink of beer and grabbed another piece of pizza. "Still with me, Jer?"

"Yeah," he said, "considering nothing you've said so far is new to me."

"Wow," she said. "You've got a keeper there, Mags."

Maggie laughed and patted his leg. "He's all mine, for better or worse."

Tanessa shook her head. "I'm sure the 'better' will come along soon enough. Anyway, here's some new stuff for you, Jer. I called a contact at the cell company and got information on their towers in the Charlotte area. Once I had that, I compared Shane's records to the towers, and there are definite gaps. The data indicates he bypassed locations he shouldn't or couldn't have."

"Right," he said. "Can you explain it in simple terms?"

"I thought I was."

"Simpler."

"Okay. If the phone was with Shane and was turned on, the data would indicate it transferring from one cell tower to another as he moved. The phone would be looking for the strongest signal on a fairly regular basis even if he wasn't using it. Each time the cell registers with a new tower, the system records the event so if someone calls or texts, the carrier knows where to send the communication."

"But if he turns the phone off, the network assumes he's still within range of the last tower he registered on?"

She winked and pointed at him. "Exactly."

"So how does that help us? None of the data matches the dates and times of the killings."

"Yeah, but here's the thing. At those times, his phone was registered somewhere far away, right? Maybe home or work or anyplace except the scene. But, in twelve of the fourteen accidents or murders or whatever we're calling them, the next tower doesn't make sense."

He peered at Maggie, then back at Tanessa. "I'm not following."

"Let's say you're driving from your home to the office. As you travel, you'll bounce from tower to tower in a fairly regular progression. His phone didn't. First, he's over here, then he's over there. The towers in the middle are missing."

"But couldn't that be because of the cell company's algorithms?"

Tanessa whistled. "I'm impressed. Sure, it could be, but the odds of that occurring at the exact times you're looking at? In a dozen different cases? I wouldn't take that bet. Plus, the algorithm should only kick in when the tower is at max capacity, damaged, something like that. I've got a call in to check the carrier's maintenance records to confirm, but I don't believe that's what's happening. Our guy's obviously turning off his phone in one location, doing whatever it is he's doing and turning it on again when he's far away."

"But only on twelve of the accidents?"

Maggie tapped his knee. "Twelve not good enough for you? Maybe Shane had nothing to do with the other two, or maybe his route worked out so the tower progression was what it should be. Who knows? What we've got is evidence of a pattern."

"I don't know, I mean, I get what you're saying, but will a judge agree it's enough for the search warrant? I don't see how. At least not without some proof these men were murdered and didn't die in an accident."

"Sorry," Tanessa said. "Best I can do so far, and it's enough to convince me Shane's involved in these men's deaths."

Jeremy rubbed his eyes. "That's great work, Tanessa, and please don't take this the wrong way, but how does it help us move forward? This information doesn't even reach the level of circumstantial evidence. No one's going to act on it."

"You sure about that?" Maggie asked. "No one?"

Tanessa nodded. "One person will. Share this information, and it'll be like lighting a fire under them."

Him? Pronger? Why would this … no. Not the detective. "Shane? Maybe it gets him all worked up, but beyond that? I dunno. It might be too early."

"You want to tell him?" Maggie asked.

"Nah," Tanessa said. "You found her. Go ahead."

Jeremy stretched his fingers. "You two can be infuriating, but you already know that. Who did you find?"

"Brenda Clancy," Maggie said.

"Who?"

"We saved the best for last. Brenda Clancy's husband is—was—one of the twelve men we can tie Shane's cell gaps to. Horrible accident in his shop. Burned to death."

"And that helps us how?"

Maggie held his hand and smiled. "Brenda Clancy works for Shane Kingston."

CHAPTER FIFTY-SIX

S hane hopped out of the car into the darkness. He had the itch. It'd been too long since he'd rescued the accountant's wife. He couldn't save them all, but the longer he waited between killings, the more women suffered. The dance between being careful and being efficient had worn on him for years, but now Winter had tilted the scale and limited the options. Stop rescuing women or get caught far sooner than expected.

But stopping now would be selfish and show he cared more about himself than others. That he was a coward. And that he was no better than his father.

Tonight would be a rarity. A killing after work instead of before. Charlie Selowosky was employed as a second-shift employee at a chemical plant almost an hour north of Charlotte. As per his nightly routine, when the man clocked out, he'd stop at a bar and down a few too many before heading home. His route would take him on Enochville Road and across the bridge that ran just over the surface of Kannapolis Lake. Shane wasn't sure of the water's depth there, but it looked plenty deep, and the concrete guard along the side was low and thin enough that it wasn't going to withstand a solid hit.

He'd planned as well as he could and removed the battery from his phone before leaving work. Some things remained beyond his control though. If there was other traffic nearby, he'd have to postpone. If he didn't identify his target's car as it passed, he'd have to try again another day. A GPS tracking device could have solved that problem, but he feared they might find it when they pulled the car from the lake. The vehicle had a broken headlight on the passenger side, and the yellow running light on the driver side didn't work either. That should allow him to identify it, as long as Charlie was sober enough to turn on his headlights.

The biggest risk of all was the man's reaction. The spotlight—the world's brightest, according to the ad on Amazon, and only $75, thank you very much—should blind him. No matter which way he swerved, he'd go into the water, but there was a chance he could also angle toward the light … and Shane. It didn't make sense that anyone would turn into the bright beam, but who knew what a drunk driver would do?

He checked the time. Just after two a.m. The bar was closed, and Charlie was within minutes of arrival on the bridge. Timing would be everything. Turn on the light too early, and the car would swerve off the bridge into trees instead of water. Of course, depending on speed and impact, that might be enough. Turn on the light too late, and the driver might be past Shane and the lake before he even reacted.

He jogged to the far side of the bridge and climbed over the rail onto the tree-lined shore, then crept toward the water, glancing behind himself occasionally to make sure he ducked if any vehicles appeared. From this low vantage point, he could see any traffic, but when it came time to act, he'd have to climb back up onto the road to get the spotlight high enough.

After a few minutes, headlights swept into view as a vehicle passed the last of the big houses and took the curve toward the lake. Shane glanced back, saw no other lights, and hopped onto the bridge. He spread his legs wide and held the spotlight as if it was a pistol. Broken passenger headlight. Check. Broken driver running light. Check. This was his guy.

Judging speed and distance turned out to be more difficult than expected. If he'd been a math major, he could have plotted out everything before tonight to determine the perfect spot to stand and the perfect distance to turn on the light. Better to operate on instinct though. It had served him well in the past. Maybe do like Luke Skywalker when he blew up the Deathstar. *Use the Force, Shane.*

The car would be on the bridge within seconds, and the window of opportunity was narrow. Three, two, one, now.

Shane triggered the spotlight. The area lit up as if the sun had decided to peek in and see how the moon was doing. For a moment, it was hard to see the car as his night vision disappeared in the flash. The light didn't affect his hearing, however. Instead of hitting the brakes, whether by accident or on purpose, the car's engine roared as Charlie accelerated.

Shane's heart raced as seconds seemed like minutes. If he didn't move, the car was going to plow over him. The screech of metal on concrete sounded as Charlie finally cut the wheel hard to the right. The vehicle impacted the barricade, spun so it now faced away from Shane, and the driver's side smashed against the low barrier, sending concrete, car, and Charlie into the water.

Shane killed the light and jumped back off the bridge. His ears rang from the noise of the crash, but there was no other sound. No splashing, no calls for help. Nothing. He waited ten minutes to be certain. Some sort of small delivery truck passed and never even slowed. It might be daylight before they found Charlie.

He stood, jogged back to his car, and tossed the spotlight into the trunk. Tomorrow, he'd leave a five-star review for the gadget.

CHAPTER FIFTY-SEVEN

Jeremy took advantage of the amenities at Shane's apartment complex and made a second loop around the hiking trail, this time without his cane. Several walkers and joggers were out this morning, some bundled in hooded jackets, others in shorts and T-shirts. He opted for his normal jeans and an untucked button-up long sleeve shirt. The mid-morning chill would soon burn off to a warm Charlotte afternoon.

He'd stopped at the spy shop on his way down to buy a GPS tracker. If the salesman recognized him from his prior purchase of the electronic lock pick, he had the good taste not to mention it. The tracker now sat securely tucked inside its magnetic case on the underside of Shane's vehicle. A $25 monthly fee allowed Jeremy to immediately access the car's location anytime he chose. Plus, an alert on his phone would notify him if the vehicle moved.

At the end of his second lap, he returned to his car to consider his options. Shane was still home but trying to talk with him there wouldn't go well. A public location, one where he'd want to be calm, suited the situation. Someplace like his work.

Jeremy checked the time. Four hours to go before then. What to do in the meantime? Too much energy for a nap and sitting around his motel room was too tiring. Another day, another coffee shop.

His phone directed him to the nearest not-a-national-chain coffeehouse, and he selected an overstuffed pleather chair in the corner. The barista brought his dark Sumatran blend to him in an oversized mug. Nice, except the large surface area meant the drink cooled too fast. He smiled and thanked her.

Overhead, a TV replayed the local morning newscast. He watched with the curiosity of a person with no skin in the game. Area politics, the weather, new construction downtown, rising crime rates. Interesting stuff if you lived here. Not so for outsiders.

One story showed a video of a car being lifted out of a lake by a small crane. A couple of divers watched from a boat as the vehicle dripped rivers of water onto the bridge before being lowered. Jeremy touched his coffee with the tip of his tongue. Already getting cold.

His phone buzzed, and he pulled it from his back pocket. Maggie checking in.

"Hey there," he said. "How's your day?"

"Charlie Selowosky. He's dead."

He sat his coffee on a side table. "Who is Charlie Selowosky?"

"One of the three we've been monitoring. You know, they were charged with domestic abuse and their names were made public." She coughed and cleared her throat. "Sorry. They're the only three we know of since you found Shane's file. This guy died last night in an accident. Apparently drove off a bridge."

Jeremy motioned to the barista. "Can I get one of these to go, please?"

"Sure," she said. "Be an extra two-fifty."

He nodded and turned his attention back to Maggie. "Got any details? Might be what I'm looking at on TV right now."

"Working on it. I'll text you the location of the accident as soon as I hang up. And you're not going to complain about paying extra for a refill?"

"No. Besides, what's the point? Won't change anything."

She chuckled. "Like that's ever made a difference with you? Anyway, Tanessa's already seeing how fast she can get her hands on Shane's updated cell records. Too bad you couldn't get the tracker on his car yesterday."

"No kidding. Not sure about the legality of it, but that's for others to worry about. Send me the specifics on the location, and I'll head there."

"Will do. Keep in touch, okay? If we learn anything on this end, I'll let you know."

He stood and strode toward the counter. "We're close, Maggie. He's about to be backed into a corner. That's when he'll make a mistake."

"Just be careful that mistake doesn't cost you," she said.

"You forget who you're talking to? I'm the king of careful."

"Right, and I'm the queen of, of, help me out. I'm drawing a blank."

He dropped a five on the counter and grabbed his to-go coffee. "Queen of me. I'll call you later. Love you."

. . . .

Jeremy stood on the bridge and reconstructed the accident in his mind. The driver had been coming from the east, lost control of his vehicle, and hit the concrete berm, sending him into Kannapolis Lake. Safety cones lined the gap in the bridge's edge, and a chatty local cop told him repairs would be done within a couple of hours.

Maggie had emailed with links to Charlie Selowosky's arrests. Two DUIs, three disturbing-the-peaces, and one domestic abuse charge. No doubt the man's alcohol level would explain the accident. Another drunk driver fatality. They happened every day all across the country.

Except this one also happened to beat his wife and that activity was public record, making him a prime candidate for Shane Kingston's brand of justice. Jeremy backed away from the crash site to the opposite side of the bridge.

The problem was that this death left a lot to chance. How could someone cause the accident to happen at exactly this spot? Kingston wouldn't have been in the vehicle. He could have put something in the road to direct Selowosky's car toward the water, but what if another vehicle came along? No, it had to be something simpler. Something portable and easily concealed.

Kingston would know the man was inebriated and his reactions were sluggish. He'd have to be in front of the car and somehow cause the drunk driver to steer the vehicle off the road. It was such a short span of bridge though. The timing to make this work would have to be flawless. Combine that with the unknowns, like which way Selowosky would swerve and what would happen when he hit the concrete berm, and no judge or jury would ever believe this was intentional. Not without physical evidence to prove otherwise.

He took a last look around, then moseyed back to his car. Shane Kingston was very good and very lucky. If Jeremy hadn't dug into Holly's and Miranda's deaths and spoken to Georgia Harding, he'd never have found Shane's secrets. The killer could've kept on doing this as long as he wanted. No one would ever know.

But Jeremy did know.

He knew William Kingston killed Holly and Miranda.

He knew either William or Shane or maybe both, killed Rachel Anderson.

And he knew it was time to finish them both.

CHAPTER FIFTY-EIGHT

Jeremy parked in a spot designated for visitors and made his way into the building. His GPS tracker worked perfectly. When Shane left his apartment, an alert came through on Jeremy's phone, and he watched in real time as the vehicle moved directly from the home to the office.

A receptionist looked up as he entered. "May I help you?"

He glanced around the lobby. Elevators off to the left. No security guard. He smiled and approached her desk. "Yes. I'm here to see Shane Kingston."

"And is he expecting you?"

"No, but I don't think he'll be surprised I'm here."

She poked her lips out. "Are you visiting or …?"

"Not really. I'd say this is more of a business issue."

Her face brightened. "Oh, are you here for an interview?"

Sure. Why not? "I am."

She placed a binder on the counter and flipped it to a page near the back. "If you'd just sign in and put this visitor's badge on for me … great. The elevators are right there, and if you'll head on up to the second floor, Arthur will meet you and get you where you need to go. And good luck on your interview."

"Thanks," he said. "Been looking for a long time, you know?"

Arthur, early forties, heavyset, and wearing a security guard outfit—no gun though—greeted him on the second floor and directed him to Shane's office. Jeremy thanked him and meandered through the cubicles toward the opposite side of the room. Besides the elevators and stairs in the area behind him, emergency exits were located at each end of the building. A low hum of voices combined with overworked printers and copiers to generate a steady drone. Most of the workers ignored him as he passed, but a few smiled or nodded.

Shane sat inside an office with his attention directed to a stack of paper on the desk. Jeremy watched for a moment before tapping on the door.

"Mind if I come in?"

Shane jerked back in his chair and took several heavy breaths before responding. "What are you doing here?"

Jeremy stepped inside. "I told them I was here for an interview. Door open or closed? Which do you usually do?"

"Neither. Get out before I call security."

"Closed it is." He shut the door and sat. "How have you been? Since the funeral, I mean? Everything going okay?"

Shane picked up the phone. "Last chance. Leave before I have you arrested."

"Wouldn't be the first time." He brushed imaginary dirt off his jeans. "Wouldn't be the last either, I suspect. And I don't think Arthur would be in too much of a hurry to get over here, do you? Anyway, Charlie Selowosky. That name mean anything to you?"

"No, now get—"

"Huh. See, I've got this theory. Goes like this." He pointed at Shane. "You're out there running around killing people and making it look like an accident. Poor Charlie was the latest, but I can't prove anything." He pointed at himself. "I'm out there knowing who killed my wife, oh, and your mom too, but can't prove that either. Not yet anyway." He intertwined his fingers. "So my problem is how do I mesh what I *know* with what I can *prove*?"

"Interesting dilemma." Shane smirked, hung up the phone, and slid a legal pad in front of him.

"Like to take notes?" Jeremy asked.

"I do during interviews." He clicked his pen several times. "Tell me a little about yourself, Mr. Winter."

"I spent a long time with the FBI. Specialized in serial killers. Not by choice really. I kind of fell into it, and my bosses thought I was pretty good, so there you go."

Shane nodded and scribbled a note. "*Lacks direction.* What would you say you enjoyed most and least about that job?"

"Oh, now that's an easy one. Hated the cases we couldn't close. There weren't many, but they stay with you."

"And I suppose the best part of the job was capturing these killers?"

Jeremy scooted to the edge of the chair and tapped his finger on the desk. "That's what I tell people. It's what I used to believe too. Not anymore though. I figured out a while back that the thing I liked best wasn't when I caught them." He lowered his voice. "It's when they died."

Shane tilted his head and dotted his pen on the paper. "And why is that?"

"I've asked myself that same question and never came up with a good answer. Maybe it's relief that they'll never hurt anyone again. Or maybe because I think they'll finally get what's coming to them." He shrugged. "Or maybe it's just that some people don't deserve to live."

Shane smiled and wrote another note. "*Intelligent.* We're not going to play that game, Mr. Winter. The one where I start to commiserate or wonder if we're somewhat alike. Despite what you believe, I've never killed anyone. If you had any evidence to the contrary, a member of law enforcement would be here, not you. Your theory doesn't stand up to the test of reality."

"No," Jeremy said, "it doesn't. But, if you'll bear with me for just a moment, I think I can clarify things for you."

Shane turned his palms upward. "By all means."

"Great. You're a smart guy. I know that, and you certainly know that. We both understand that getting away with murder's really not too hard. Not if you plan it correctly. None of that heat-of-the-moment passion to screw things up. But that's if you only kill once. If someone wanted to do it more often and not get caught, then it becomes quite a bit trickier."

"I suppose."

"Of course it does. Think about it. Every murder gets investigated, right? Patterns emerge, evidence is discovered, suspects are ID'd. But fatal accidents are different, aren't they? No one's looking for a murderer. As long as there's a reasonable explanation for the accident, something that makes sense, story over." He shrugged. "Someone who was smart enough would know that if they spread things out over time and a large geographic area, they'd never be caught. Not unless they did something stupid."

Shane shook his head. "*Delusional.* Nobody's that smart, Mr. Winter."

Jeremy laughed. "Of course they are. I could do it, and I bet I know a dozen other FBI agents who could too. The only reason we don't is we're not psychopathic killers with daddy issues."

"Nice. Daddy issues. *Antagonistic.* Sorry. Doesn't elicit an emotional response."

"Really?" Jeremy said. "I bet it would if your father was here instead of me."

Shane stood and stuck his hand across the desk. "Thank you for your time, Mr. Winter, but I'm afraid you're not a good fit for any of our current openings."

"Really? This is a collection agency, isn't it?" Jeremy grasped the man's hand. "I'm very good at collecting what's due. One day soon I'll show you."

"Best of luck. You'll see yourself out?"

"I will. Thank you for your time, Mr. Kingston. You've been most helpful." He opened the door and paused. "I wonder if you'd do me one favor though?"

"Not likely."

"I understand. No problem. I'll ask someone else for directions."

"To where?"

"Want to make sure I get this right …" He pulled a piece of paper from his shirt pocket. "Ah, yes. Directions to Brenda Clancy's desk."

CHAPTER FIFTY-NINE

S hane accompanied Arthur as he escorted Jeremy out of the building, then waited until the ex-FBI agent got in his car and drove off. The meeting had not been unexpected, but the timing was far sooner than he wanted.

In a way, the conversation offered both validation and relief. Despite what Winter said, the two of them did share a bond. After all, their mutual inability to tolerate delayed justice was what brought them together. Deep inside, Winter knew Shane was a good man, even though he could never say so.

Arthur hitched his pants higher. "Everything okay now?"

"Yes. Some people just don't want to hear that a job is not right for them."

The elevator doors opened, and the security guard stepped inside. "Coming up?"

"Um, no. I think I'm going to take an early lunch. Will you let the other supes know?"

"Sure thing. See ya later."

The doors closed, and Shane turned toward the parking lot. "No, Arthur. No, you won't."

. . . .

The first stop was the storage shed. He raised the overhead door and yanked the tarp off the 2001 black Ford Taurus, purchased off Craigslist a few years back. For a couple of grand and a promise to update the tags and title, he'd obtained the final piece of his operational requirements. Another weakness had been removed from his SWOT analysis.

Inside the vehicle's trunk was his go-bag filled with cash and clothes, an empty cardboard box, and a slew of bubble wrap and packing peanuts. The plates, stolen months ago, still had time before they expired. All was as it should be.

He swapped the positions of the two cars, locked the shed, and headed to the apartment to grab some toiletries and his laptop. Then all that was left was to get Buzz ready to travel.

Chemistry, like all of the sciences, had never been interesting to Shane. Molecules and atoms and bonds and compounds and blah, blah, blah. All so complicated and boring but necessary. Especially for what Winter called his "daddy issues."

Deciding which explosive to use had been remarkably easy. Search Google, with a VPN and, incognito mode of course, for "unstable explosives," and the first thing you find is a little number called triacetone triperoxide. TATP for those in the know. And not only was it unstable, the compound was easily manufactured with household chemicals, which made it a favorite of terrorists the world over and earned it the nickname Mother of Satan.

The problem with TATP, or *benefit* depending on your point of view, was its sensitivity. Even if you did everything right, losing a finger or two during the mixing process wasn't out of the question. Once made, the powdery substance could be packed inside the appropriate container, such as a hollowed-out Buzz Lightyear, until ready for use. Any movement of the item risked detonation as the crystals rubbed against each other.

Adding to the uncertainty was the belief that as the powder aged, it became more unstable due to the crystals becoming larger and creating more friction surfaces. One day you might be able to handle the bomb, albeit gently, and the next, boom. Kind of like a game of Russian roulette where every so often you'd add a bullet to the chamber. It'd been years since Buzz had been loaded with the chemical. His chamber had to be almost full by now.

The amount of TATP in the toy would create a rather small explosion. Unless you were nearby when it went off, say within three feet or so, you'd most likely survive. Inside that radius though, death was a certainty. Shane decided long ago that when the time came, Buzz would ride next to him in the car. It was only fair. A detonation in the trunk wouldn't accomplish anything. And if the two of them made it to their destination safely, the final decision would rest with Buzz.

Explode or don't explode. Either way, Shane's days of rescuing women would be behind him. He'd never see the outside of a prison again.

But as long as Buzz opted for infinity and beyond, at least there'd be no more daddy issues.

. . . .

Jeremy yawned and brushed the back of his hands against the car's roof liner. How much longer was Shane going to be in there? The storage facility was surrounded by empty fields, no doubt the reason for its location. Buy the land cheap, toss up some metal buildings, and voila. A ready-made business.

The open spaces meant there was nowhere to park and observe without being spotted. Not a big deal. The GPS tracker solved that problem. Jeremy sat more than a mile away at the far end of a grocery store parking lot.

Stakeouts were the worst. He checked the time again. Almost two hours since Shane went to the storage shed. What in the world was he doing? Clearly he had no intention of returning to work tonight, or maybe ever. But if he was running, why spend so long in town? Why not hop on the interstate and disappear before anyone even realizes you're gone?

He turned down the radio's volume. Shane was a planner. It's how he'd managed to avoid being noticed, much less caught, for so long. He'd plan for the possibility that one day he'd need to get out of town in a hurry. Spending so much time at the storage shed didn't make sense. Whatever was in there would've been ready to go.

He pounded his fist on the window and cursed.

Whatever was in there would've been ready to go, including a different vehicle.

CHAPTER SIXTY

Jeremy's drive to Shane's apartment complex took half the time it should have. Risking a speeding ticket was better than letting a killer escape into the night. He'd been parked here for nearly thirty minutes, but without knowing what Shane was driving, there was no way to be certain whether he was home. Jeremy had phoned Maggie on the way, and she insisted on staying on the line.

"I'm going in," he said.

"Give it another fifteen. By then Tanessa will know if any other vehicles are registered to Shane. You won't have to go inside if we have another way to look for him."

He stepped outside. "We both know she's not going to find anything. I should've realized what was happening at the storage shed. Stupid."

"Not stupid, and we haven't lost him. We just don't know where he is right now."

"Kinda the same thing, isn't it?"

"We'll find him."

He moved toward the staircase. "I've waited long enough. If he's home, he's asleep."

"Or waiting for you. Could be a trap, and he'd have every right to shoot you. An intruder in the middle of the night? Please, call the cops and report a suspicious odor or too much noise from the apartment. Let them at least come knock on the door."

He ignored the complaints from his leg and took the steps two at a time. "Shhh. I'm going quiet until I'm inside and know I'm alone. No talking, okay?"

"Be careful."

He picked the lock and eased the door open far enough to trace his finger along the jamb and check for wires. Nothing.

Inside, the apartment was dark except for the usual tiny starbursts of electronic gizmos. He waited for his eyes to adjust before moving farther. No sounds or indication of movement. After covering his phone with his hand, he turned on a flashlight app to get a hint of light, then shuffled down the hall, dragging his feet slowly with each step. If anything was on the floor, he didn't want to disturb it.

The bathroom appeared empty, and he peeked behind the shower curtain to be sure. Across the hall, nothing seemed to have changed in the office, but the laptop was gone. Chances were Shane was too, but Jeremy had to be certain.

The door to the bedroom was open, and he peered into the darkness of the area around the bed. The covers remained tucked tightly in place, and the pillows were neatly arranged.

He flicked on the light, knelt, and checked under the bed before opening the closet. "You still there, Maggie?"

"Yeah, you okay?"

"Shane's not here. The laptop's gone so he must've stopped by after the storage facility."

"Anything else missing?"

"It's going to take a few minutes to check, but … hold on. He took his Buzz Lightyear with him."

"Like his security blanket or something."

He shuffled through the clothes hanging there. "Maybe."

"What are you going to do now?"

"What *can* I do? Finish up here then try to figure out where he's gone."

She sighed. "I really think it's time to get the police involved. When you lay out everything we know, it's a pretty strong case."

"To us maybe, but we're not the ones who have to prosecute him. Besides, by the time we convinced anyone to look into Shane, he could be on the other side of the world."

She clicked her tongue several times. "Go someplace you can talk without worrying about being caught on a B and E. Text me, and I'll set everything up."

"Set what up?"

"You've been out of the real world too long. You've forgotten. Nothing jumpstarts ideas and momentum like a conference call."

"We've talked about this," he said. "Leave the sarcasm to the experts."

. . . .

Jeremy waited in his car outside the motel room. He was packed and ready to go as soon as he had an inkling of which direction to head.

"Okay," Maggie said. "I think I've finally got everybody. You there, Tanessa?"

"Uh-huh."

"Detective Pronger?"

"I'm here."

"Jeremy?"

"Conference calls haven't improved, I see."

"Be nice," Maggie said. "Thank you everyone for joining on such short notice. I know it's the middle of the night, but this couldn't wait until morning. Before we proceed, I need to make one thing clear. What's said on this call is private. It is not to be shared with anyone else. Things may or may not be discussed that border on, um, illegal. If you want to hang up and not be involved, now's your chance."

"I assume you're talking to me," Pronger said. "I'll stay."

"Thank you, Detective. Jeremy, you want to bring everyone up to speed?"

"Sure. Long story short, I screwed up, and Shane Kingston is in the wind. I met with him and laid all our cards on the table. How we knew what he was doing and that his father killed Holly. I wanted to increase the pressure and force him into a mistake. I guess it sort of worked because he bolted, but I have no idea what he's driving or where he's going."

"Quit saying you screwed up," Maggie said. "We had a GPS tracker on Shane's car, and he switched vehicles on us. You can't anticipate everything."

"She's right," Tanessa said. "This guy's no idiot. I'm sure he's tossed his phone too. But if you still want to play the blame game, do it *after* we've nailed him."

"Fine," Jeremy said. "So let's hear your thoughts. Shane ran what I'd say was a very successful operation in Charlotte. Truth of the matter is that even if we find him, I'm not sure what happens next. But is there anyone on this call who isn't a hundred percent convinced he's a vigilante serial killer?"

Several seconds of silence followed before Pronger spoke. "I don't have all the information the rest of you have, but I'm going to assume you'll catch me up later. For now, if you believe it, I do too."

"Good enough," Jeremy said. "And we know that serial killers don't stop until they're caught or they die, right? They may take breaks, sometimes decades long, but they always kill again. Shane's no different. He will murder more people, and possibly increase his pace based on the success here."

"We'll monitor his Social Security number for any hits," Maggie said. "I'll see what I can do about getting access to his bank accounts and credit cards too. I doubt any of that will help, but it's worth a shot."

"Agreed," Tanessa said. "I'll do the same with his phone records."

Jeremy nodded. "He had this all planned. He's got a destination in mind, so I guess the question is where would you go if you were him? As far as we know, he never took vacations anywhere specific and never made contact with old friends."

"Home?" Tanessa said. "He could go back to Frederick."

"I don't think so," Jeremy said. "He seemed to hate the place. Nothing but bad memories. You there, Pronger? Any ideas?"

"Yeah, just thinking. You know the one thing that's always stuck with me about him? 'My father killed her, and she let him.' That's what Shane said when I interviewed him. Like he blamed the mother more than the father."

"Okay," Jeremy said, "but even if that's true, where does it lead us?"

"To a guilty conscience," the detective said. "William Kingston abuses his wife, right? Shane watches this for most of his childhood and decides enough is enough. Dad's not going anywhere, so Mom has to. Bam. She ends up dead."

"I can see that," Maggie said. "Abusers always say it's the other person's fault, right? Shane blames his mother, maybe even kills her. That still doesn't point us anywhere though."

"I cheated on my wife," Pronger said.

No one spoke for a moment.

"Um, okay," Tanessa said.

The detective cleared his throat. "Swore I would never do that. Not after watching what my old man did to my mother. Serial adulterer is probably what they'd call him today. I've got other names for him. The point is, I didn't want to be my father. I knew firsthand the pain he caused."

Jeremy rested his head against the seat. "And Shane doesn't want to be his father."

"Right," Pronger said. "But he couldn't help himself, and now he wants to atone for whatever he's done. Tell himself that he's the good guy in his life's story." He sighed. "I don't know; maybe that's all psychobabble."

"Maybe," Jeremy said. "But it's a whole lot better than anything else we've got." He started the car and shifted into reverse. "And if Shane thinks he's the good guy, there has to be a villain, right?"

"William Kingston," Maggie said.

The car's tires squealed as Jeremy pulled away from the motel. "Shane's going to kill his father."

CHAPTER SIXTY-ONE

Jeremy climbed the stone wall surrounding William Kingston's community and dropped to the ground behind a row of evergreens. He landed harder than expected, and a spasm of pain shot through his left leg. His criminal skills weren't improving any.

He leaned against the wall to rest and orient himself. It'd been a short night followed by a long day. Three hours of sleep after getting home from Charlotte, then right to work. Detective Pronger phoned William Kingston shortly after the conference call ended and issued a vague warning to be on alert because his son may have dangerous intentions. William muttered "what's new?" and hung up the phone.

The group debated informing the local police but ultimately decided against doing so. No one actually heard Shane make any threats and at best, a written report would be taken. That would do nothing to stop whatever he had planned, assuming he was even in Baltimore.

Jeremy's breathing slowed, and he focused on Kingston's house. Maggie texted twenty minutes ago to let him know the man had just pulled out of the parking garage at his office. Assuming no stops on the way, another half hour before arrival was a safe bet. The few streetlights that dotted the community already flickered on, but the darkness would soon compress their effectiveness into a smaller circle. Kingston's home, a two-story behemoth with four columns along the front and a garage tucked to the side, remained unlit. There were surely exterior lights that could be automated, but like most of the other residents, he opted to leave them off.

The thing about gated communities was their double-edged sword of security. They might deter crime, though opinions on that were divided, but they definitely offered a false sense of refuge to the homeowners. This wasn't an island of sanctuary in a sea of danger. More like a leaky rowboat on the *Titanic* except the passengers don't see the holes.

Using stone for the wall made for a great appearance but also provided plenty of footholds for anyone wanting to climb over. The nearby trees beautified the area while offering a hiding spot for would-be miscreants. And the gated entrance, operated by a keypad, was only as good as the people using it. Twice today he'd followed vehicles through the gate before it closed. If the residents really wanted security, their community would resemble a prison.

He glanced at his phone. Time to get into position. A straight walk from here to there would be eighty yards or so, but he'd use the various trees and bushes dotted around the landscape to maintain his stealth. More for practice than usefulness. No one was going to spot him. Anyone at home had their blinds and curtains pulled tight.

Four minutes later, he stood with his back against the side of Kingston's garage. This was far too simple. If a middle-aged guy with a bad leg could do it, Shane could too. And probably a lot faster.

Jeremy squatted as headlights approached and the garage door began to open. Kingston was home. He stopped at the streetside postbox, then continued up the driveway and into the building. Jeremy peeked around the corner and watched as the man exited his vehicle, shuffled through the mail, and hit the button to close the garage door as he stepped inside his home.

No challenge. Kingston maintained no sense of awareness. No clue of the danger nearby. This was the most likely place to attack. Jeremy could have easily killed him if he wanted to.

Easily.

If he wanted to.

CHAPTER SIXTY-TWO

This was the third morning in a row Jeremy followed the routine. There was no other choice. He tailed William Kingston's vehicle as it drove away from his neighborhood and headed for the office.

Shane still hadn't turned up anywhere. No hits on his phone or financial accounts, though it would have been a shock if he'd been so clumsy. And, at least as far as Jeremy knew, no contact with his father.

A horn honked, and Jeremy swerved back into his lane. How much longer could this go on? He wasn't responsible for William Kingston's safety, was he? Wouldn't that be the irony of ironies? Protecting the man who killed your wife. He cracked his window and let the cold morning air bathe his face. If Shane wanted to kill a killer, who was Jeremy to stand in the way?

That thought crossed his mind regularly. With no evidence of any crime by either of the Kingstons, the best thing to do might be to sit back and let things run their course. And if Shane did murder his father, would Jeremy's conscience explain the guilt as a death he could've stopped, or one he should've taken care of himself? Would he care?

Maggie guessed his thoughts. She offered to take time off work and handle the surveillance, but he refused. Don't worry, he told her. He could defend Holly's killer from Shane if it came to that.

She knew that, she said. Her question was whether he *would* defend him.

His answer sounded better than it felt.

....

Shane watched as a security guard unlocked the front doors of the Dependable Guaranty Insurance headquarters promptly at seven. Third morning, same routine. The receptionist would be the first to arrive in about fifteen minutes. From that point until nine o'clock, other workers would make their way into the building. Dad would show up sometime between seven-thirty and eight.

This afternoon, the process would repeat itself in reverse, concluding with a different security guard locking the doors at six, thirty or forty minutes before Dad left. Various workers would straggle out of the building for the next couple of hours, each in a hurry to get to the parking garage and their vehicle. The last to leave would be a middle-aged woman and a younger man with bleached blond hair, him first and her discreetly after. Two evenings in a row so far. Maybe they weren't having an every-night fling, and if not, he'd have to wait until they were in the mood again.

No security guard remained on-site, but once every hour a rent-a-cop would pull up front, tug on the doors to make sure they were locked, and drive away. A cleaning crew appeared sometime around midnight and left three hours later.

There were a few unknowns inside the building, so he'd have to think on his feet. Be flexible and adapt. A key management principle. And he already had an employee's badge, stolen from the car of a worker while she dined at Arby's. The photo on the ID was of a thin African-American woman, but no one would notice.

He'd execute the plan tonight. The preparation was shorter than most of his operations, but time was of the essence, and his confidence was high. Very little could go wrong as long as Buzz kept his cool.

CHAPTER SIXTY-THREE

S hane watched from the parking garage as the young man, his tie in his hand and his nearly white hair mussed, hurried from the lobby to his car. The tryst had continued for a third night.

He stepped out of the vehicle, slid his hands under the cardboard box containing Buzz, and walked toward the office building. The employee ID badge flopped against his shirt with each step, and he forced himself to slow down. Had to time this just right so he wouldn't be waiting at the door when the woman exited.

His heart pounded, and he realized he'd been holding his breath. He slackened his pace even more and licked a bead of sweat off his upper lip. Nervous energy and excitement. That's all this was. No fear. Buzz and he had taken many journeys together.

As he approached the building, the woman came into view in the lobby. For the briefest of moments, the two made eye contact, but she quickly averted her gaze. She pushed hard on the door so it swung as far as possible, thereby relieving herself of any self-inflicted responsibility to hold it for him. She stared downward and avoided looking his way.

Shane stuck his foot out and propped it open. "Thanks," he said. "Forgot some files."

She didn't respond and was soon out of sight.

He stepped inside the lobby and pushed on the door to ensure it closed completely. Step one completed. Now to the fifth floor and Dad's office. If it's unlocked, Buzz could go ahead and take his position, but Shane would still have to hang around until the cleaning crew left. Wouldn't want someone to think they needed to dust under the toy.

He rode the elevator to the top floor and paused in the entranceway. Very nice. Not unlike he imagined his own boss' office. A tad ornate for his taste, but if you've got it, flaunt it, right? Of course, none of these executives paid for the grandeur out of their own pockets. They'd tell you they actually hated the ostentatious display of wealth, but it was important to impress the clients.

Right. More important than taking care of the employees.

He shook his head. Now's not the time for a lecture on worker motivation and retention. If he had his bearings straight, Dad's door would be the one on the far right. He moved close enough to read the gold nameplate. William Kingston, CXO.

Chief Experience Officer. Jeremy Winter was right. They were making stuff up now. He grasped the doorknob and tried to turn it without success. Locked. One of the unknowns he knew he'd have to deal with.

If the cleaning crew's pattern held, they'd be here in two or three hours and work their way down from this floor to the first. All Shane needed to do was find a comfortable spot on a lower level to wait, then stroll back in here when the vacuuming and dusting were in full swing. They'd assume he had a key to get in the building. As long as he looked like he knew where he was going—and he did—no one would pay him any mind.

He found a closet full of old file boxes on the third floor and settled in. From the looks of things, this space didn't get dusted very often. He'd probably be sneezing his head off by the time he got out.

He placed Buzz's carton on the floor and sat next to him. Sneezing his head off. What do you think about that, Buzz? One good ah-choo while I'm carrying you and that's probably not far from what will happen.

We've come this far though. Time to finish.

. . . .

Three hours later, he stood and arched his back in a lengthy stretch. The cleaners arrived a few minutes ago, and by now they should be busy at work on the fifth floor. The thought occurred to him that they might not have a key to the executive offices, but he'd disregarded the idea immediately. People at the top of the company weren't about to walk into a dirty office every morning, and the cleaning service wasn't stupid. They started there to make sure that even if nothing else in the building was clean, these rooms would be.

He flexed his fingers and lifted the box off the floor. One last trip. Ready?

The elevator opened on the fifth floor, and he walked immediately toward his father's office. Two women vacuumed at a frenetic pace, and he nodded. They smiled and continued their work.

He moved past Dad's admin's space and into the executive office. Another woman flitted about the room, her duster flying. She had her back to him and headphones on, and her movements obviously mimicked whatever beat pounded into her ears. He maintained a safe distance—wouldn't be good if she was startled around Buzz—and waited until she turned his direction.

She saw him and jumped back, one hand on her chest and the other pointing her duster at him. Her face flushed as embarrassment swept over her. Shane smiled and pointed at his ID badge. She freed one ear from the headphones.

"Sorry," she said. "You scared me."

"Didn't mean to. You looked like you were pretty far into your dance routine, and I didn't want to interrupt."

She laughed and resumed her dusting. "I'll be done in just a moment."

"That's okay," he said. "I have to replace some of the network wiring, so if you don't mind ..."

"You're sure? You want them to vacuum in here?"

"No, that's okay. As long as the trash gets emptied, everything will be good."

"Already got it." She walked to the door. "Have a good evening, sir."

"You too." He moved to the desk and eased the box on top of it before hurrying to close and lock the door.

Finally. Time to take a breath.

The layout of the office was as he expected, no surprise since he'd been able to scout most of it from the parking garage's upper level. He'd watched Dad swivel his chair and talk on the phone and work at his computer. To his credit, the man did seem to stay busy.

Shane stood near the corner of the desk and stared out the window. In a few hours, he'd be parked out there, waiting for Dad to get to work. Buzz would complete his mission.

Or not.

He'd thought the anticipation of it all, the ending of his work, the nervousness over Buzz's cooperation, the impending loss of his own freedom, would generate a sense of excitement, or at least imminent doom.

Instead, he felt nothing. Hollow.
Like he was about to lose his only friend.

CHAPTER SIXTY-FOUR

Unknown caller. Jeremy held the phone at eye level and glared. If this is another telemarketer … he answered but didn't speak, waiting for the automated voice to tell him they were calling about his credit card or a free vacation.

"Hello?"

Jeremy's adrenaline flashed. "Shane?"

"Yes, Mr. Winter. I hope you're well."

Why was he calling? He shook his phone and crossed his fingers that the recording app still worked. "Where are you?"

"Well, I'm not camped outside my father's community waiting for him to leave for work."

Jeremy glanced in all directions around his car. "No, I guess you're not. What's going on? Why are you calling?"

"Always with the questions. I have to be honest though. I did enjoy our talks. It's not often I have someone to speak to who understands me. Maybe even appreciates me."

Play along or not? "I'm afraid you give me too much credit. There's a difference between knowing who you are and understanding what you do."

"Is there? How can you have one without the other? Look at yourself. You're a man who seeks justice. Your entire life revolves around it, even before your wife was killed. But now there's a problem. After so many years, you have the chance to get the very thing you want, but not without risking what you already have. I understand that predicament."

"If you called just to chat, you're wasting—"

"I once had the same dilemma. I won't bore you with the details but suffice it to say things worked out in the end. Would you like to know the solution to your problem?"

He gripped the steering wheel. "Do I have a choice?"

"It's a simple answer. You have to remove part of the equation. One has to go away. Either the chance to get what you want or the risk to what you already have. I chose the second option. Once I realized that my freedom would be taken from me at some point, no more quandary."

Jeremy licked his lips and glanced in the mirror. "What are you planning to do?"

"Uh-uh. That would spoil the surprise. Do you trust me, Mr. Winter?"

"I think you know the answer to that."

"I'm sorry you feel that way. I want you to know I trust you."

You shouldn't. "Is that supposed to make me feel good?"

"My father won't be leaving home for at least another half hour. I assure you that no harm will come to him at his residence. There's a Starbucks not far from there. You pass it on the way to his work."

"I know where it is."

"Fine. Go there, and we'll talk. I'll call you in ten minutes, from a different phone, of course."

"I don't suppose you're going to tell me what's going on?"

"Roll the dice, Mr. Winter. You won't be sorry. Oh, and please hurry. We have much to discuss before a more urgent matter requires my attention."

Jeremy sped toward the Starbucks, briefing Maggie along the way. She insisted he was all kinds of stupid for playing along and should get the police involved. He'd answered that nothing had changed as far as proof against Shane, and whatever plan he had was already in motion. Their best chance of stopping it was getting him to reveal what was going to happen.

He pulled into the coffee shop and parked. On cue, his phone rang, and he glanced at the time. Two minutes early, which meant Shane could probably see him. "Okay, I'm here. What now?"

"See the two guys sitting outside wearing suits?"

"Yeah, I see them."

"There's a walkie-talkie taped under their table. And no, they have no idea it's there. Go get it."

Jeremy stepped outside and moved toward the men. "Then what?"

"Then," Shane said, "you get back in your car, and we finish our interview."

Jeremy hurried to the table, apologized for the intrusion, and retrieved the device. The men stared speechlessly as he turned and jogged back to his vehicle. After taking a second to compose himself, he keyed the mic on the walkie-talkie. "Why are you in Baltimore?"

"Can we be honest with each other, Mr. Winter?"

"That's entirely up to you."

"I feel the same way about you, so let me begin by asking an easy question. Do you want to kill my father?"

A car horn sounded through the walkie-talkie, and Jeremy studied his surroundings. Shane could be close or miles away. "I'm not going to kill your father."

"*Evasive*," Shane said. "That's not what I asked. Do you *want* to kill my father?"

Jeremy stared at the rooftops of the nearby buildings. "I don't know. My preference would be that he is convicted for my wife and daughter's murders, but that's not going to happen, is it?"

"A partial truth is not the truth."

"I don't know if I want to kill your father, but I do know that he needs to pay for what he's done."

"I think you're holding back, but fair enough."

"Is this where you ask the 'what kind of tree would you be' question?"

"*Sarcastic.*"

"If you're keeping notes, you might want to underline that one," Jeremy said.

"Mr. Winter, if you want to be a collection agent, you'll have a great deal of interaction with people who won't want to speak with you. How do you think you can handle that situation?"

"I've pretty much made a career of it."

"Can you elaborate?"

"No."

"I see. *Weak interpersonal skills.* I'll be honest here. Things aren't looking too good for you right now. Why would anyone hire you?"

Jeremy smiled. "Because I know how to get the job done. Maybe it's not always pretty, but it is finished. My turn. I'll ask again; why are you in Baltimore?"

"And why do you ask questions that you already know the answer to? Today's your lucky day, Mr. Winter. You will come visit me, won't you?"

"You turning yourself in?"

No response came. Jeremy keyed the mic again. "Shane, are you still there?"

What did he mean by 'his lucky day?' A jolt of adrenaline rocketed through him, and he slammed the car in reverse before speeding toward William Kingston's home. A diversion. That's all this was. An excuse to get Jeremy away from Kingston.

Now the son would kill the father.

And nothing Jeremy could do would stop him.

CHAPTER SIXTY-FIVE

Jeremy pounded his fists on the steering wheel. Kingston's car was not at his house, and there was no sign that anything unusual had occurred. He yelled toward his cell lying in the passenger seat. "He's not here. Tell Tanessa to try calling Kingston again."

Maggie's voice sounded from the phone's speaker. "She's been trying, but he's not picking up. Maybe he's on his way to work?"

"Maybe." He pulled away from the residence. "I'm heading there now. This could all be some sort of bluff, but if it is, I don't see the point. Shane sounded serious. Something's going to happen today."

"We need to contact the police. There's no more time."

The cops would send a squad car to Kingston's office building. That might be enough to deter Shane, assuming that's where he planned to kill the man. Jeremy ran the back of his hand across his forehead. His urgency answered one question. Saving Kingston's life—not taking it—consumed his thoughts. "Do it. Call the police. I'll head for …"

His phone beeped twice, and he picked it up. "Maggie, I've got to go. Warn Kingston's admin too. Incoming call from an unknown number. I think it's Shane."

. . . .

Shane sat in his car on the upper level of the Dependable Guaranty Insurance parking garage. From here, he had a clear view into his father's office. After removing his seat belt to get more comfortable, he dialed Jeremy Winter's number.

The man answered on the second ring. "Shane? That you?"

"I love my dad, Mr. Winter. That may not make sense to you, but I do. The chance to see him one last time was too much to pass up."

"Have you tried to visit him? Does he even know you're in town?"

Shane straightened and leaned into the steering wheel. "He's about to." He watched as William Kingston sat in his chair and swiveled to peer out the windows. "Dad had an early appointment this morning. Did I fail to mention that?"

"Listen to me," Jeremy said. "Whatever you're about to do—"

"I'm not about to do anything. He is."

"I don't understand."

"I left a gift in his office. An item that's very personal to me."

"Shane, you don't—"

"Just a simple toy from a happier time. Before I understood … things." He shook his head. "I don't know. Symbolic maybe? He broke Buzz like he broke our family? What do you think? Am I overanalyzing things?"

"Buzz Lightyear?" Jeremy asked. "The one from your closet? Will he even know it's from you?"

William Kingston turned back to his desk, shuffled a few papers off to the side, and froze. He reached behind his lamp and lifted a white object, about a foot tall, with two arms and two legs.

Shane grinned. "He knows."

Kingston turned the toy around and gave it a quick scan before shaking his head and dropping Buzz Lightyear into his trashcan and sending him off to infinity.

CHAPTER SIXTY-SIX

Jeremy stood among the throng of emergency personnel remaining in the building's lobby. Had to be fifty police cars and half that many fire trucks out there, not to mention the dark FBI sedans lining the street. He spotted a bobbing mass of red hair and waved both hands over his head. Maggie returned the wave and veered his way.

"You made quite a mess," she said.

He hugged her and kissed the top of her head. "Could've been a lot worse. One fatality, no other injuries."

"Where's Shane?"

"The Bureau's got him. The bombing moved it into federal jurisdiction. Once they're done, I guess North Carolina can start their process."

She placed a hand on his chest and pushed away so she could see his face. "You okay?"

Was he? "Why wouldn't I be?"

"Kingston's dead. Is it enough?"

He breathed heavily. Enough to erase the desire for vengeance? "William Kingston paid the price. Shane thought he was doing me a favor too."

She bit her bottom lip. "And was he?"

"I don't know. Not yet. Maybe not ever."

She wrapped her arms around him and squeezed. "You do know. You're just not ready to admit it. Or too stubborn."

"I wish I had your confidence in me." He dragged his fingers through her hair. "So where do we go from here?"

She gave him a quick kiss and stood on her toes to whisper in his ear. "Home, Jeremy. We go home."

CHAPTER SIXTY-SEVEN

Jeremy waited in one of the jail's interrogation rooms. Next to him sat an attorney from the Public Defender's office. The man wore earbuds and focused on his cell phone, glancing up now and then to make sure Jeremy was still there.

It had been three days since William Kingston's death, and the investigation into Shane was moving rapidly. Stories popped up in the news daily regarding his exploits in North Carolina. A tiny but vocal minority clamored for the charges against Shane to be dropped based on their belief he was actually performing a community service by getting rid of the domestic abusers. Jeremy shook his head. Such was the world today.

The door opened and Shane, dressed in prison orange and shackles, shuffled into the room, smiled, and sat across the table. "Hello, Mr. Winter. It's good to see you. And I'm happy to see my attorney is also present."

"First off, I'm not your friend, Shane. Chances are this is the last time we'll speak. I brought your lawyer only to prove to you this meeting isn't being recorded. Anything you say will be subject to attorney-client privilege." He nudged the lawyer and waited for the man to nod.

"Fair enough," Shane said. He rested his elbows on the table. "Then we'd better be thorough. Now, what is it I can help you with?"

"You once asked if we can be honest with each other. I'm hoping that now that things are, um, resolved, we can speak freely."

"Regarding ...?"

Jeremy touched his fingertips together and stared at them for a moment. "Regarding your father. More specifically, his death. Why kill him after all this time, especially since you had to know this is the first place we'd look for you? Why not disappear and start over somewhere else?"

"Are you disappointed you didn't kill him before I could? Remember, we're being honest here."

"Disappointed? No. Not now. I believe he deserved to die for what he did to my wife and daughter."

Shane nodded. "And my mother and daughter."

What? Jeremy forced his breathing to remain calm. "I wasn't aware you had a child."

"I don't. Didn't. Whatever. But I could have. Dad and, since we're being honest here, Mom to some extent, made sure that didn't happen."

"I'm sorry. I don't understand."

"Ancient history, as they say." Shane shrugged. "I got a girl pregnant in high school. My parents were livid. I think more so because of her than the baby. Said she was white trash and would hold me back. Ruin my life." He laughed. "Yeah, because things turned out so great without her."

Jeremy swallowed hard. "What happened?"

"Miscarriage. Look, I don't know if the baby was a girl or not, but I like to think she was. My folks pretended to be sad, but we could tell it was an act. The pressure they put on us, the stress and anxiety, we always figured that was the cause. Might not have been the reason, but to a couple of teenagers, it sure seemed like it. After that, Georgia and me just drifted apart. Never talked about the baby again."

Georgia Mayer Harding. "Tough way to grow up," Jeremy said. "How did Georgia deal with the breakup?"

"As well as can be expected, I guess. I'd see her around school and stuff, but I mostly tried to avoid her. Too much pain there, you know? I loved that baby, Mr. Winter, but I didn't love Georgia. I'd have done the right thing by her, but it wouldn't have lasted."

Something ... something wasn't right. Ms. Harding never mentioned being pregnant. Was that because her husband was with her that morning at Denny's? Was it even important? Jeremy squeezed his eyes shut and tried to focus. Think. Whatever *it* was, it wasn't coming. Not here. Not now. He tapped the lawyer on the shoulder and stood. "I'm sorry, but we'll have to do this another time."

Shane tilted his head to the side and narrowed his eyes. "Was it something I said?"

"I, um, I need to look into a few things." His brain wanted to explode as thoughts jetted in all directions. He stepped out the door, hurried back through security, and ran to his car.

CHAPTER SIXTY-EIGHT

Jeremy sat in the recliner and stared out the front window of Georgia Harding's living room. According to the new GPS tracker he'd placed under her car an hour ago, the woman would be home from work in a few minutes. If her husband showed up too, that shouldn't be an issue. He rested his hand on the Glock in his lap.

Yesterday's meeting with Shane triggered something that ate away at Jeremy. Sleep last night was out of the question. He'd spent today making phone calls, asking questions, reviewing all his notes. A little over two hours ago, he found what he was looking for.

Maggie knew, but no one else. Not yet.

A car pulled into the driveway, and the woman walked to her porch. A key slid into the lock, and she stepped inside and closed the door.

Jeremy waited until she dropped the keys back in her purse. "Good afternoon, Ms. Harding."

The woman screamed and turned back to the door.

"Please don't do that," Jeremy said.

She froze for a second, then looked over her shoulder. "Mr. Winter?"

"Yes. Please, come in. Sit down."

"I ... I don't understand. How did you get in here? What's going on?"

He sighed and pointed his gun at her. "Sit. Down."

She moved to the sofa, never taking her eyes off the weapon.

"Thank you," he said.

"I'm not sure what this is all—"

"It was the crib, you know. There were other things, like why you never mentioned you got pregnant with Shane. You must have hated his parents too. Really. So why go to his mother's funeral? It wasn't for Shane. You never even spoke to him. Yeah, other things." He shifted forward in his chair. "But mostly it was the crib."

Ms. Harding slid her purse into her lap. "What crib? What are you talking about?"

"You'll want to put your purse on the floor now. Then push it to me with your foot." He waited until she complied. "Thanks. Just want to keep everyone safe, right? Now, since you're doing so well, take a look at this." He handed her a copy of a photo.

She stared at it for a moment. "This is from your wife's murder, isn't it? I recognize the shopping cart and baby stuff."

"Yes. The diapers, crib, all the things you mentioned that morning you and your husband met with me at Denny's. Remember that?"

"Of course I do. But what does any of that have to do with—"

He used his gun to gesture toward the picture. "Where's the crib, Ms. Harding?"

She blinked rapidly, and the photo shook in her hands. "It's here. Under the basket. There's a car seat and a crib."

"Yes, there is. The car seat is on top of the crib, which is in a brown cardboard box. I'm curious as to how you knew it was a crib though. I mean, look at the box. No visible images. No writing. How did you know?"

"I didn't. I mean, you just told me, so I assumed that's what was in there. That morning at Denny's I never said I—"

Jeremy held up his hand. "Uh-uh. We're not going there." He pulled his phone from his pocket and punched a button.

Ms. Harding's voice sounded through the speaker. "I'm walking past the little strip mall, the one where your wife ... where it happened. The place is nearly deserted. I see this woman, your wife, pushing a shopping cart packed with baby stuff. Diapers, crib, things like that."

Jeremy stopped the playback. "That's you talking, right?"

"You had no right to record that conversation. I told you not to. It's illegal and will never be, uh ..."

"Never be what? Admitted in court?" He shrugged. "So what? The only way you could've known about the crib is if you'd seen Holly in the store. You stalked her. Followed her to the car. You were pregnant, right? When you killed Holly? She had baby stuff. You wanted baby stuff. Kingston was never even there, was he? Just another lie to protect yourself." His voice deepened, and he shifted forward in the chair. "You murdered my wife and baby, then panicked and took off. Intentional or not, makes no difference to me."

She jumped to her feet. "Get out of—"

The sofa pillow at the opposite end of the couch exploded as Jeremy pulled the trigger. His ears rang, but not so much he couldn't hear Ms. Harding's scream. After a few seconds, he touched the shell casing to make sure it wasn't still hot, then slipped it into his pocket.

"Sit down," he said. "The next shot won't be a warning."

Her breathing came in staccato bursts as her mind struggled to accept what had just happened. She peered at the remnants of the pillow and placed her hand over her mouth.

"Yeah," Jeremy said. "You're probably going to want to replace that. Might be able to repair the couch though. Oh, and since you're wondering, that was a hollow point. Flattens out on impact to do more damage. One side effect is that it makes it harder for CSI to identify the weapon it came from. Not impossible, just harder. Still, none of that matters, does it? Because you're not going to report any of this."

She swallowed hard. "Are you going to kill me?"

"Uh-uh. You don't get to ask any questions. Not yet." He sniffed the air. "I love the smell of gunpowder, don't you? Anyway, clarify something for me. I have a theory that you killed Shane's mother. Am I right?"

"No," she said. "I've never killed anyone."

"Uh-huh. See, I think you couldn't deal with the fact Shane was headed off to college and leaving you behind. His parents hated you, right? Were afraid you'd screw up their only child's future? Easy enough to blame them for everything. First, you lost the baby, and now you were losing Shane too."

Wrinkles creased her forehead. "We weren't even together then. Hadn't been for nearly two years."

"So you're patient. You've got the motive, you've got the means, same gun you shot Holly with … oh, that reminds me. Did you steal William Kingston's revolver or did Shane give it to you? I hate loose ends."

One corner of her lips turned up. "Got it all figured out, do you?"

"Convince me I'm wrong."

"I'm not going to prison, Mr. Winter."

"There are at least half a dozen people behind bars who told me the same thing, Ms. Harding."

"Everything you've said is speculation. I have never agreed to being recorded, so none of that will ever get into court. You have no proof of anything. Your only way out of this is to kill me, which would surely lead to your arrest and conviction. You wouldn't let that happen."

"Finished?" he asked. "You have no idea what I will or won't do. Honestly, sometimes *I* have no idea. So I'll ask again. Did Shane give you the gun?"

She crossed her legs and sighed. "Shane didn't have the guts to do anything. Not then. If half what I see on the news is accurate, I guess he's changed, huh?"

"Have you changed, Ms. Harding?"

She intertwined her fingers and stared at the ceiling. "It was an accident. Your wife, I mean. Believe it or not, I still have a lot of guilt over her. Shane's mother though, she deserved what she got. His father too."

"It must be terrible living with that guilt." He stood and frowned. "Sorry. My fiancée says I need to cut back on the sarcasm. Hard to change after so long, you know?"

She exhaled and focused on his gun. "What happens next?"

"Entirely up to you," he said. "Of course, my preference is that you go to the police and tell them everything."

"That's not going to happen."

"I figured as much." He walked to her and pressed the Glock's barrel against her forehead. "Funny. I don't think I'll have any guilt over killing you."

Her eyes widened, and she began to hyperventilate. "You can't ... they'll know it was ... please don't do this."

He pulled the weapon away and slipped it into his holster. "Not today. But I *will* kill you, Ms. Harding. I learned quite a bit from Shane, like how easy it is to make a murder look like an accident. But you'll know. When it happens, I promise that you'll know it was me before you die."

He opened the front door. "Might want to let the place air out for a while. Get rid of the gunpowder smell. Three days, Ms. Harding. Three days for you to go to the police. Ask for Detective Pronger. I'm confident you understand the repercussions if you don't."

He stepped onto the front porch and inhaled deeply. "Please don't try to run. I'll be watching. Oh, and Ms. Harding?"

She stared at him and remained silent.

"Hobby Lobby has a sale on couch pillows. Everything in there is always thirty percent off."

CHAPTER SIXTY-NINE

Jeremy maintained a safe distance behind Georgia Harding's vehicle as she drove through the darkness. Less than an hour after he'd left her home, she'd thrown a suitcase in the trunk and headed north on I-81 through Pennsylvania, headed for Canada most likely. Wonder if her husband knows what's going on?

Harding stopped twice, once in Frackville for gas and again in Wilkes-Barre for food and a bathroom break. He could have taken her at either location if he wanted but held back. Let her get a little farther down the road. Start to feel safe. Maybe drop her guard.

They crossed into New York shortly before midnight. Another five or six hours before she reached the Canadian border. He shook his head. Like that was going to do her any good. He propped his knees under the steering wheel and stretched his arms behind him. His adrenaline wore off long ago, which meant hers had too. They were both running on fumes. He had the advantage of experience in these situations, but she had something better to keep her going. Desperation.

Finally, at one-fifteen in the morning, she pulled off the interstate in Cortland and stopped at the gas pumps outside a convenience store. After topping off with fuel, she hurried inside and headed straight for the restroom.

Jeremy parked on the other side of the gas pump and leaned against his car while his tank refilled. Above the store, three video cameras pointed across the parking lot. Assuming they worked, and these days most did, whatever he did next would be recorded. Fine by him.

She'd be out in a few minutes, ready to make her final push north.

That wasn't going to happen.

Once his car's tank was full, he waited until he spotted her in the store.

She had a giant cup of some sort of beverage and was perusing the snacks. No sense of urgency at all.

When she headed for the cashier, Jeremy walked to the front of her car, laid on the oil-and-gas-and-water-and-who-knows-what-else-stained concrete, and scooted on his back until he could retrieve the GPS tracker. The heat from the undercarriage carried the smell of hot rubber and oil, and his stomach grumbled against the odor. He slipped the GPS device into his pocket and stared toward Georgia Harding as she exited the store.

When she was fifteen or twenty feet away, he maneuvered from under the car and grunted as he pushed himself off the ground. "Good morning, Ms. Harding."

The mega beverage fell to the concrete and sent a tidal wave of soda over her legs. She stammered to find words. "How ... you ... I can't ..."

He smiled and walked back to his car. "You shouldn't have run. I told you not to."

She swallowed hard and placed her hand on her car's hood to steady herself. "What ... what were you doing under my car?"

"Oh." He scratched his chin for a moment and dug a quarter out of his pocket. "Dropped this and it rolled under there. Can't afford to lose money, not when I'm retired and all." He opened his car door. "Have a *safe* drive, Ms. Harding. I don't think we'll be talking again."

"Wait!" She knelt and looked under her vehicle.

Jeremy laughed. "Looking for a flashing red light or something? Come on, now. Give me some credit, will you?"

She stood and glanced back toward the store. "What does that mean? That you didn't do anything or that you're smarter than to make it so obvious?"

He eased his door closed and moved to within inches of the woman, then frowned and took several heavy, deep breaths. "You killed my wife and daughter over a couple of hundred dollars' worth of baby stuff."

She backed away. "I told you I didn't mean to."

"And that's supposed to matter to me? Maybe if you'd come forward back then. Told the truth about everything. But not now. I gave you a chance and look what you did. You ran." He rubbed his hand on the hood of her car. "You won't run much farther, Ms. Harding."

She choked back a sob. "We can fix this. I'll go to the police. Tell them everything. I swear it."

"Too late." He pointed to the store's video cameras. "You'll say it was all coerced. That I threatened you. Even fired a gun in your home. That's a chance I'm not willing to take."

"But it's NOT coerced. I'll make them believe me. I know I can."

He shook his head and strode to his car. "I'm going home."

"I know what was in the bag." She stared at the ground. "The bag your wife was carrying. I know what was in it."

His heart leapt, and he glared at her. "Go on."

"That was never made public, right? I mean, no one except the police knows. Socks and bibs and some pajama things with zippers on the front. Lots of pink on everything."

He clenched his jaw. "And you know this how?"

"I was in the store. I watched her, and when she left, it was just ... I was only going to rob her." She wiped her hand under her eyes. "I didn't mean to do it. I swear I didn't."

"And you'll tell all this to the police?"

"I will. I swear it. Give me another day to get everything in order. Please."

"How much time you have is not up to me." He twisted his neck to work out the kinks, then stared into the sky. "I didn't do anything to your car. Promise. You can go anytime you want. Take my car if you don't trust me."

"You ... you won't follow me? How do you know I'll—"

"I've got everything I need." He pulled his phone from his pocket. "You get all of that?"

She tilted her head and squinted. "Get all of what?"

"Oh, sorry. Not you. I hate these things." He pressed the speaker button on the phone. "You still there?"

"Yes," Maggie said. "I heard everything."

Georgia Harding stiffened. "You can't record me. It's not admiss—"

"It wouldn't be," Jeremy said, "if we were in Maryland or Pennsylvania. But we're in New York. Turns out their law says only one person has to consent. And for the record, I do. Consent, I mean."

"You coming home now?" Maggie asked.

"I don't know," he said. "You already notify the cops?"

"Yeah, they'll be there in a few minutes. I told them Ms. Harding had something she wanted to get off her chest. Of course, if she doesn't, well, we'll know soon enough. Oh, and the border patrol's already got her info."

Jeremy nodded. "I'm not going to hang around. I'll call you when I get close to home, okay? Maybe meet you and Beks for breakfast somewhere."

He hung up the phone and tossed it into his car before walking slowly toward Georgia Harding. "What happened here tonight," he said, "was a second chance for you. Me too maybe. It would be a mistake to interpret that as weakness."

He leaned closer and her breathing accelerated.

"Maryland doesn't have the death penalty," he said. He tapped his forefinger between her eyes. "I do."

Flashing blue-and-red lights bounced around him, and he glanced up as a patrol car drove down the street.

"Have a good evening, Ms. Harding." He hurried to his car and cranked the engine, then pulled toward her and lowered the passenger window. "I'll be watching."

EPILOGUE

Jeremy, Beks, and Pronger sat at the Purple Penguin diner waiting for Maggie and Tanessa to arrive. Two days earlier, Georgia Harding confessed to Detective Pronger and now sat in the Frederick jail waiting for her trial date to be set. Her husband had not stepped forward to arrange bail.

In the time since then, Jeremy had been busy with other plans and tonight was the result. Maggie and Tanessa showed up fashionably late and were already giggling by the time they made it to the table.

"What a day," Maggie said.

Tanessa widened her eyes and blinked. "Jer, I've been laughing for like six hours straight. You have got to get Mags to tell you—"

"Where's Janice?" Maggie asked. "And hello, uh, Pronger. You really don't want me to call you something else?"

He shook his head. "Pronger's fine."

"Can I go get her now?" Beks asked.

Jeremy nodded. "Be careful in the parking lot."

Maggie's eyes narrowed. "What's going on?"

"Nothing," he said. "A little surprise."

"Why do I feel like my day just got—Grayson?" Maggie squealed, jumped from her seat, and hugged the old man.

Grayson Wynford, the pastor of the First Baptist Church in Pleasant View, Texas, became a friend during the Talbot investigation. While Beks and Jeremy recovered in the hospital, he was an everyday presence, and they'd spoken somewhat regularly since then.

"Easy now," Jeremy said. "Let him breathe."

Maggie put her hands on her hips. "Janice, how long have you known about this?"

The woman grinned. "About a week. I picked him up at the airport yesterday, and we've been sightseeing ever since."

Grayson smiled. "Couldn't ask for a better tour guide."

Janice touched his arm. "Hush with that nonsense."

"Don't take this the wrong way," Maggie said, "but why are you here?"

"My idea," Jeremy said. "I decided a justice of the peace was a tad too informal, so I gave Grayson a call and flew him up. I hope that's okay?"

"What? Of course." Maggie squinched her nose. "Does this mean we're getting married soon?"

Grayson winked and waved his hand around the table. "Sit, everyone. Let's get something to eat. And Jeremy, I still owe you that steak, so get a big one."

The waitress jotted down their order, and the group discussed possibilities for when and where to do the ceremony. Janice already took the preacher to the courthouse and got him squared away on the paperwork, so the sooner and the simpler, the better.

"We don't have the rings yet," Jeremy said.

Maggie shrugged. "We'll get them later. That's not a requirement to be married."

"But it won't be … I mean … are you okay with that?"

"*You* called Grayson, remember? You're not looking for a reason to delay this, are you?"

He opened his mouth wide and pointed at himself. "Me? Of course not."

"Mama," Beks said. "What was so funny?"

"When, baby?"

"When you got here Miss Tanessa said—"

Maggie's face turned beet red. "Maybe later, dear."

"Uh-uh," Tanessa said. "Not happening. Today your mom had to teach a class of new recruits. I won't go into the gory details, but basically she had to explain how to deal emotionally with crimes that are especially heinous. You know what that means, sweetie? Heinous?"

The girl nodded. "Really, really, bad."

"Right. Well anyway, your mom thought—"

"I thought the *h* was silent."

Jeremy spat his water onto the table while Tanessa erupted into laughter again. Grayson was nearly doubled over and slapping his hand on his leg while Janice rubbed his back and told him to stop and take a breath. Pronger brushed away tears while Beks gaped at everyone.

"What?" Maggie said. "It was an honest mistake."

The waitress stopped by to say their food was on the way from the kitchen and if it wasn't a problem, could they please take the noise down a notch?

After a few moments, everyone caught their breaths, though the occasional chuckle threatened to start the whole ordeal over again. Grayson cleared his throat. "Would you folks mind if I asked the Lord to bless our meal?"

"Of course not," Maggie said.

The group bowed their heads while the pastor said grace. After a round of amens, with Beks' being especially loud, they dug into dinner.

"We're really going to do this?" Maggie said.

Jeremy nodded. "We are. The paperwork's in order, and the fees are paid, and you don't need anything else. Paperwork and money. The government's daily bread."

They ate in silence for a few minutes, each desperate to avoid eye contact lest they start laughing again. Jeremy dunked an onion ring in ketchup and stared at it. What if …

"Let's do it now," he said.

Maggie peered at him. "Do what now?"

"The wedding. Let's do it now. Why not?"

She wrinkled her forehead. "I'm supposed to tell people we got married at the Purple Penguin?"

"Everyone we'd invite is already here."

"I don't know. I mean, this is kind of a public place, isn't it? People are eating, and the restaurant is—"

"Uh-uh," Jeremy said. "It's your wedding and, like it or not, you'll be the center of attention. In fact, I may get on one knee and—"

"Don't you dare," she said. "I don't want to have to help you back up." Her face reddened, and she peered at Beks. "What do *you* think?"

"Can we get dessert when you're done?"

Maggie rubbed her fingertips together. "We can. Grayson, is it all right with you?"

The old man used his napkin to dab around his lips. "This is your wedding, not mine. Whatever you folks want is fine by me."

"How would we do it?" she asked. "Here at the table or ..."

"Yep," Jeremy said. "How long will it take?"

"Depends on if you want to say anything," Grayson said. "If you don't, couple of minutes maybe."

The waitress stopped by to check on them, and Jeremy asked if it would be okay to have a marriage ceremony in the restaurant.

Her mouth hung open for several seconds before she spoke. "You want to get married here?"

"We do."

"I'll have to check with the manager. When did you want to do it?"

"Now," Maggie said.

The waitress glanced around the half-full restaurant. "I don't know. I mean, I don't want to interrupt anyone's dinner, and I could get in trouble if—"

"Miss," Grayson said, "do y'all sing Happy Birthday here? Bring out a cake and all of that?"

Beks perked up. "Is it your birthday, Mr. Grayson?"

He smiled, exposing his yellowed, crooked teeth between the gray whiskers of his mustache and beard. "No, honey, it's not."

The girl slumped back in her seat. "Oh, man."

The pastor turned his attention back to the waitress. "So don't you think all that singing and commotion interrupts meals? I promise you, the wedding won't take more than a couple of minutes."

"Can I ask the supervisor on duty?"

"Sure you can. We don't want to cause any problems. It's just that these two here have been itching to get hitched together for quite a while now. I think it's time we let them."

After she'd hurried off to ask permission, Jeremy leaned forward. "Hey, Beks. I need you to listen to me for a minute."

She scooted her plate until the fries were out of his reach. "Okay."

"Remember when we talked about me marrying your mom?"

"Yeah."

Maggie cleared her throat and arched her eyebrows at the girl. "Excuse me?"

"Yes, sir."

"Well," he said, "I want to say it one more time. I love you, and I love your mom. I want to be part of your family. Is that okay?"

"I thought you already were."

Maggie smiled. "He was. Is. This just makes it official. Is that all right?"

"Do we still get dessert?"

"Of course," she said. "What about it, Jeremy? You want your dessert here or would you rather wait until we get home?"

"Do we have ice cream at the—"

Maggie widened her eyes and tilted her head. "Listen closely. I'm offering you *dessert at home.*"

"Yeah, I know. You already said ... oh." His face flushed, and he took a sip of water.

"Jer," Tanessa said. "I believe you are the most clueless man alive."

Grayson laughed. "Ain't never met a man who wasn't when it came to women."

The waitress returned and said they could have the ceremony as long as it was quick, but if any of the other customers complained, they'd have to stop.

"Fair enough," Grayson said. He stood and tapped his fork against his water glass several times until most of the patrons were looking at him. "Folks, if I could have your attention for just a second. These two here"— he gestured toward Maggie and Jeremy—"want to get married."

A smattering of applause broke out and the pastor held up his hand. "And they don't want to wait, so we're having the ceremony right here, right now. Won't take more than a minute or two, and I guess what I'm saying is, if anyone has any objection to that, let them speak now or forever hold their peace."

The restaurant grew silent except for the kitchen noise. Someone near the back shouted, "Go for it!" and several people turned their chairs to face the pastor.

Grayson gestured toward Jeremy and Maggie. "You two ready for this?"

Jeremy took her hand, and they stood before him. He glanced down, expecting to see his heart pounding through his shirt. "Ready. Wait. Beks, will you stand with us?"

The couple released hands and ushered the girl between them, then took her hands in theirs.

"Okay," Maggie said. "Now we're ready."

Grayson tugged at his beard and raised his voice. "Let's make this short and sweet so these people can get back to their dinner. Do you, Jeremy Winter, take Maggie Keeley to be your lawfully wedded wife, to have and to hold from this day forward, for better or for worse, for richer, for poorer, in sickness and in health, to love and to cherish from this day forward until death do you part?"

"I do," Jeremy said.

"You do what?" Beks asked.

Maggie shushed her and nodded to the preacher. He repeated the phrase for her and the customers laughed when she paused and said she was making sure he left out the "obey" part before saying "I do."

The pastor rubbed his hands together. "Before God and all those assembled here, I now pronounce you husband and wife. Jeremy, you may kiss your bride."

Maggie threw her arms around his neck and pulled him to her. They kissed for a moment, hugged, then both squatted and repeated the process with Beks. More applause came from around the room as chairs scooted back to their original positions.

Grayson raised a hand. "Thank you, everyone. Now go on and eat before it gets too cold. And dessert's on me tonight."

Jeremy grinned. "No thanks. I'm having my dessert at home."

AUTHOR'S NOTE

Thank you for reading *Winter's Fury*. I'd greatly appreciate it if you'd take the time to leave a review of the book online when you get the chance. Other than buying their work and recommending it to friends, the best thing you can do for an author is write a short review.

Is there more to come from Jeremy Winter? Yes. Maybe. But there are definitely more stories coming your way soon. If you want to be among the first to know the latest news (and maybe win a free book), you can sign up for my newsletter at www.tomthreadgill.com. You'll receive an occasional short email with things like publishing dates and special offers. I promise not to spam you or give your email address to anyone else.

Thanks again and keep reading!

Made in the USA
Columbia, SC
24 November 2020

25417398R00181